Summer Tour

B. Elizabeth Beck

SUMMER TOUR

Text copyright © 2020 by B. Elizabeth Beck
First published in the United States of America
ISBN: 9798636244875
Imprint: Independently published

Cover images copyright ©by Kat O'Sullivan
Cover Design copyright © by Carter R. Neumann
Caslon CP Font permission obtained from Claude Pelletier

For Carter, the sun; ah, my son

Summer Tour

1

I come unglued while in midair and land to reform
Limb by limb
And I am taken far away

"Limb by Limb"
Anastasio, Marshall, & Herman

"Please don't clip your toenails on the floor. Use the trashcan," I said to my pain-in-the-ass roommate, Chip. The guy had no manners.

He grunted but reached for the can. I was about to complain it was too late when I heard the knock. I got up to answer it since Chip was engrossed in his grooming. Seeing Dad in the doorway freaked me out. He never just randomly showed up.

"What's wrong?" I asked as a greeting.

"Pack your room, and let's get to the airport." He held two duffel bags to demonstrate his point. "I've made arrangements with Aunt Karen. You'll be staying with her until September."

"Okay, but what's going on? I still have finals," I said. My heart was pounding, wondering what could be so important he would pull me out of school a week early.

"I've got to go to China for a few weeks. It's unavoidable," he said. Dad was a steel broker who traveled a lot of the year. It's one of the reasons he sent me to boarding school. He continued, "I've already cleared that with the headmaster. I've arranged your finals as take-home essays, so you can finish them and submit them from Ohio. But you only have two weeks to complete them."

1

I exhaled with relief. It wasn't an emergency. No tragedy. Business. That I could handle. Because I had never been to Aunt Karen's house, and since Dad never took any goddamn time away from his company, I knew better than to argue. Even though I was reeling from the idea of take-home essays as finals, I couldn't wait for any opportunity to blow out of St. Philips, where I'd suffered prep school for the past three years. I just thought I would have to endure one last year before escaping to college. I needed this break, even to just go to Ohio. If Holden could take off to New York, I could find adventure in Maywood.

Holden Caulfield was the first literary hero I had ever encountered. I mean, *Huckleberry Finn* was just ridiculously hard to read and so outdated, I don't know why the English teachers still adored it. All the guys in *A Separate Peace* were pretty much bullies, and there were already enough of those pretentious assholes here. I didn't need to read about others. So, when Mr. O'Donnell assigned *The Catcher in the Rye,* I was hooked from the start. Finally, a character with balls, even though I had yet to understand what point Salinger was making. Sometimes you can find clues, but only if you're ready for them or if you know how to spot them. Reading can be like that, like following a map of sorts. Or maybe I'm just the only one who finds connections between my own life and the books I read. Or lack of connection, in the case of most of the stupid books assigned by boring teachers at this boarding school, an all-boys academy *preparing young men for life.* Anyway, when he showed up unexpectedly that random Thursday in early June, I was nowhere near the carousel

2

scene in Central Park. Not that it would have made any difference. I mean, when you are legally still just a minor, you don't always choose your fate. A lot of life spirals beyond your control, and if you just hold tight, you may be surprised where you land.

Between layers of clothes, I tucked my laptop, journal, a framed picture of my mom, and *The Catcher in the Rye* into my bags. The first thing I planned to do when I got to Ohio was to buy a red hunting hat. Surely, they had those for sale in Maywood. I didn't have the least idea of what to expect, though. I had never been there before. I assumed there were cornfields and hunters because it's in a southern rural area of Ohio. Like both Salinger and his character Holden, I grew up in Manhattan and still go back home to the city every summer. Regardless of the setting, I was ready for whatever adventure presented itself. Perhaps just having the right mindset was key to what I would discover, but I didn't know that yet. I didn't see a lot of things. All I knew was that I was sick of the same guys in the same school doing the same things. It just never occurred to me that there was an escape out of this maze.

Walking down the hallway, I was so excited, I had to suppress my urge to yell, "Sleep tight, you morons," but I knew Dad wouldn't get it. Not to mention, he would probably be pissed. Besides, since I was returning to school with the same guys for yet another year before graduation, perhaps just yelling the sentiment in my head and not aloud was a smart decision. They're still a bunch of goddamn phonies, though.

2

It was not yet evening as we drove the rental car from the Columbus airport. I watched dusk descend on endless flat fields of farmlands, a first for me. Growing up, we never visited Ohio. Aunt Karen always came to New York, something I had never questioned before.

"Why didn't we ever come here?" I asked my dad.

"Your mom didn't fly," he replied. "You know that."

"Yeah, but why? And was it always?" I asked. "Didn't she study in Europe or something?"

"Ever since 9/11. She just refused to fly. One of her many limitations," Dad said bitterly. "I accepted it. Just I like accepted—"

"What?" I pushed, but he just turned on his blinker and didn't respond. Only a moment passed before an inevitable business call conveniently interrupted. I inserted my earbuds in response and zoned out the rest of the two-hour drive. Because I was only three months old when the attacks on 9/11 happened, I spent my entire childhood under that cloud. I was too tired to sift through those memories right now.

The exit from the highway didn't take us through the town of Maywood. Instead, Dad followed the GPS down more country roads to a barely paved lane, which led us to what Aunt Karen calls her Calico House. It sat on a pond surrounded by acres of land. Aunt Karen had painted the exterior of the house in a rainbow-colored way that nobody else would ever think to do. There was even a smiley face splashed on one side, a Cat-in-the Hat chimney, and elaborately scrolled details as trim to make the house look even more whimsical. Aunt Karen was a painter. She said her home reflected her art.

I had only ever seen pictures of the house. It was crazy, an artist's home for sure. The house looked like a friendly version of a Gingerbread House from the fairy tales; only Aunt Karen was not an old witch. She was still young-seeming, slim with brown hair cut to her shoulders, kind of a natural-looking lady. She's my mom's younger sister. In the three years since Mom died, I had only seen her only a few brief times and only in New York, like for holidays.

Aunt Karen skipped onto the porch, bare-footed, and in a long patchwork skirt. She wore silver earrings that jingled when she moved. Aunt Karen moved a lot, used her hands to talk, and liked to laugh. When she smiled, I could see the resemblance to my mom.

"Hello, Andrew." Aunt Karen greeted Dad with a handshake, and then pulled me into a suffocating hug. She said, "Sam, honey, I'm so happy to see you. We are going to have a lovely summer together."

I smiled, despite my vow to always seem bored any time I was around my father. No matter, though. He wasn't paying any attention to us. As she led us into the house, Aunt Karen shooed some of her chickens from the kitchen, much to my father's disdain. I knew he didn't approve of chickens in the house any more than he approved of Aunt Karen's house itself. Hell, I didn't think Dad even liked Aunt Karen, so I thought it a bit weird he insisted I stay with her for the summer. I guess that was because he had no choice.

Aunt Karen reached up to tousle my hair. She said, "You've gotten so tall, Sam. You're almost as tall as your dad now, but you still look the same as you were when you were a baby," she said. I knew that wasn't true. I looked like a sumo wrestler as a baby. As if there were rubber bands on my arms and legs, they were so fat. Now, no matter how much I eat, my body stays lean. I guess I'm just lucky like that. Dad is tall and slim, too.

The kitchen smelled of incense and a faint hint of garlic, mixed with the scent of flowers arranged in a mason jar placed in the center of the kitchen table. Aunt Karen poured tea for us while Dad checked his messages. He was always on the phone. Always. He did *unplug* long enough to accept the tea, asking Karen about her latest art projects in his distracted way before he rose to leave. I thought about what Holden would say. Dad was precisely a goddamn phony.

"Okay, Son, so I'll plan to see you parents' weekend in October if not before. Call or text if you need anything." Then he turned to Karen and said, "Thank you. I appreciate this favor."

She said, "No worries. Have safe travels." Aunt Karen waved Dad away and turned to smile at me.

She said, "So, let me show you around, and you can settle in your room for a bit before it's time to take off. We're going to my friend's art show this evening, okay?"

We walked from the kitchen into her living room. One wall was dedicated to floor-to-ceiling shelves stuffed full of books, sculptures, and framed pictures. There were two worn leather sofas in front of the fireplace and a window seat full of pillows. Attached to the living room was a sunroom, divided by open glass doors. The sunroom was exploding with plants. The only furniture was a sofa covered in a corduroy cover, draped with quilts in front of which a wood trunk served as a coffee table. A dining room big enough to hold a table large enough for twelve finished the central space of the house.

"What's most special is the porch," Aunt Karen said, leading me to walk the span of the covered porch that wound around the entire house. Arranged in clusters were wicker furniture was arranged, and there was a hanging porch swing big enough to lie down on, with a collection of pillows and a throw pillow on its bench, inviting me to nap.

"Tomorrow, I will show you my art studio and the chicken coop," she said. "When it's light. But that's it. This is the Calico House."

I grinned at her. "I love it. Thank you for letting me stay here this summer. It is going to be good."

"You are more than welcome, my dear," Aunt Karen said as we turned back into the house.

Upstairs, there were three bedrooms. She pointed out the hall bathroom that would be mine for the summer before directing me to the room I would use. I could see from the two large windows framed with blue and white striped curtains that it faced the backyard. There was a brass bed, nightstand, dresser, closet, and desk. A gray rug broke up the hardwood floors that ran through the entire house.

It only took a minute for me to drop my duffle bags on the bed in the room and open my backpack to remove my books, journal, and laptop. I searched for an outlet for my chargers as I ran my hand through my hair, which never lay flat the way I wished. Instead, the cowlick above my left eyebrow caused the front of my hair to stand straight up perpetually. I looked down at my CBGB t-shirt, sniffed under my arms to be sure I didn't stink, and hoped my jeans were okay for wherever we were going.

Aunt Karen detailed her friends who were involved in the show as we drove toward the outskirts of Mayfield. It was some kind of co-op studio space, so more than one artist was showing their work. She pulled into the parking lot of a small shopping center. A restaurant anchored one end, and a pharmacy stood at the other. In between were a hair salon, a tattoo place, two boutiques, and a coffee shop. The art studio building looked like a converted garage. One wall was all glass and looked like it could open like a garage door. There were a lot of potted plants in garbage cans and hanging from macramé plant holders. Mounted to the walls were various paintings, and canvases leaned on easels in the main space. I walked around, pretending to understand the art, but it was some whacked-out stuff, not like the art we study at school, that's for sure. One sculpture was funny, though. It was an old television. In place of the screen were plush fabric breasts. A little card read, "Boob Tube." I was standing in front of it when two kids my age approached me.

"Cool t-shirt," the girl said. "You must be Sam. Karen told us to look for you. I'm Claire, and this is Christopher."

I was stunned for a minute. Literally stunned. Claire was the most beautiful girl I had ever met in person. Long, curly blonde-hair framed her face, and she had the darkest brown eyes I had ever seen. It was quite an unusual combination. I know it sounds stupid, but Botticelli's Venus came immediately to mind. Before I could regain my composure, Christopher barked a laugh. "I know, dude. I'm always telling her she should model. Don't you think she could be a model?"

"Shut up, Christopher. That's just because you're my brother or at least my almost brother." Claire mock punched him in the arm. "He's my step-brother to be completely accurate. His mother is my step-monster".

Christopher shook his head to shift the grimace on his face to a smile for my benefit. "Don't listen to her," he said. "And you can call me Chris."

"Or Captain," Claire said just before she squealed and clapped her hands, seeing two girls who were jumping up and down across the gallery. They all ran into a big hug.

I looked at Chris, who stood as tall as me but seemed lankier somehow. He wore several woven string bracelets around his bony wrists and a big glass pendant on a hemp necklace. A big poof of curly brown hair made his head seem even more prominent on his long neck, and his beak nose stood out from bright blue eyes. He wore torn jeans and what boarding school kids called a drug rug, which was a woven cotton hoodie stoners and hippies wore.

"Captain?" I asked him.

9

"It's a stupid nickname. I go by Chris. Only Claire calls me Christopher to bug me, and some people call me Captain, but it's only a joke," he replied. "Have you seen Claire's work yet?"

"No," I said. "She's an artist?"

"Yes," Chris said. "An artist she may be, but a genius she is not."

"What?" I asked, confused.

"Don't tell her I said this, but she is really good. This isn't even her first show. Come. I'll show you."

I followed Chris from the main space into one of the smaller studios where a sign read, "Reinventing Barbie and the Evolution of the Dollhouse." Around the perimeter of the room were at least a dozen white columns holding different Barbie dolls. Behind the columns hung framed photographs, and in the center of the room was this huge dollhouse. We began walking clockwise around the space, as directed by another little sign. Modified somehow to appear to have gained weight enough to look no longer like a supermodel was the first Barbie doll. Instead, she was more pear-shaped and dressed in just a shirt and pants. Behind her, the stark black-and-white photograph was of several plus-sized women, naked, but modestly covering their breasts and private areas with their arms and hands.

The next column held two Barbie dolls. One was dressed in leather, and her hair was cut close. The other wore a striped-shirt and pants, but also a dog-collar around her neck whose chain was held by the butch Barbie. The photograph behind that was of a rainbow flag. On another column, Barbie was naked. Her breasts were removed, and a tattoo bra was painted in replacement. The photograph behind it was one large nipple, taken so close-up it almost looked like a huge sunflower.

I think the most shocking Barbie was one that wore low-cut denim cut-offs only. Her hair was curled and long, and she wore make-up and diamond-looking earrings. She looked most like the typical Barbie from her head up. Scrawled across her breasts and torso in black graffiti styled lettering were the words:

Don't tell me how to dress. Tell them not to rape.
The photograph behind her depicted four men whose eyes were blind-folded, and hands tied behind them, execution-style.

We walked to the center of the room. The exterior of the dollhouse looked like any other fancy dollhouse with white clapboard and a black shingled roof. Pink gingerbread molding defined the roof. Electric lights worked little candles in every shuttered window, and even little lights flanked the front door. Miniature climbing wisteria wound the porch. There were also low potted plants holding small flowers, except every single stem was broken, leaving the blooms to hang, facing downward, the only imperfection of the otherwise fairy tale rendering of a dollhouse cottage.

We stepped around to see the inside of the house. There were three floors. The bottom floor was one big space instead of being divided into individual rooms. Wallpapered as a black and white collage on all three walls were faces of children whose eyes were large, haunted, pained. Black curtains covered the windows. The floor was painted black. In the center of the story were a life-sized pacifier and disturbingly, an empty Trojan condom wrapper.

The second floor divided into separate rooms. Scattered around the furnished living room were miniature crumpled beer cans. An overflowing ashtray, a little mirror, and a small razor lay on the coffee table. In the kitchen, miniature books, notebooks, pens, and a coffee mug sat on a Formica table. The bedroom held an unmade bed with rumpled sheets stained with a dark red blotch. The bathroom looked unremarkable until you looked a second time. Hanging from the shower curtain was a noose.

Exposed beams and little cobwebs hung in the corners of the ceiling of the top floor attic. Tiny trunks and cardboard boxes filled the space. Suspended from the center of the attic was a little white lace gown on one small little hanger. The dress looked like the white communion gowns Catholic girls wore in second grade.

I wanted to connect how all the images worked together as a cohesive unit now that I had experienced the story or whatever as it unfolded the first time through. Knowing that the center of the show focused on childhood sexual abuse changed my perception of every Barbie doll and photograph. It made it all seem more sinister and threatening. I didn't even notice the column supporting a Barbie doll with an erased face and whose body appeared to be melting until this second walk-through. The photograph behind this doll depicted a 1970's styled family portrait with an X scrawled across it, and the dad's face scratched out, as if with a pin.

I turned to Chris and said, "This is a powerful exhibit. I don't think I've ever seen anything like it before."

"You need to tell that to Claire. I mean, you're from New York so she'll take your compliment seriously. She's all things, New York, these days," he said. "It's her first choice for college. Either NYU or the New School. She's hoping this feminist work is good enough to include in her portfolio."

Claire returned and said, "Come on, you guys. Let's blow outta here. We've made our appearance, so to speak."

I asked, "Where are we going? Maybe I should tell my Aunt Karen?" Great, now I felt even more idiotic, asking permission like a little kid or something. I wish speaking was like writing, and there was a delete button or an eraser, at least.

But Claire said, "That's cool. Karen won't mind. I've known her since I was in diapers, practically. Karen is amaze-balls. I wish I could live in the Calico House."

Aunt Karen was holding a plastic cup of wine and talking to a dread-headed guy when we approached. She hugged Claire, greeted Chris, and said it was okay for me to go with them. As soon as we walked out of the studio, I blurted out, "Do you guys know where I could buy a red hunting hat?"

Claire turned to me, her eyes glowing. "Ah, the great Holden Caulfield, huh? That's cool. I fucking love that book. Remember, Christopher? Last year? Mr. Taylor's class?"

"I wasn't in that class last year. Remember, Claire," he said sarcastically. "Not all of us were in honors English."

"Oh, that's right. If it's not *Growing Up Dead,* it's not worth your time," Claire said.

"Exactly," Chris said.

"What's *Growing Up Dead?*" I asked.

"The book that changed Christopher's whole life," she mocked.

"It's definitely my inspiration," Chris said. "It's written by Peter Conners. I'll lend it to you if you want."

"Cool," I said.

"Back to *Catcher,*" Claire said, "Are you reading it now? What part are you on?"

"He's traveling around the city right now, bugging a cab driver about some ducks. He's just left school, basically," I said.

She frowned. "You aren't very far at all. You're gonna love it, though. Holden is my hero."

"Mine, too." I felt like something had been settled. I wasn't quite sure yet what that was, but the fact she read the book felt a little less disorienting to me, considering not even twenty-four hours ago, I was at school in New Hampshire and not getting into a car with kids I barely knew in I-don't-know-exactly-where Ohio.

Chris said, "Are you guys coming or what? Let's get a six-pack and go to the trestle." Chris opened the car door for Claire. I got in the back. I wasn't quite sure what a trestle was, but there wasn't an opportunity to ask since Claire commanded the car stereo to blast Prince, singing along at the top of her lungs. She turned back to me, her hair whipping around from the open window. "Don't you love Prince? I love everything about the '80s, don't you?"

"What? The 80's? I guess."

"I think I was born in the wrong era or something. If I were my age in the '80s, I'd be in New York, hanging out with Madonna and Keith Haring and Basquiat even." She kept her gaze steady on me. "I mean, you must, right? Like, get it, I mean. You get it. Your t-shirt? I mean, as soon as I saw you, I just knew you'd get it."

I had no idea what the hell she got, but I wasn't going to disagree with anything she said, so I nodded along. I wasn't going to admit to her I was wearing one of my mom's old t-shirts. That was a bit too personal, and I think, sounded weird. It's not a girl's shirt or anything. It was just a damn t-shirt.

Chris pulled into a corner store's parking lot and jumped out. "Want anything else?"

"I want those hard lemonades, Chrissy." Claire smiled, kicking her Chuck Taylors on the dash. "We have to come out here to buy liquor. The only other store is in town, and Mr. Brown knows all of us. It is the only place Chris can use his fake i.d. I think the owner knows it's us Maywood kids, but he is kinda shady himself, so he just turns a blind eye. Isn't that a funny expression, *turns a blind eye*? I'm heavy into Atwood these days. Do you read her work?"

I watched as Chris walked up the two steps, pulled on the glass door and entered the store before I turned back to Claire to answer her. "Umm... I think I saw some of the episodes of *The Handmaid's*

Tale, but I've gotta admit, I didn't read the book like I was supposed to."

"The show is nothing like the book. Atwood is a genius. I hope to be half as smart when I grow up. That's another funny expression, *grow up*. I feel as fucking grown up now as I'm ever going to be. Don't you? Do you think we'll actually change when we grow up or whatever? A person is a person."

"I think we're more a sum of all of our experiences, so I don't know. Maybe the more you experience, the more you change," I said.

"But do you think your core nature will ever change? I mean, I can't imagine just saying one day, 'Okay, I'm done acting like Claire. I'm going to respond in an entirely different way to every life experience I have'. I mean, it just doesn't work that way. People are who they are."

Chris saved me from responding when he returned to the car with a brown paper bag he put in the backseat next to me.

He threw a Juul to Claire and said, "They're still out of mango."

"Did you ask for mint?" Claire said.

"Yes, but they're still out of mint, too. Enough of this shit," Chris said as he changed the music.

"At least make it, *What's the Use*," Claire said. Then, she turned to face me in the backseat. "This is the summer of Phish."

"Fish?" I repeated back to her, brow furrowed.

"The band, Phish. Have you heard of them? Grateful Dead, Phish. Jam bands," she clarified.

"Oh, Phish," I said, embarrassed at my misunderstanding. I had heard of the band. A few guys at boarding school listened to jam bands.

"You're going to love them," Claire promised as Chris cued the music and pulled out of the liquor store parking lot. It only took less than ten minutes before Chris turned off the main road and parked next to a group of other cars. We all got out and walked to what I assumed to be the infamous trestle. To be honest, I would have followed Claire off a cliff at this point. Not only was she beautiful, I had never heard a girl talk so much about I don't know what before in my life.

3

Claire's best friend, Taylor ran over about two seconds after we got out of Chris's car. She was a tiny girl with light brown skin and friendly brown eyes. She looked like a kid, her freckled-face bare of make-up and an eager smile in place as she shook my hand as an introduction. Claire protectively wrapped her arm in the crook of mine as we walked together across the clearing to the trestle, which I soon found out was an old, abandoned train track that ran across Lake Juniper. When we got to the edge, about a dozen or so kids were hanging out, drinking. Someone had brought a portable speaker to play music, and a few girls were sitting on the trestle, dangling their legs toward the lake below. It was a pretty chill scene, but I was happy to accept the beer Chris offered.

"Not much of a scene, but it's all we've got," Claire said. "I can't wait to graduate and get to New York. You're from New York, right? I think that's what your Aunt Karen told us, or am I wrong?"

"I grew up there before I left for boarding school in New Hampshire. But I go back to New York on holidays," I said.

"That's perfect. Oh, I knew you were perfect. First of all, I've gone to the same school with the same group my entire fucking life. I mean, boring. Beyond mundane, really. There's nothing left to talk about, really. And then, Karen told me you were coming for the summer, and I just knew. And then your t-shirt. Where did you get your t-shirt? Oh, I know. The first thing we'll do is go immediately to Washington Square Park and get a latte from Café Reggio and walk around the Village. Is that what you did? Walked the Village? When's your birthday?" she asked.

She spoke so fast, I was disarmed, so I just laughed and took a slug from my beer. I wasn't sure where to start, so I just said, "July. I'll be eighteen July sixteenth."

"Perfect." She threw her arms around my neck. I could smell her perfume, which was spicy like geraniums.

She said, "We'll get to celebrate it together. The end of your childhood, Sam. The end." She twirled away from me and ran over to the girls sitting with their legs dangling. Claire held her arms out like a trapeze artist and walked one track of the trestle across the lake. The moon was almost full, and the light reflected on her curls made her seem to glow. She was radiant. I had to follow.

The trestle still had rails, so it wasn't like we were going to fall off suddenly, but it did feel like floating to be on the tracks above the lake at night. Once we reached midway, Claire turned around. "See the lighthouse?" she asked.

I looked across the lake to see the small point of light. It made me think about Gatsby. Claire could be Daisy, but I would probably be more like Nick. I always felt like an outsider looking in. I glanced back at the kids hanging out at the end of the trestle. I still heard the music, saw them laughing, but there wasn't anywhere else I would rather be than alone with Claire. She took my beer from my hand, drank the rest of it, and said, "Come on, let's jump."

"Where?" I was confused.

"Into the lake. It's no big deal. We do it all the time. Come on," Claire said as she grabbed the railing and began straddling it. I looked down. It seemed like a pretty significant drop, and I couldn't be sure the lake was deep enough for us to jump.

She asked, "Don't you trust me?" She reached out her hand for me. I took it. I remembered something Dad once said to me when I had gotten into some kind of trouble in school, some prank or something. He said, "If you were a lemming, would you follow these idiots off a cliff?"

I guess the answer was yes.

4

Claire and I balanced on the ledge outside the railing for just a moment longer before she yelled, "In omnia paratus," let go of the rail and jumped. I followed immediately. It was as long of a fall as I feared. When I thought we should have landed into the water, we were still falling. Finally, we hit the surface and sank below. Luckily, that part of the lake was deep enough, or I wouldn't be telling this story. It was cold, though. Claire laughed when we came up for air. I laughed partially with relief and somewhat because her laughing made me laugh. A bunch of kids ran down the trestle and yelled and cheered for us. She threw her arms around my neck and kissed me full on the mouth before turning to swim to shore.

Soaking wet and shivering a bit, we climbed our way up the scrubby hillside back up to the trestle. Chris met us at the top with blankets to throw around us and another beer for me. "In omnia paratus," he said.

"I don't know what that means," I admitted.

Taylor ran over to us, yelling, "In omnia paratus!"

"You did it, Sam." Claire smiled at me. "You are ready for all things."

"Rory Gilmore would be proud," Taylor said.

"Rory, who?" I asked, confused.

"*The Gilmore Girls*," Claire said to clarify, but it didn't explain anything to me.

We walked to the picnic area away from the trestle where a fire was burning in the fire pit. I looked around the clearing to see a few picnic benches, grills, and realized it was a park area. Still shivering, I put my hands to the fire to warm. It was pretty stupid to jump in wearing jeans. They were cold, wet, and heavy, and I forgot to take care of my shoes, which squished as I walked. Not that I even had a moment to think, though. I privately congratulated myself on my spontaneity and bravery.

"I have track pants in the car," Chris said. When I looked puzzled, he continued, "I mean, if you want to change outta those jeans, you can borrow them."

I decided to take him up on his offer instead of freezing in wet denim, so we walked back to his car. Good thing Chris and I were about the same height even though he was skinnier than me. I hoped the elastic of the track pants would stretch enough for me to wear them. He opened the trunk, retrieved the pants from a gym bag, and handed them to me. Then, he gave me a hooded sweatshirt, as well. Once he walked back to the fire pit area, I quickly stripped down and changed, looking around first to be sure I was utterly alone. I slid on the borrowed track pants but kept on my wet boxers. There was no way I was going to rub my junk against some other dude's pants. I pulled on his sweatshirt before I trudged back to the fire. The track pants were that itchy kind of nylon, but I was grateful to be dry and, hopefully, warm up. I walked barefoot, carrying the blanket over my arm to give to Claire, who was still in her wet clothes.

Music blared, and more kids had gathered around to party. Claire was dancing with a guy I hadn't seen before. He must have just shown up while I was changing. I took another chug of my beer.

"Here's the copy of the book," Chris said as he approached me. I looked down at the rainbow cover of a bright green VW bus. "Claire can joke all she wants, but she'll be having the last laugh in just a few weeks when we are on tour."

"Last laugh?" I asked, confused.

"Well, maybe not last laugh exactly, but our fam is ready to roll June eleventh, man." Chris sat on a fallen log and motioned me to join him as he picked up a frisbee and began crumbling weed from a baggie to roll into what was the largest joint I have ever seen. As he lit the fattie, he said, "Just because it's Phish and not the Dead doesn't mean we can't get on the bus, too."

"Your family is going to see Phish?" I asked, taking the joint from him.

"Yeah, exactly," he said excitedly. "Me, Claire, Taylor, who you just met. Alex and maybe Drake, we'll see."

He saw the confused look on my face and continued. "That's what we call ourselves. Our family. Our *real* family if you get what I mean. I've been working on an RV I bought in March, and it's almost ready. We plan to load up and take off as far as we can on tour. Phish tour."

"How long will you be gone?" I asked, feeling a bit let down. I had just met these kids, and it would suck if they were going to be gone all summer.

"Well, we'll have tix for St. Louis, Blossom, and Camden, but the goal is to make it to Alpine. We're bagging on Bonnaroo, though."

That didn't answer my question, of course. It was like he was speaking in some kind of code I'd yet to understand. I opened the cover of the *Growing Up Dead* book. Maybe I needed to drop *Catcher* and skim this so I could talk to Chris.

"June eleventh can't get here soon enough," Chris sighed.

Taylor approached us, her hand reaching for the joint. She took a deep drag, exhaled, and said, "We've got extras for St. Louis. Maybe he could come with us."

Chris frowned in response, so I said, "That's okay. I know you've got your plans, so..."

Taylor looked pointedly at Chris and said, "It's only two nights. He could come along, and we'll see."

Chris nodded. He stood up from the log and said, "You're right. Strangers stopping strangers and all that. You should come, man. The more, the merrier. And I do mean, merry."

Claire approached us, threw her arms around Chris from behind, and said, "That's you, oh captain, my captain. The merriest of Merry Pranksters."

"Ha!" Chris barked, untangling himself from Claire's embrace. "Damn straight. Long live, Kesey."

"Did you smoke without me?" Claire asked with a pout, pulling her arms across her chest.

"We did indeed, but where there's a need, there's always more..."

"Weed!" Claire and Taylor chimed in.

"You guys are funny," I tried to say, but I think I was higher than I realized. My tongue felt thick.

"Watch it there, buddy. You alright?" Claire asked as she sat next to me on the log. Or hot dog. Was I sitting on a hot dog or a log? How could that be, though? The log did feel like a hot dog, but I realized that probably didn't make any sense, which made me laugh.

"Is this a hot dog?" I asked.

"This joint?" Claire answered, holding up yet another fattie. She laughed. "Oh, yes. It is a very tasty hot dog."

"I think I need to lie down," I hoped I managed to at least croak.

"Here," Chris said, reaching down to pull me up by the hand. "You can crash in the car, dude. It's cool."

I didn't worry about whether anything was cool or not as I pushed off the hot dog log and followed him to the car. "Sorry," I was able to mumble.

"No worries, man," Chris said.

I curled up on the backseat and felt so grateful to close my eyes. Before I did, I saw the red lights flashing and the blue scarf from the corner of my memories. I must have passed out, but I woke up and felt relieved when Christopher pulled up to the Calico House. Aunt Karen left the front door unlocked and a few lights on. It was a weird night, and I just wanted to go to bed. I felt cold, tired, and hungry, but mostly disoriented. I had that feeling I got during finals week, pulling too many all-nighters. I passed the framed family pictures hung on the walls, arranged on the bookshelves, and clustered on tables to tiptoe to my room, where I quietly closed the door behind me.

5

All alone the life you lead
A silent diner where you feed
Bow your head pretend to read
This one is for you

"Brian and Robert"
Anastasio & Marshall

The moment I awoke, I reached for *The Catcher in the Rye*. I do that sometimes, read the moment I wake up, still in bed. I don't even brush my teeth or anything. I just read. After Holden left the two girls in the bar, I put the book down and thought about why I liked this character so much. He was as lonely as me. He kept wanting to call somebody but, like me, didn't have anybody to call. And that Ackley character was precisely like the asshole Chip, my roommate. Just as gross with his nail clippings. Weird.

I remembered my mom taking me out to lunch when I was much younger. She always made me take a book with me to the restaurant, and while we'd eat, we'd both read. Dad said it was rude and bad manners, but now I realized why she did it. She said, "So when you grow up, you will never be lonely. As long as you have a good book to read, you can eat anywhere alone yet never feel lonely." I understood what she was trying to teach me, but I couldn't help it. I still felt lonely all the time. Even when I was in a room full of people, I was profoundly alone. She also insisted on another ritual when Dad joined us at restaurants for dinners. Instead of reading, we all had to order different dishes so we could share. We all ate bites from each other's appetizers, dinners, and even desserts. She said that was so we could sample more of the menu, something that inexplicably delighted her. Dad would scowl but go along with it. I had forgotten about that. Thinking about food made my stomach protest in hunger, so I put my book down and shook my head to rid myself of memories.

I got out of bed and tromped downstairs to find Aunt Karen. The house was empty except two chickens I shooed off the counters. However, Aunt Karen left the coffee pot on, so I helped myself to a mug and filled it with two heaping spoons of sugar before I added the coffee. I walked around the house a bit, ready to study the old family photos. I lingered over Mom and Dad's wedding picture with *Andrew and Maggie* scrawled across the white frame. I wasn't used to seeing so many pictures of my mom. I only had one photo I kept in my sock drawer at school. I know that sounded weird, but when you lived at boarding school, you needed to keep your private shit private. When I looked out the window, I saw Aunt Karen outside, sitting at her easel painting. I gazed at her for a moment before deciding to interrupt to ask about breakfast.

"Good morning, Sam." Aunt Karen looked up as I approached. I studied her landscape painting depicting a lady was floating above a lake with chickens painted bigger in scale than the woman below. It kind of reminded me of that painter, Chagall, in a way.

"That's beautiful. It reminds me of Chagall." I sipped my coffee and looked out over the pond, spotting groups of ducks, like little families, and I wondered if I should ask Aunt Karen where her ducks went in the winter.

"That is a lovely compliment. Chagall, huh?" Karen stood up and put her paintbrush into a pickle jar of water that sat on a tree stump next to her easel. Another pot held a collection of well-used brushes, and her paints were in a wood toolbox at her feet. "I'll bet you are starving. When is the last time you had fresh eggs? Let's go in. I'll cook for you."

I followed her into the house, almost bumping into her as she paused to pick up a basket of eggs she had collected from the chicken coop earlier this morning while I was still reading in bed. Aunt Karen dropped the basket on the counter and turned on her stereo before she reached for a cast-iron skillet. The Grateful Dead played from the speakers as she began sizzling bacon in the pan and cracking eggs into a blue and white flecked ceramic bowl. I helped myself to more coffee and offered to help, but Aunt Karen insisted I sit. From the refrigerator, she pulled another ceramic bowl, this one pink and white flecked that was full of cut fruit. She set a plate, fork, and napkin at my place and instructed me to eat. As I worked my way through the fruit, she added the bacon, and then eggs, and finally pulled muffins from the oven. It was a feast, and I wasn't shy about eating. Aunt Karen nibbled on fruit as she kind of danced around the kitchen in her bare feet.

"After breakfast, I thought we'd ride into town. I need to drop off some things for the farmer's market and see a friend. I can show you around a bit, too. Did you have a good time last night with Claire and Chris?" Aunt Karen asked.

"We went to the trestle," I answered. I rose to clear my plate and rinse it in the sink. "I jumped in."

Aunt Karen laughed. "You did? Your first night? Good for you, Sam. Oh, it's been years since I've been to the trestle. Do all of the kids still get together there?"

"I guess so. Yeah, there were a lot of kids. I met Claire's friend, Taylor," I said.

Aunt Karen smiled as she sipped from her mug. "Claire is a talented artist. Did you see her work last night? Potent stuff."

"Yes," I said. "It was shocking. Good, but I'm not even sure what to make of it. Some of the images were disturbing."

"Well, that's the point. Claire is delving into political art, and it will be interesting to see what develops from here. Her first feminist work. Exciting." Aunt Karen stood to rinse her mug. "Go get showered and dressed so we can take off."

Before I could ask her any more questions, Aunt Karen retreated to her bedroom. So, I did what she asked: took a quick shower, toweled my hair dry, and dressed in a pair of jeans and a plain t-shirt. Messages on t-shirts were taken seriously around here, and I didn't want to be misunderstood again. My damp clothes from last night were still hanging on the back of the desk chair where I left them, but I remembered to fold Chris's track pants and sweatshirt to return to him. I debated taking them with me but doubted we would see them at the farmer's market, so I just left them behind.

Aunt Karen was ready when I got downstairs. She had loaded the backseat of her car with baskets of eggs, lettuce, and basil, maybe. I don't know shit about gardening. We drove the few miles into the center of Maywood, a town so small it could be considered a hamlet. There was a village green with a white gazebo in the center, a courthouse with an old bell tower at one end, and small buildings on either side that housed the town's banks, the library, and businesses. A diner and two churches flanked the town square, and there was a Dairy Queen where a baseball team of little boys lined up for their cones.

Aunt Karen pulled into the farmer's market. She jumped out, greeted a guy who had a table full of produce and began unloading, handing me baskets to carry.

The guy smiled and introduced himself. "You must be Sam. Your aunt talks about you all the time. I'm Luke." He took the load from my arms and began unpacking everything onto his table.

"These eggs look beautiful, Karen," he said.

A few people were walking around the market: mothers pushing strollers and an old couple holding hands, but nobody around my age. I looked across the green space and spied what seemed to be a general store. I asked Aunt Karen if I could walk around.

She said, "Just be back in a half-hour. I don't want to be here all day. I just wanted to drop this stuff off before it got too late," a comment that made Luke laugh for some reason. It was only just afternoon, but I had a feeling the farmer's market opened much earlier in the day.

I walked across the green to the entrance of the store, reaching to feel my back pocket to make sure my wallet was there. Surely, this store would have hunting hats. A little bell jingled when I opened the door. I took my time walking around what looked to be a grocery but also had a counter behind which displayed guns, ammunition, fishing poles, and lures. There was a rack of plaid jackets and shelves of stacked jeans and t-shirts. Next to the cooler with a sign that read *Live Bait*, I spied the red hunting hat and reached for it immediately. There it was: the hat Holden wore in the book. I took it to the counter where an older man sat behind the cash register, reading the newspaper. He barely looked at me as he rang up my purchase. Didn't even say a word as I handed him a twenty from my wallet, and he returned my change.

I walked back out of the store, feeling satisfied. Although it was already almost eighty degrees and sunny, I pulled the hat down on my head. Before I could walk back to the farmer's market, Chris and Claire pulled up. Guess I should have brought along his clothes.

"Nice hat," Claire yelled from the open window. "Get in, *Holden*. Wanna go to the club with us? We came to invite you."

I walked up to the car and leaned in to see them better. "What club?"

"Sorry, I didn't bring your track pants. I'll wash them and these trunks and return them to you later," I said.

Dude, no worries. We'll see you this summer," he said.

"Cool. Well, thank you," I said.

He opened a locker where I stuffed my jeans and red hunting hat for safety. I guess it was a good thing we were similar in height and weight. I should just feel grateful, but I had to admit, wearing his clothes made me feel even more ill at ease. It wasn't as if I had never been to a country club. My paternal grandparents lived in their country club, practically. I guess I just didn't think Maywood was big enough of a town even to have a country club. Grandpa liked to golf, and Grandma played bridge. Dad and I usually spent Easter Sundays with them at their club, indulging in their vast buffet. Dad's like me, though. Instead of playing golf, he plays tennis. Last summer, we got park passes and played several times a week when Dad got home from work. The courts were close to our apartment, and afterward, we would sometimes go to a local pub for pastrami sandwiches and a beer. Well, okay, Dad would have a beer. I drank a soda or whatever.

It just goes to show no matter how small a town, some people liked to belong to exclusivity. I didn't think I'd ever join a country club when I grew up, though. It's just not my scene, although I wasn't quite sure what my scene was anymore. I guess I'd always thought of myself as a New Yorker, regardless of my time at prep school. My heart was in the city. I think I always assumed I would return there after college.

When we returned to the pool area, Claire had already reserved three chaise lounge chairs under an umbrella to one corner. She looked sophisticated in her black bikini, earbuds in place, and a *Vogue* magazine at her painted toenails. Chris threw himself on one lounge, so I sat on the edge of the other. Within minutes, a guy in a crisp white polo shirt holding a tray came over to ask what we would like to order.

"Bloody Mary's all around," Claire said, removing her earbuds. The server laughed. "Claire, you know I can't serve you alcohol. Do you want any food or anything?"

Claire looked at him and frowned. "Okay, three Virgin Mary's then."

"And one order of fries," Chris added. The server nodded and walked away.

Claire winked at me. "Don't worry. I brought a flask." She reached into her striped canvas bag and pulled it out to show me. "We'll mix our own bloodies."

"Better not let Mom see you with that. You know she will probably come by after her tennis game," Chris said.

"Miss Nipples can do whatever she wants. I'm not worried about her." Claire rolled on her side to face me. "She's had so many boob jobs; her nipples are no longer symmetrical. I swear, Sam. When you meet her, be careful not to stare too long at her breasts. It may be unavoidable, though, but do your best."

I didn't know what to say, so I just kind of laughed.

Chris said, "God, Claire. Sometimes you can be such a bitch."

"No, Christopher. That would be all of the time, actually."

"You're telling me," he said. "Are you sure Taylor isn't coming?"

"Christopher, give it up. The answer is no, and anyway, I thought it would be a nice idea to hang out with Sam today. Get to know him better. You really need to move on."

The server brought our mocktails and Chris's french fries. As soon as he turned to walk away, Claire pulled her flask out and emptied vodka into our drinks, first taking a long sip from each cup to make room, all the while staring directly into my eyes. I stared back, unable to look away until she raised her glass, said "clink" and drank. I did, too. Chris took the flask from Claire, drank straight from it before chasing it with his own Bloody Mary.

It's not as if we guys didn't drink at school, we did. Sometimes a guy filched a bottle from his parents' liquor cabinet and brought it back. A few of the older guys had fake IDs and bought beer and shared with us, underclassmen. But these two seemed to take drinking to a whole new level almost. Maybe it was true what books and stuff say about country kids in the midwest. There wasn't much to do, so they drank and drove around cornfields. Or, in this case, hanging out at country clubs.

Chris leaned over. "Jesus, it's already really fucking hot. I'm going to take a dip. Anyone care to join me?"

I would have, except at that moment, Claire handed me a bottle of sunblock and asked me to help her with her back. Chris just sighed and got up from his chaise, walked to the edge of the pool, and

make a big fuss with a tent and a band. It's catered, and thank God; there's an open bar, at least."

"I don't know. I mean, I just got here and haven't spent any time with my aunt. I feel bad, you know. I should probably spend some time with her. Thanks for the invite, though."

"That's fine. Maybe Christopher and I will see you once we've done our duty, that is. Boots and Daddy put on this show of one big happy family and parade Christopher and me around. But then they pretty much forget about us, like always, so we can probably sneak away. I'll text you, okay?"

We were interrupted by a voice calling softly, "Claire. Psst. Claire."

I looked up and saw the same guy with whom Claire was dancing last night standing outside the chain-link fence.

"Drake," Claire said, standing up while reaching behind to tie her top. "Wait there. I'll come out."

I watched her as she walked away. Of course, I did. In that bikini? I couldn't not watch. In a moment, she returned with Drake in tow.

"Where's Chris?" Claire asked.

"I don't know. Swimming, maybe?" I said.

"This is Drake," Claire introduced us. "Drake, this is our new friend, Sam. He's here for the summer."

Drake reached over to shake my hand. He seemed like an ordinary guy. Our age. Short with glasses and shaggy blonde hair. As we exchanged greetings, Chris returned from his swim. He reached for a towel to drape around his shoulders and frowned at Drake.

Claire said, "I invited him to come. It's time you two talked it out."

"Here?" Chris asked.

"Why not here? It is just as good as anywhere," she said. "Come on, Sam. Let's swim."

I followed her to the pool and into the water, which felt great, not too warm. I dunked underwater a few times to clear my head from the heat, vodka, and Claire's body. I looked back to see Drake and Chris sitting opposite each other, talking intensely.

"What's that all about?" I asked Claire.

"Taylor," Claire replied. "It's always about a girl, right?"

I smiled. "Sometimes," I said.

"Well, we are down to the last ten days before we leave on tour, and those two need to figure it out. They've been best friends since first grade. Like Taylor and me. We've all known each other forever, which is why we all need to come together already. We've been planning this tour for a year, practically. Chris has been working on his RV all spring."

I noticed this was the first time Claire didn't call him Christopher. Perhaps the first time I've ever seen her serious.

"We're a family," she concluded. "Families need to work shit out."

I wish that were true, but instead of continuing this conversation, I ducked under the water again and began to swim. I

41

made my way past kids playing to the other side of the pool, where I stayed until Claire got out and joined Chris and Drake. When she waved me over, I leisurely swam my way back before climbing out. The sun was still beaming, and I wondered if it was always this blasted hot in Ohio. It was only early June. What would it be like in July or August, even? I guess I was here to find out.

7

It was a good thing I declined Claire's invitation because Aunt Karen was hosting what she called a "gathering." I ducked inside to take four aspirin before I helped her devil eggs, chop onions for the potato salad, and set up tables in her back yard where everyone would place their potluck dishes. A giant clear plastic tub sat on the table, warming sun tea. Aunt Karen had me slice lemons to float on the top. Prayer flags and paper lanterns hung from the covered porch that held outdoor wicker furniture, and The Allman Brothers floated from the speakers. I stood looking at the ducks on the pond as the sun began its shift to the west for a moment before Aunt Karen's guests started arriving.

Aunt Karen's friends were a completely different crowd from the country club, that's for sure. Most of the people were what I guess you would call hippies. Karen introduced me by their trades, though. Musician, artist, sculptor, farmer, and then their first names. I met Mason, a bearded banjo player who also happened to be a French translator and his wife Jenni, a potter. Jenni offered to teach me to throw clay on her potter's wheel if I wanted. Mason introduced me to Josh, a stretchy yoga teacher and his partner Lauren, a Reiki healer. They owned the local yoga center. They invited me to come by for wheatgrass tea, and Lauren offered to read my chakras, whatever that was. Everyone brought a dish to share, and as I wandered around, people were perched everywhere, eating from plates resting on their knees and drinking tea or wine or beers, whatever they had brought to

"What happened?" I had never heard these stories before.

"Nothing happened. Your mom was always a brainiac, read everything she could get her hands on, like you. Anyway, she scored damn near-perfect SATs, got into Radcliffe to rebel against her bohemian upbringing, met your dad, again another act of rebellion, ha, just kidding. Then, she and your dad settled in New York and had you. Grandma died when you were just a baby and Grandpa shortly after. Maybe because that was just how they were, they met when they were teenagers themselves and did everything together. They farmed this land. Not chickens, though. That's me. I'm the friend of the chicken, even though they're so ill-behaved," she said, shooing one from her porch before continuing.

"Grandpa worked as a carpenter, and Grandma was an English teacher before she homeschooled us. On tour, they would sell the tie-dies and patchwork skirts and dresses Grandma made really, though they could afford their lifestyles. Grandma came from a rather affluent family, so they lived on her trust fund. Trustafarians, they were called back in the day. Not that you would know from looking at them, of course. They looked like the rest of us crazy hippies. But, when Maggie got into Radcliffe, they were able to pay for her tuition, and they did a great job of raising us, in my humble opinion. I miss them every single day. That's why I love living here in the Calico House. It's my only link left to my family. Except you, Sam. My beloved nephew. Except you."

"But you went away to school, too, right?" I asked.

7

It was a good thing I declined Claire's invitation because Aunt Karen was hosting what she called a "gathering." I ducked inside to take four aspirin before I helped her devil eggs, chop onions for the potato salad, and set up tables in her back yard where everyone would place their potluck dishes. A giant clear plastic tub sat on the table, warming sun tea. Aunt Karen had me slice lemons to float on the top. Prayer flags and paper lanterns hung from the covered porch that held outdoor wicker furniture, and The Allman Brothers floated from the speakers. I stood looking at the ducks on the pond as the sun began its shift to the west for a moment before Aunt Karen's guests started arriving.

Aunt Karen's friends were a completely different crowd from the country club, that's for sure. Most of the people were what I guess you would call hippies. Karen introduced me by their trades, though. Musician, artist, sculptor, farmer, and then their first names. I met Mason, a bearded banjo player who also happened to be a French translator and his wife Jenni, a potter. Jenni offered to teach me to throw clay on her potter's wheel if I wanted. Mason introduced me to Josh, a stretchy yoga teacher and his partner Lauren, a Reiki healer. They owned the local yoga center. They invited me to come by for wheatgrass tea, and Lauren offered to read my chakras, whatever that was. Everyone brought a dish to share, and as I wandered around, people were perched everywhere, eating from plates resting on their knees and drinking tea or wine or beers, whatever they had brought to share. A lot of people were smoking pot; not just dab carts guys smoke at school. These folks were smoking flower in glass pipes or rolled into joints. A couple of women were swaying to the music in the living room, but most everyone else had retreated outside to enjoy the summer evening. Luke, the guy from the farmer's market, was loading wood to build a bonfire for later. I decided to make myself useful and offered to help.

When we had finished, I was parched, so I grabbed a mug to fill with sun tea. A friendly, bearded Latino guy handed me a bottle of water. "Drink this instead unless you want to be tripping balls. That's mushroom tea, man," he said.

I accepted his water and took large gulps before I could even speak, I was that parched. "Mushroom tea?" I asked.

"Psilocybins, you know. Magic mushrooms," he said.

"Thanks," I said and drank the rest of his water. "I was loading wood."

"I know. I saw you with Luke. I'm Alex." He shook my hand.

"Sam." I looked at his full beard with envy. I wonder what it felt like to have such a big beard. I mean, I have to shave, of course. But, at almost eighteen, I don't have a full beard growth yet. This guy seemed a little older but younger than most of the crowd here. I wondered what his trade was since Karen had taken such pains to identify everyone else, a thought that made me laugh.

"What's so funny? You didn't drink some of the tea earlier, did you?" Alex asked.

"No. But thanks for telling me. It's just weird, I guess." I swept my arms for emphasis. "I've never been to a 'gathering' or whatever before."

Alex said, "Hey, listen, drink the tea if you want to. I'm not judgmental. I might drink some later, but I like to pace myself, you know? I have to ride my bike home."

"Like a motorcycle?" I asked.

"No, a bicycle. I cycle everywhere I can. I just like it," he said. Alex gestured over to where he had parked his bike. He looked like a cyclist, actually; lean, not very tall. He was a Latino guy who wore jeans, a My Morning Jacket concert t-shirt and a chewed-up, tweed cap perched on his head. When I told him I liked that band, we started a conversation about music. Alex had been to so many shows and music festivals.

"I can't wait until St. Louis, man," he said.

"You're going, too?" I asked.

"On the bus," he said. "With Chris and Claire."

"You, too?" I repeated.

Alex laughed. "Yea, man. There aren't a lot of us in Maywood, but we're a tribe. You ought to consider coming with us. Let's talk about that. But now I wanna climb that tree," he said.

I followed Alex down the lawn.

"This is only the world's greatest Siberian elm. I mean, have you ever seen such a beautiful tree?" he said.

Before I could answer, he had already swung into the lowest branches and started climbing his way up. "Come on, Sam. The view is going to be great up here. Don't you want to see the sunset?"

I followed his lead. I wasn't going to admit that I had never climbed a tree before. Maybe because I was raised in the city and it was illegal to climb trees in Central Park. Nobody climbed trees at St. Philips, but nobody jumped from trestles at prep school, either. As we approached the massive trunk, I thought briefly about that short story we read in class. The one where the writer says something about a nine-year-old boy's concept of time, how it stands solid like a tree you can walk around and around and look at. It was how I pictured that tree when we read the story. Warren, I think the guy's name was. Not the boy, the author. I grabbed the bottom branch, hitched my legs up, and began to climb.

Near the top, Alex and I perched on branches and watched the sun descend over the pond and then fade, leaving pink streaks in the sky before it seemed to sizzle on the horizon. Alex sighed. I heard people below clapping. It was a perfect moment in time, one you wish you could capture in a snow globe to remind yourself later.

8

After we wound our way down from the tree, I decided to load a plate of food from the potluck while Alex wandered to the tea. It's not like I'm against drugs or anything, obviously or I wouldn't have smoked weed last night, but I had never really done anything except drink alcohol and smoke a little bit at school even though all the guys were into vaping. I didn't vape. It just seemed stupid to me. Besides, I already felt high from climbing the tree, a sentiment too sappy to say out loud. I found Aunt Karen sitting on her porch next to Luke when I walked up the stairs. Crosby, Stills, Nash & Young was playing from the speakers. I recognized Aunt Karen's music because my mom played the same music. Even if you hadn't heard a song in years, it seemed to come back really quickly.

"Mushroom tea?" I asked Aunt Karen directly, raising an eyebrow.

"Don't be such a moralist, kid. It's not a bad thing to expand your mind. You didn't drink any of it, though, did you?" she replied.

"No." I laughed. "Did you?"

"Not tonight. Luke and I are sitting this one out. I'm glad you're here this summer, Sam. I know your mom ran away from this house; this life a long time ago, but I think Maggie would have liked you to come here to... I don't know. See what her life was once like, I guess. Before Andrew. Before you. I mean, if you think we're hippies, you should have known your grandma and grandpa. Maggie and I were at Woodstock as babies on their backs. Grew up in their VW bus, homeschooled between Grateful Dead shows," she said.

"What happened?" I had never heard these stories before.

"Nothing happened. Your mom was always a brainiac, read everything she could get her hands on, like you. Anyway, she scored damn near-perfect SATs, got into Radcliffe to rebel against her bohemian upbringing, met your dad, again another act of rebellion, ha, just kidding. Then, she and your dad settled in New York and had you. Grandma died when you were just a baby and Grandpa shortly after. Maybe because that was just how they were, they met when they were teenagers themselves and did everything together. They farmed this land. Not chickens, though. That's me. I'm the friend of the chicken, even though they're so ill-behaved," she said, shooing one from her porch before continuing.

"Grandpa worked as a carpenter, and Grandma was an English teacher before she homeschooled us. On tour, they would sell the tie-dies and patchwork skirts and dresses Grandma made really, though they could afford their lifestyles. Grandma came from a rather affluent family, so they lived on her trust fund. Trustafarians, they were called back in the day. Not that you would know from looking at them, of course. They looked like the rest of us crazy hippies. But, when Maggie got into Radcliffe, they were able to pay for her tuition, and they did a great job of raising us, in my humble opinion. I miss them every single day. That's why I love living here in the Calico House. It's my only link left to my family. Except you, Sam. My beloved nephew. Except you."

"But you went away to school, too, right?" I asked.

She said, "I did. I studied art before I returned home after graduation. Grandma had gotten sick, and I don't know, it just seemed right to me. Maggie settled in New York with Andrew, and you were just a baby. So, I moved back, and Grandpa built my studio, and I guess I've been lucky. I began selling my paintings enough that I can afford to stay here and continue this lifestyle. I'm glad to offer it to you as another home, Sam."

"I'm glad, too," I said.

Luke got up during our conversation to light the fire. I heard the sound of drumming. A few people dragged their wooden drums I would later learn were called djembes, around the fire circle, and started a rhythm. A little away, four women were hula hooping, and one woman was dancing with fire.

"Those are poi," Aunt Karen explained before I could ask. "I tried to study it once, but when I burned my hair, I decided it wasn't worth it." She laughed. "Let's go join the fun."

We walked together to the fire to end the evening. I even drummed a little on a small bongo drum Alex handed me with a nod. I just tapped along and watched the women hula hoop and dance poi as the fire burned long into the night.

9

The summer queen flies by and sees
Her realm of butterflies and bees

"Winterqueen"
Anastasio

It never occurred to me throughout the evening to check for texts from Claire. I knew she asked me to text her, but I had to admit, I wasn't used to being accountable to anyone, but myself and I'd only known her for three days. So, I was a bit perplexed by the multitude of messages I scrolled through. When I awoke around noon, Aunt Karen and Luke had already been up for hours cleaning, and there was still a lot of work to be done, something I didn't mind in the least. It was a beautiful June day, one of those blue-sky days where the air was just bright, and everything seemed so sharply defined. Warm, no humidity and a slight breeze cooled us as I helped Luke cut and stack more wood to replenish what we had burned. All the while, I gazed at the elm tree I had climbed. It was majestic with its enormous trunk and wide-reaching limbs. I felt oddly proud of myself and somehow connected to that tree.

Robert Penn Warren, I suddenly thought. That was the name of the writer. The story was called *Blackberry Winter.* I didn't remember much else about it other than the dead cow floating on the creek after the flood, but the first passage about the concept of time killed me, it did, which is how I remembered it. I looked out at the pond, which reflected light in more sparkles than Mrs. Cutler's diamonds, a thought that propelled me to retrieve my phone from the bedside table where I had left it when I had gotten home from the club the day before. I didn't know what to do. Should I text back or call Claire or not respond at all? She was beautiful, but I would only be in Maywood for the summer, and she was leaving for Phish for most of it. What was the point?   Regardless, I grabbed my phone, my laptop to work on the take-home assignments, and my copy of *The Catcher in the Rye* and trudged back down the stairs.

I wandered my way to Aunt Karen's studio building, where she was working. When I opened the door, the first thing I noticed was silence. Everywhere in Aunt Karen's house, speakers played music seemingly incessantly, so the quiet was noticeable. She stood in her smock with a paintbrush in hand in front of a sizeable half-painted canvas. A lot of Aunt Karen's paintings were larger than life. I think she must stretch them herself for them to be so big, but I don't know for sure. I stood there quietly until she turned her attention to me. I know she heard the door open, so I waited, inhaling the scent of oil, glue, and turpentine. I saw her Chagall chicken painting propped up against the wall, waiting to be completed, next to the collapsible wooden easel she carries to the pond to paint outdoors.

"It's quiet in here," I said, walking up to inspect the painting more closely. What I liked about Aunt Karen's paintings was that when you got close, you saw details that you couldn't see from far away. It's like there were two paintings in one. Walk back away, and the composition formed again. It's like optical illusion art. I knew she

51

liked to adhere fabric to the canvas before she began to layer the paint and then finished with tiny paint markers to create almost invisible lines. Like in this painting, I saw the outlines of columns and a garden bench when I got close. She called her work mixed-media collage.

"I like silence when I paint. The compositions have a rhythm I need to hear, you know. And time seems to stand still and quickly move all at the same time. So, if there's music on, I'm too conscious of linear time, and I don't like that. Instead, I keep a little clock here to keep track of time when I need to," Aunt Karen said.

"I can come back later if you like," I said.

"No, what's up? Has Luke gone yet? He needed to get back to his studio. You know he's a furniture maker, right? He's such a great carpenter. In fact, he helped me with the detail work on the Calico House," she said.

"I didn't know that. But, yes, I think he left. We finished with the wood," I said.

"That was kind of you. What would you like for dinner tonight? Or should we go out? There's a perfect pizza place in town. Does that sound good?" she asked.

"Pizza is great. I need to ask for your advice, though. See, I forgot that Claire was going to text me last night and by the time I looked at the messages, it was today and boy, is she mad. I mean, like mad. Should I text her or call her or what?" I asked.

Aunt Karen put her paintbrush down. "Well, I don't understand why she would be so mad, considering you only met her a few days ago. Did you have definite plans with her? Is that it?"

"Well, not exactly. Her folks were having a party last night, and she invited me, but I told her I wanted to spend time here. And then, when I got home, you had the gathering, and I guess I just got caught up last night and forgot to check for messages. It didn't even occur to me."

"I would be a little cautious with Claire. She's a nice girl, of course, but a little wild," she said.

"Wild, how?" I asked.

"Oh, maybe I shouldn't say *wild*. That sounds a bit dramatic. I mean, what teenaged girl doesn't struggle, right? Her mom and dad divorced when Claire was young before they moved here to Maywood even. It must have been hard for her to grow up without a mother. I'm glad to see her progress as an artist. Years ago, she used to come here for painting lessons when she was a little girl. So cute. God knows you'll be a better influence on her than that Drake kid. He doesn't seem terribly bright, but I guess I shouldn't say that maybe. Aren't *they* still a couple or am I so old, I'm out of the loop?" she asked.

I was startled. "What? No. I think he goes with Taylor."

"Taylor?" Aunt Karen frowned. "I thought Taylor was with Chris. I know they were together, at least at some point. They went to prom together. I saw pictures on social media."

"Okay, but like, should I call her?" I asked.

She said, "Why not? I'll finish in here in a bit, and then tonight, we'll go out for pizza, okay?" She turned back to her canvas, a signal for my dismissal, so I respectfully closed the studio door behind me. A few chickens were pecking around the entrance, but I walked past them down to the elm tree to sit while I gazed at the ducks on the pond before I summoned up my courage to make the call. I really needed to ask someone about those ducks.

Instead of calling, though, I took the easy way out. Well, maybe not the easy way, but I just texted, "I got your messages. Sorry about last night. Karen had a gathering." But then I realized Claire would probably be angry for missing a gathering, so I deleted that last part. Not that I knew Claire very well, but I knew enough to understand she would probably feel left out. So, I just left the sorry part, hit send, and picked up my book to read. I decided it would be better to just keep to myself than to get involved with potential friends who were planning to leave for the summer. What would be the point? Although I must admit, my mind wandered into little fantasies about going away with them. How great would it be on the road for a while, accountable to only ourselves and the next show? I wondered what the RV looked like and contemplated dropping *Catcher* to read *Growing Up Dead.* I had to finish other assignments as well. Geometry. American History and these take-home finals weren't going to write themselves. And the sooner I submitted them, the sooner I could read for fun.

The afternoon melted away as I sat under the tree. I finished my math and got half-way through my history research, so I turned to the summer reading. I got to the part where Holden met that prostitute who called him a crumb-bum. That cracked me up. I had never heard that before. Crumb-bum. That Salinger had a way with words. I didn't get any further in my reading before Aunt Karen called for me. I guess it was already time to get pizza. I still hadn't heard anything back from Claire, though. On the drive into town, I thought about what Aunt Karen said about Claire's mom. Maybe Claire and I had more in common than I thought. Neither of us still had our moms.

10

Mellow Mushroom was the name of the pizza joint, and it looked as psychedelic as it sounded with crazy paintings of Jerry Garcia's head inside a sun and murals of VW buses. There was even a plastic tree with a face at the hostess stand. The music was loud, and there was a crowd drinking beer at the bar. Aunt Karen and I sat, looking at pizza names like *Kosmic Karma* and *Magical Mystery Tour*. There were even gluten-free pizzas. Luke entered a few minutes later, just as our drinks arrived. He sat next to Aunt Karen and put his arm around the back of the booth. I guess they were a pretty serious couple, judging by how often I'd seen the guy in just a few days.

After we placed our order, Luke and Aunt Karen talked about the piece of furniture he shipped today. It was going to a loft in New York. Luke asked me if I knew the address.

"I know the neighborhood, but our apartment is east of that." I took a drink of my soda.

"I'll bet you're glad to be out of the city during summer," Luke said. "I hear it's pretty brutal in terms of heat and humidity. Not that it doesn't get down-right soppy down here, but at least we have the pond to swim, grass, trees. The trestle."

"It's not too bad. Most summers, Dad and I play tennis a few evenings a week after work, which is the best time. Not as hot. But you're right. Spending the summer here is turning out to be great. I do miss the park, though." I said.

"Central Park?" Luke asked.

"No, Gramercy Park," I replied.

Luke turned to Aunt Karen. "Isn't that the park where you need a key?"

"Yes," she replied. "It's the space where they installed the Janey Waney sculpture."

I must have looked sad at the mention of the sculpture because Aunt Karen was quick to switch subjects. "Sam already jumped the trestle," she said just as our pretzel appetizers were delivered. I dug in. They were good.

"I've never been to Manhattan," Luke continued. "I wonder if I'd like to live in a city like that?"

"Somehow, it just doesn't sound much like you." Aunt Karen leaned into him. "But we could visit if you'd like. Maybe we'll go see Sam and his dad for the holidays this year."

"I'm glad you brought up the topic of home and the holidays. It reminds me I need to work on my finals. I have to submit them to school soon." I frowned, thinking of the work I still needed to do. Meanwhile, the server brought over our pizza straight from the oven. I was glad it was so huge; I was still starving. I put down my half-eaten pretzel and helped myself to a slice.

"Relax," Aunt Karen said. "I mean, you just got here, and it's been a busy few days. Don't worry. It will be quiet for a bit while I finish the last pieces for my show. You'll have plenty of time to work if you want it."

I said, "Sure, if I stay away from jumping off trestles, climbing trees, drumming around fires, and hanging out at country clubs with crazy girls."

"What crazy girls?" The voice behind me made me jump up from the booth a bit. I turned around to see Claire standing behind me, hands-on-hips.

"Busted," Luke muttered as he took a swig of his beer.

Aunt Karen straightened her back. "Hello, Claire, dear. Care to join us?"

"Don't mind if I do." She pushed her shoulder to make room on the bench before grabbing my slice of pizza and eating off the corner. I love the corner, so I frowned at her and then helped myself to a new slice.

"I only wanted a bite." She pouted.

"What are you doing here?" I asked as I pointedly took a bite from the corner of my slice.

"Christopher and I ordered a pizza to take out, and I just happened to see you, so I thought I'd come over." She waved behind me. I looked to see Chris standing at the delivery bar. He gave me a half-wave, and I nodded in return. "So, thank you. I just wanted to say hello. I'm going back now. Good to see you, Karen. Luke."

"Good to see you, too," Aunt Karen called out as Claire sauntered back to her table.

Luke winked at me. "Man, have you got troubles." He chuckled.

"I thought you were going to call her?" Aunt Karen kept her voice low.

"I texted her." I grabbed another slice of pizza.

After a moment, Aunt Karen resumed her conversation with Luke, asking about his furniture and their plans for the weekend. I kept eating and wondered how Claire knew I was here. Was it really coincidence? I guess it was bound to happen in a small town, there were only so many places to go, right? I wished I could follow them. I wondered again about the RV and thought about how these kids had all been friends their entire life. I felt a pang thinking about Joel, my best friend in New York. He and I stopped spending time together once Dad shipped me off to boarding school. Even before I left, it was just me and Joel, not a whole group of friends who called themselves family. I felt a pang of envy for that security.

By the time Luke had finished a second beer, and I had stuffed myself with all the pizza I could eat, when we rose from the booth, and I turned around, Chris and Claire were already gone. At least she hadn't called me a crumb-bum, I guess.

11

The next few days fell into a rhythm. I rose about nine or so each morning, but even still, Aunt Karen was always up before me. Unlike the first morning breakfast of bacon and eggs, we usually ate toast or cereal and fruit before she went into her studio, and I took my school stuff down to the elm tree to work. At lunch, we'd break to eat together. Sometimes Aunt Karen wanted to walk before returning to the studio, so I'd join her on a trek around the pond on her property. Other times, she barely ate an apple before racing back to finish her work.

Consequently, within a few days, I had most of my take-home finals completed. In between, I made my way through my summer reading. The more I read, the further Holden got into trouble and even more *troubled*, as Aunt Karen would say. I found myself worried about him, especially when that pimp beat him up. I don't know what I'd do if I found myself in that sleazy hotel in that crazy situation. In between, I couldn't help myself. I started reading *Growing Up Dead.* The first page hooked me. It led me to research wormholes, learning about the Beat culture and the Grateful Dead. Mostly, I loved the narrator's voice. I wanted to learn how to get on top of a trip, play like a prankster, travel around with a group of friends and then, write about the whole experience like Peter Conners. I also looked up *Gilmore Girls.* Apparently, it was a popular television show, but I had never heard of it. I'm still not sure what it had to do with in omnia paratus. Hopefully, I'd have another chance with Claire so I could ask her.

Alex pulled up in a red pick-up truck Friday afternoon as Aunt Karen and I had finished lunch of turkey sandwiches loaded with avocado, tomatoes, and lettuce on whole grain wheat bread. It was good to see his bearded smile again, so I smiled in return.

"Wanna go hiking? I got off work early today and thought I'd swing by and see if you were free," he said to me. "A free afternoon is a rare thing in my life, man. My family owns *Miss Elva's Cocina*, the only Mexican restaurant in town. Miss Elva is my mom. My dad has all of us kids working there almost every waking moment of our lives, me, my two sisters, and my brother. It's a Latino tradition that the family works together. Seriously."

"That sounds nice. A whole family working together," I said.

Alex laughed. "Yes, there are good parts to it, I suppose. You should come by soon. Everyone loves my mom. She will want to feed you until you can't move. Anyway, do you want to go?"

"Sure," I said. "Where are we going?"

"Let's hike up Mt. Gibson. That trail should only take a few hours up and back, so we can make it down before it gets dark. I know that trail like the back of my hand. Go grab some good boots or shoes and a bottle of water, and let's take-off man," he said.

He didn't have to tell me twice. I couldn't wait to hike. We drove only a half-hour before the entrance to the state park. The mountain wasn't a mountain, more of a rolling hill, but as soon as Alex took off, I had to hustle to keep up. He must hike all the time to keep that pace. It was beautiful. A hot day, but the trees on the hillside provided ample shade until one turn lead us up past the treetops. Looking down was dizzying. Like the entire world was spread out below us. Once we reached the top, Alex and I drank huge swigs from our water bottles. I used a bandana to wipe my brow. Alex hadn't even broken a sweat. He grinned at me and then took out a camera from his backpack. I remained silent while he shot photos of the landscape and even one of me, smiling back at him. I thought about how Holden's brother had died and wondered what was worse, having a brother who died or not having a brother at all. I decided on the latter. It was hard enough having your mom die like mine. I wouldn't want to suffer the loss of a brother. Maybe that's why Holden felt so sad and lonely. Perhaps he was still grieving.

"I like you," Alex said suddenly. "You know how to be quiet."

"Thanks, I guess," I replied.

"No, it's a good thing. Seriously, most people feel the need to fill up space with meaningless chatter. I feel there is a lot is going on in that head of yours, even though you don't speak much," he said. "Of course, coming from a Mexican family means there is never a moment of peace. Everyone talks over each other all the time. In both English and Spanish. It can give you a headache."

"I'll bet. I guess it's true that I am quiet. I read a lot. And I come from a small family. I'm an only child."

Alex laughed. "An only child? That was my fantasy when I was a kid."

"Oh, I know what I wanted to ask you. Do you know what happens to the ducks in winter?" I asked.

"What ducks?" he replied.

"Like, any ducks. Like the ducks at Aunt Karen's pond or the ducks in New York. What happens to them in the winter?" I persisted.

Alex laughed. "You are a hilarious dude. Ducks? Nothing happens to them. What do you mean, what happens to them? They just hang out."

"Like all winter? They don't freeze?" I asked, confused.

He said, "No, man. They're ducks, equipped to handle winter. They huddle, I guess. I mean, maybe the New York ducks head a bit further down south like geese, but I don't think so. I think they just hang out. Don't worry about them too much. Ducks are resourceful little things. Ready to head back down? See the sun? It's going to fade soon, and I want to make sure we make it back by sunset."

Even though I didn't get my answer, I followed Alex. We hiked back down the hillside. The temperature was much cooler now that the day was fading. It was only early June, but the Ohio summer had already proven to be humid and hot. I had to admit; I wondered about ducks the entire hike down. I guess it was sort of a weird obsession of Holden's. I wonder why it had also become an obsession of mine, too? I mean, I've never worried about ducks before. I shook my head just as we rounded a bend that ended in a creek. I looked up to see a blue heron perched on a rock. It was prehistoric-looking and made a weird squawk at us before spreading its enormous wings to take flight. I had never seen a heron in real life before. It was cool. Maybe I should worry about herons instead of ducks.

12

A dream it's true
But I'd see it through
If I could be
Wasting my time with you

"Waste"
Anastasio & Marshall

Claire was sitting on the porch with Aunt Karen when Alex dropped me off. He didn't have time to come in, though. He had to get going to see this band he loved called The Tall Boys. He said he would have taken me with him, but the band was playing at Joe's Bar, and I wasn't old enough to go to a bar, so I just thanked Alex for the hike and jumped out of his truck. I took a deep breath and greeted Claire and Aunt Karen, who excused herself so Claire and I could be alone to talk. I hadn't dated many girls, had only taken a few to dances at school, so I wasn't quite sure what Claire expected from me. I didn't even know if we were "dating," especially since we'd never actually been on a date alone yet. She looked beautiful, though. She smelled of that geranium perfume, and her hair and face just killed me. I wanted to both stare and look away at the same time. I felt my face flush just thinking about her in that bikini the other day, so I tried to remember the flood of text messages and her weird behavior at Mellow Mushroom instead. I still felt torn between being attracted to her and being a little disarmed by her altogether. The way she showed up at different times, unannounced, was a way of keeping me off-balance, though.

She said, "I've missed you. I guess I came by to see if you ever wanted to see me again."

"Why wouldn't I want to see you?" I asked.

"You didn't respond to my texts, and then you were so weird at Mellow Mushroom. I guess I thought you weren't interested in me," she said.

"I am," I insisted. "Interested in you. In getting to know you."

"Well, you sure have an odd way of showing it," she said.

"You're right. But it doesn't matter, though. Does it?" I asked.

"What do you mean?" she asked.

"You're leaving, right? Getting on the bus?"

She laughed, "I see you've been reading."

"A little," I admitted. "It's interesting."

"We want you to come with us to St. Louis. It's only two nights, and it will be good," she said. "You can tell your Aunt Karen you're going for a college visit with us. It's at the university."

I laughed. "I don't have to tell her that. She'll get it. I guess my grandparents were Deadheads. They raised her and my mom on tour."

"Are you serious?" Claire asked.

"That's what Aunt Karen told me. You should see the pictures. There's an album, even," I said. I had just discovered the album the night before. Between reading *Growing Up Dead* and seeing my family pictures, I felt proud that I was already part of this world I was just discovering. I excused myself from the patio and walked into the house to retrieve the album. When I returned with it,

Claire exclaimed over almost every picture, so it took nearly an hour to sift our way through.

Claire leaned over and kissed me. At first, the kiss was tentative, but it quickly gained momentum. Suddenly, she stood up and offered her hand to me. "Let's go walk by the pond. I mean, I don't want your aunt to walk out here at any moment. I want to be alone with you."

Of course, I followed. It's what I did, followed Claire. She reached for my hand as we walked to the elm tree where I usually read. Once we had settled at the base, facing the pond, we resumed making out. It got heated quickly. I ran my hands down her sides, not sure if I should try to reach under her blouse or not. In answer to my unspoken question, Claire pulled away and lifted her shirt over her head. She wasn't wearing anything underneath. I felt a little self-conscious, though. I mean, Alex and I had just hiked, and I worried I smelled a little ripe, but that didn't seem to bother Claire the further we went. It was difficult for me to think, but I did stop just before, as I realized I didn't have a condom with me. I didn't usually carry condoms, but I owned some, more for form's sake than anything else. Our school nurse handed them out like candy, practically. The last thing our school wanted to be the scandal of unwanted pregnancies. Not that the school condoned sex, but I think they were just practical. Besides using them as water balloons to drop out of dorm windows, I didn't know how many of them were used as intended. I mean, guys bragged all the time, but you knew most of it was bullshit.

"Claire?" I pulled away. "Should we, like, slow down? I mean, I don't have anything with me."

"Oh, I do. Here." She handed me a condom from her back pocket. Suddenly, I didn't feel like continuing. I knew most guys would have jumped at this chance, but I was suspicious. Did she carry condoms all the time, or did she plan this? It wasn't like I was a chauvinist or anything. Girls were supposed to be as sexually responsible as guys, but aside from making out with Margaret Reed at the freshman mixer, I didn't have much more experience than that.

She asked, "What's wrong? It's not like you have to worry about my virtue. I'm not a virgin."

Before I thought, I spoke, "That's what kind of bothers me, though." Wow, was that the wrong thing to say. Claire's eyes blazed, and she quickly pulled on her shirt.

"Maybe I had the wrong idea about you," she said. "Maybe this was all a big mistake."

"I'm sorry. That wasn't what I meant. I like you a lot. I mean, I like you."

We started making out again. Without hesitation this time, I took the condom and used it. I wished I could say it was an earth-shattering moment, but the truth was, it was much like every other cliché of a guy's first time. It was over in a matter of seconds. As I lay on top of her trying to catch my breath, I whispered, "I'm sorry."

Claire nudged me off her and dressed. "You seem to say 'I'm sorry' a lot, Sam. What is it they say? Love means never having to say,

'I'm sorry'? Because I think I'm falling in love with you. Do you have feelings for me?"

"Of course, I do. I'm very attracted to you. I think you're beautiful," I said.

She sighed. "Beautiful. Yes, I guess that will have to be enough for now. But give me time. I'll make you fall in love with me."

That was such a startling remark, and I had nothing to say. I just knew I had a sinking feeling. Of course, I felt a sense of responsibility for this girl. We had just had sex, and I didn't think I was the kind of guy who would ever be a player. And then, I laughed at myself. I don't need to overanalyze every single thing to death. Maybe I should just relax and let this run its course. I mean, it was only for the summer, and then I went back to school, and life would resume as normal. How serious could this all be?

Claire rolled over and sighed. "I'm glad our first time is at the edge of the pond. I just love anywhere the earth meets the water."

"You mean the shoreline?" I asked.

"Yes. It doesn't matter which body of water. An ocean. A river. A lake. This pond. Anywhere the earth meets the water is the same earth even when it's a different body of water. Makes me feel less disjointed. Comforted knowing it's the same earth that touches the edges of any water."

I thought about the East River I walked a million times in my childhood versus the Atlantic Ocean where we'd vacation in South Carolina versus this pond. Claire was right. It is comforting to think it's the same earth no matter which body of water it meets. I looked at her with newfound appreciation. I had never met anyone who thinks like her.

13

The next day, I wrote. I keep a journal, but I hadn't written anything since I arrived at Maywood. Because I had a lot to say, it wasn't until late afternoon that I even moved from my usual spot at the base of the elm tree. When I stood to stretch, my back cracked in about a million places. Because Aunt Karen was still working in the studio, I decided to try to make dinner. I can't cook much, but I could boil pasta and add spices to a jar of marinara. She entered the house as my sauce was bubbling nicely, garlic bread was browning in the oven, and I was chopping up vegetables for a salad.

"You're making dinner, Sam?" she asked, smiling.

"An attempt anyway," I joked. Then I asked, "Should I set a place for Luke, too?"

Aunt Karen said, "Yes, thank you. He should be here within the hour. You like him, don't you?"

"Of course, I like him." I felt flattered she asked my opinion. I asked, "So, you guys are serious?"

"As serious as we'll ever be," she said. "No. It's good. We both have careers and stay busy. He runs the farmer's market, as you know, as well as his furniture business. I've got my art and the chickens and now, you. We're happy, I guess."

"I'm glad," I said. "You deserve to be happy."

"As you do," Aunt Karen said. "Claire makes you happy?"

I laughed. "I'm not sure yet, but it's cool. She did ask me to go with them to St. Louis next week. So, I wanted to talk to you about that."

"Oh, so your dinner isn't just a nice gesture, but more of a bargaining tool?" she teased.

"What? No," I said. "Well, not entirely, anyway."

We laughed. She opened a bottle of wine and lit the candles on the table as Luke walked in. I served, and we ate. It wasn't the best pasta I had ever eaten, but I was proud to have cobbled together a dinner. We were just finishing when Claire rapped on the back door.

"Claire, come in," Aunt Karen stood to welcome her. "Are you hungry? Sam cooked tonight."

"And it was good," Luke said. "Thank you, Sam."

"No," Claire replied. "I've already eaten, but I appreciate it. I came by to see if Sam would like to come over to see the bus. Or RV, but Chris insists we call it a bus."

"Chris has an RV? When did he get that?" Luke asked.

"In March. It was a big production, but Dad finally agreed, so they drove up to Troy to buy it," Claire said. "But he's been working on it for months, and we're finally ready. Good thing, as we leave first thing Tuesday morning. St. Louis is over a seven-hour drive."

"So, Alex is going, too?" Aunt Karen asked.

"Yes. Alex, Chris, Taylor, maybe Drake, me and Sam, if he can go," Claire said.

"I guess it should be alright. Two shows and then home, right?" Aunt Karen said.

"Exactly. We'll definitely be home after St. Louis. The next show we're planning isn't until the following week. June nineteenth at Blossom," Claire said.

"Oh, I love Blossom," Aunt Karen said. "That's my childhood venue."

"It is?" Claire said. "I was planning to create an installment there, in the lot. But at the rate I'm moving, the pieces probably won't be ready, so I will just install it at SPAC."

"What's SPAC?" Luke asked.

"Saratoga Performing Arts Center," Claire answered. "It's the only other venue that has enough green space for the project I'm creating. Camden is too urban for what I'm trying to do."

"What are you working on?" Aunt Karen asked. "Your show at the co-op was powerful. I wanted to tell you that."

"Thank you. These new pieces are feminist as well, but entirely different. I'm striving to build community with the pieces. They'll be interactive, to an extent," Claire said. "Have you ever heard of Marjorie Minkin? From Boston? Her work is amazing. I've been studying it, but I don't have access to Lexan. Do you work with that material?"

"No," Aunt Karen said. "I've never experimented with plastics. It sounds incredible. What's her name again? I'll look her up."

"Marjorie Minkin," Claire repeated. "Her work isn't feminist, per se, but she is Mike Gordon's mom. Mike Gordon, the bass player of Phish. At first, I thought using Lexan would be perfect for a part of this new series, but I'm not sure I want to risk trying to use a new material I've never worked with before. These pieces are too important. I want to include them in my college portfolios."

I had finished loading the dishwasher, so I put my hand on Claire's shoulder to direct her out the door. I was anxious to see the RV. I grabbed my red hunting hat from the peg near the door and turned to Aunt Karen and said, "Okay, so I'll be home before midnight?"

"Have fun," she said, waving us away.

"That was easy," Claire said as she pulled her car out of the driveway.

"I know. Maybe too easy," I said.

"Why?" she asked. "Don't you want to come with us? It's going to be a blast. I promise."

"I do. I'll be able to submit my take-home finals soon, and I can't imagine what it would be like to be here without you. Without all of you," I said.

"Tonight is our planning night. You know. Who's going to bring what. Like to eat and stuff," she said.

"So, you're working on art to take on tour?" I asked.

"I was hoping I'd have at least the first piece done for Blossom," Claire said. "It just depends on how much work I get done and how far the pieces evolve. It's a process."

We drove through town, past even more cornfields to her parents' neighborhood, which was a gated community near the country club. I had to smile, thinking about New Yorkers' impressions of the Midwest, like Ohio, where there were supposed to be nothing but cornfields, hunters, and farmers with hayseed stuck in their teeth; meaning, provincial people who were undoubtedly not intellectual nor sophisticated. Another New Yorker's stereotype pictured the typical Midwestern suburbanite, like Claire's family. These McMansion dwelling, mini-van-driving set flooded the city during the holidays to see the tree and to ice skate at Rockefeller Center while snapping endless pictures and asking pesky directions.

In this case, the stereotype about McMansion neighborhoods in the middle of cornfields was true. Claire's house was a large two-story white brick house with a black roof and black shutters. Columns flanked the front door. The driveway curved as a semi-circle, but Claire veered right and parked in front of the four-car garage. She hit the garage door remote to reveal the RV. There it was—the bus.

Before I could say anything, though, Chris charged toward us, waving his hands back and forth. "Shut the damn door, Claire," he said.

"I will," she said. "Once we come in."

Drake stood next to Chris, shielding his eyes as if it was the middle of the day and not already dusk. As soon as we walked in, Claire hit the remote again to close the garage door behind us. "Happy?" she asked.

"Better," Chris grumbled.

There were camping chairs set up outside the RV, and Phish was playing from portable speakers. On the camping table were a laptop, cell phones, a notebook, pens, a tube of JB Weld, a roll of painter's tape, two dab carts, some screwdrivers, and wrenches.

"How long have you had this?" I asked Chris before I remembered Claire had already told Luke at the house. I had to say something, though. I was a bit surprised by how nice it was. I half-expected a converted school bus or one of those 1970's conversion vans. Not an RV, you'd expect to see old retired people or suburban families driving.

"George bought it for me in March, I think. I've been working on it ever since. The engine is good, though," he said.

"Good thing since you're not a mechanic anyway," Claire said. "But Dad knows that, or he wouldn't have bought you such a good vehicle. He spoils you, I swear."

"It's a Class C Thor Motor Coach Citation," Chris said with pride. "A Blue Tech turbo engine. Big enough for us to all fit, but small enough for me to drive."

"It's a Mercedes," Claire said.

"It might be a Mercedes, but we're calling it *Suby Greenberg,*" Chris said.

"I thought you called it *The Bus,*" I said. I wanted to show off my knowledge from reading *Growing Up Dead.*

Chris grinned at me and said, "We're getting on the bus, but this vehicle will be known as *Suby Greenberg.* And anyway, since we're going on tour with Phish, it's called *getting on the train.*"

"Okay," Claire sighed. "Train. Bus. Whatever you call it. Spill. Why the name?"

"Because when George agreed to buy this for us, for me, I mean, he told me a story about his old favorite car, which was a Subaru SVX. He loved that car, apparently, and drove it until it was held together only by duct tape and JB Weld, which also gave me this idea I'll tell you about in a minute. The point is, I thought we could pay tribute to George by calling the RV *Suby Greenberg*," Chris explained. "And, of course, a nod to Phish, too."

"So, what have you been working on?" I asked.

Chris grinned and opened the door. "This. Come on. This, you'll want to see."

I climbed in. Even though the outside of the RV looked ordinary, the inside was anything but. Tapestries draped across the ceiling, and beads separated the bed in the back from the rest of the interior space. Chris had painted the cabinets purple, blue, and green on top of which he decorated with Phish stickers. There was a lava lamp on the table in front of a sofa covered in tie-dye. It smelled like incense and patchouli, scents with which I'd become familiar in my short time at Aunt Karen's house.

Chris began pointing out features. "There's a bunk overhead, see? Two guys can easily sleep up there. The big bed, of course, but the sofa also pulls out to another bed. I figure that fits five of us easily. Now, there's a small bathroom, see?" He pulled open the door. Inside was a narrow shower, a small sink, and even a toilet. "But I think we should use that as sparingly as possible. Pee only, for sure. Otherwise, it will stink up the whole joint."

I laughed but nodded once I saw how severe Chris was.

He continued. "And if there are going to be six of us. If Drake comes—"

"I'm trying!" Drake yelled. "I told you, it's a matter of figuring it all out with my 'rents."

"If there are six of us," Chris continued, "I guess we'll have to use an air mattress and take turns. You'll need a sleeping bag."

"I'm sure Aunt Karen has one I can borrow," I said as Chris opened the cabinets to reveal the storage capacity.

"And now for the final detail," Chris declared. We followed him out of the RV. He held up the tube of JB Weld in one hand and reached for a metal disc in the other. He turned to reveal the disc as the classic symbol of the Grateful Dead, a *steal your face* emblem.

"I didn't dare paint the outside so George wouldn't freak out, but we are going to adhere this baby over the Mercedes emblem on the front," Chris said.

"Okay," Drake said. "You do know once we use JB Weld, it's not coming back off."

"That's the whole point," Chris insisted. He uncapped the tube and frowning in concentration, squeezed the glue around the rim, finishing with a solid X in the center. "Tape?" he barked.

"Right here," Drake said, holding a roll of green tape in his hand.

We all watched as Chris carefully positioned the *steal your face* over the Mercedes symbol. Drake pulled large sections of tape that Chris used to hold it in place.

"Once the glue dries, we can remove the tape, but I don't want it to slide off," Chris explained.

"Makes sense," I said. "I hope it holds."

"It will hold," Chris assured me. "Otherwise, George wouldn't have used it on his Subaru. Now, let's talk about food and supplies."

Claire grabbed the notebook and pen and settled into one of the camping chairs.

"Wait," Chris said. "I thought you had an excel spreadsheet going for this."

"I do, Christopher," she said with a withering tone. "First, I'll take notes while we plan, then I will enter it all into a spreadsheet for you, weirdo."

"There is nothing weird about being a good captain," Chris insisted.

"Where's Alex?" I asked as I leaned against the RV.

"Working," Drake responded. "He picked up an extra shift at his family's restaurant so he can leave with us on Tuesday." Drake perched on the other camping chair, frisbee on his lap, busy rolling a joint. When he finished, we decided to step back outside to smoke it. Just then, Taylor pulled up on a golf cart.

"Perfect timing," Claire said, walking to Taylor to hug her hello.

"I just got done with my workshop," Taylor said.

"She writes poetry," Claire explained.

"Not well," Taylor grimaced.

"Don't say that," Chris said. "That's bullshit. I don't even like poetry, and I love your work."

"That's because you don't know any better," Taylor laughed.

"I do so," Chris insisted. "I've been to Holler."

"What's Holler?" I asked.

"The monthly poetry reading in town," Taylor explained. "You are welcome to come to the next one, Sam. I'll have to check for sure, but I think it will be an evening after we return from Blossom."

"So, you are going to Blossom?" I asked.

"We're going as far as we possibly can," Chris replied. "The plan is St. Louis, Blossom, then down to North Carolina, back up to Maryland for the two Merriweather shows and if we are lucky, we can continue to Maine, on to Camden, SPAC, Fenway, Mohegan, and Alpine."

"Lucky how?" I asked.

"In terms of tickets, time, and permission," Claire explained. "We don't have tickets for all of these shows. I'm not sure how it's going to work, being on the road until July, and I'm not sure Dad will even let us do all of these shows."

"If we ask permission, that is," Chris said.

"Well, it's not as if we're just going to take off, Christopher, and you know that," Claire said.

Chris passed the joint to me and replied, "Let's just take this one step at a time, okay?"

We opened the garage door once we cashed the joint. Claire took notes as we decided who would bring bread, cheese, cereal, fruit, chips, and all the other food we could think to add to the list. Chris changed the music from Phish to another band he liked called Pigeons Playing Ping Pong. The upbeat tempo was an optimistic backdrop to our mood. Once Chris was satisfied we had considered everything we needed to bring with us Tuesday, Claire drove me back home. On the drive, I asked her about Chris and Taylor.

"They had been a couple since Freshman year. Pretty serious, which was strange for me because Taylor and I have been friends since day one. But I adjusted to the situation, and everything was fine until just before prom when Taylor made out with Drake. That was pretty bad; I have to admit. Taylor and Chris had it out at prom, and ever since, things have been shaky between them. Not to mention, Drake is Chris's best friend. Oh, the drama of a small-town romance," she concluded.

"Is that what they were discussing at the club the other day?" I asked.

"Yes. I talked with Drake at the trestle, and he feels terrible about what happened. It's not as if he and Taylor slept together. It was one drunken, stupid kiss. Not enough to tear our entire group apart. At least, I hope it's not."

"So, you didn't go out with Drake?" I asked. "I mean, he's never been your boyfriend?"

"No," Claire said. "What gave you that idea? He was my prom date, but just as friends." I guess that cleared up Aunt Karen's confusion. I was relieved Claire hadn't dated Drake. I mean, I'm sure she had dated plenty of guys before me. I just didn't need actually to know them if I don't have to. And I liked that Drake kid. From what I knew of him anyway.

"Is that why Drake is being so vague about coming on tour with us?" I asked. "Because of Taylor?"

"Probably," Claire said. "It could just be his parents. They aren't like my dad, who gets it or Karen, even. Taylor's parents are musicians, so they are understanding. Drake's parents are more traditional. Definitely not as open-minded. So, we'll see, right?"

"Taylor's parents are musicians?" I asked.

"Chamber music," she replied. "They both have, like real jobs. Her dad is a dentist, and her mom works as a realtor, but Taylor's mom plays the cello, and her dad plays the violin. They belong to a local chamber music group."

"A chamber group that plays Phish?" I asked.

"What?" Claire laughed. "No. Not Phish. That's funny. I mean that because they still play music, they understand us wanting to go to shows more than Drake's parents who are very buttoned-up and strict."

We pulled into the driveway of the Calico House. Aunt Karen left the porch lights on for me, but the rest of the house was dark. I leaned over to kiss Claire, and we made out for a while in the front seat.

"Do you want to come in with me?" I asked her.

"No," she sighed. "It's late. I'm going to head back home. We'll have plenty of time alone together when we leave."

"I can't wait," I said before I got out of the car.

"I'm glad you are here, Sam. I mean, I'm glad I've gotten to know you and that you are coming with us," she said as a good-bye.

"Me, too," I said and then kissed her one last time. I felt happy walking into the house. This summer was shaping up into more of an adventure than I could have anticipated, and I couldn't wait for Tuesday.

JUNE 11, 2019

CHAIFETZ ARENA, SAINT LOUIS UNIVERSITY
St. Louis, MO

SET 1: Cool Amber and Mercury, 46 Days, Stash, Nellie Kane > Free > Theme From the Bottom, Tube, Drift While You're Sleeping

SET 2: No Men In No Man's Land > Bathtub Gin > Ghost -> Piper -> Blaze On > Joy > Simple > Limb By Limb, Slave to the Traffic Light

ENCORE: Turtle in the Clouds, Character Zero

14

It's not an experience if they can't bring someone along

"Birds of a Feather"
Fishman, McConnell, Gordon, Anastasio. & Marshall

Chris arrived in *Suby Greenberg* as promised, early Tuesday morning, and I was ready. I had submitted the take-home finals to my teachers and only had the rest of *The Catcher in the Rye* to finish, which was fine. It was summer reading anyway. I brought it as well as my copy of *Growing Up Dead.* In addition to a sleeping bag, my duffle bag of clothes, and my journal, Aunt Karen had packed food, snacks, eggs, and water for us to bring. Not only did we plan to get to St. Louis in plenty of time for the show, but time was also on our side. St. Louis is an hour behind us, on Central Time, so it was like we gained an hour in our journey, which was cool, almost magical. As it turned out, Drake was not allowed to come with us. Alex sat upfront with Chris while Claire, Taylor, and I hung out in the back. We listened to Moe. and Umphrey's McGee on the drive, and upon my request, Taylor read some of her poems aloud. I hadn't read much poetry outside English class, but her work was excellent.

"Recite the Larkin poem for Sam," Claire said.

"Do you know it, Sam?" Taylor asked me. "Philip Larkin? *This be the Verse?*"

"No," I answered. "You memorized it?"

"You'll see," Claire said.

"Okay," Taylor pulled herself up straighter and launched. *"They fuck you up, your mum and dad..."*

Claire and I applauded her when she finished. I was laughing half in shock, half in recognition of the truth of those words.

"Are you going to study creative writing in college?" I asked her.

"That's the plan," Taylor said. "After attending the Reynolds Writing Program at Denison last summer, I've been inspired to take my writing more seriously."

"So, you're going to attend Denison?" I asked.

"My first choice is Kenyon," she said. "But Denison is my back up school. I liked Denison, but Kenyon has a better writing program, and *The Kenyon Review* is a well-respected literary journal. My parents want me to apply to a historically black college, though."

"They're still after you about that?" Claire asked.

"Howard, Spellman, or Wilberforce," Taylor sighed. "They say it's important since I've always lived in an almost all-white neighborhood, and was one of the only black kids at school, but I don't care about that. I only care about the best school to study writing."

"You have loved Kenyon since middle school," Claire said.

"That's true," Taylor said, then she looked at me. "I was chosen for an accelerated reading program in middle school. They assigned us all these other books, but when we went on the field trip to Kenyon and attended lectures, that was it for me. It's the only place I've ever wanted to go to college. It's my dream school."

"Where do you plan to apply, Sam?" Claire asked. "What's your dream school?"

"I'm not sure yet," I answered. "I guess I don't have a dream school, but my mom attended Radcliffe. My Dad went to Harvard for undergrad and NYU for grad school. I don't know. I guess I always assumed I'd go back to New York for college."

Claire smiled. "Maybe we can go to college in New York together."

"You're applying to schools in New York?" I asked.

"NYU and the New School are my two first choices," she said. "I'm also going to apply to RISD and The Savannah College for Art and Design."

"What does your mom do?" Taylor asked. Claire nudged her, but I answered.

"She died," I said. "Three years ago."

"Oh," Taylor said. "I'm so sorry. I didn't know."

Before I could respond, Alex interrupted. "We're here, guys! Look! You can see the tip of the arch."

Chris pulled into St. Louis's one downtown RV park. Over the buildings, I could see the tip of the arch. Alex and Chris jumped out to get our pass from the main office. Within minutes it seemed, we were parked and hooked up.

"Look," Claire said. "They have a pool."

"I don't think we'll have any time for swimming," Chris said. "It's almost three now. We need to get going if we're going to have any fun before the show."

"Okay," Claire sighed. "Taylor and I will be ready in fifteen minutes."

"What do they have to do to get ready?" Chris mumbled after them. "All I need is my backpack and our tickets."

Alex laughed. "Relax, man. That's women. The day is ours. Time is on our side. We're cool."

"I guess it gives us time to hit the cart," Chris said, leaning against the RV. "Should we open the canopy and get out the chairs?"

"I'm sure they won't be that long," Alex said. "But, you could hang the flag."

"What flag?" I asked.

Chris ducked into *Suby* and returned, holding a flag folded up in plastic. He unwrapped and unfolded it to reveal the Phish logo. Alex and I helped him push the flagpole through the end and hang it from *Suby*. We stood back to admire it. It looked great. It kind of made up for the steal-your-face emblem Chris had JB welded over the Mercedes emblem. Even though he had taped it in place, it was just a bit crooked. Chris insisted it was intentional. We knew better than to argue.

"We got these mesh bags in case all bags need to be see-through," Claire said as she stepped out of *Suby* with Taylor. The girls seemed to glow from the body glitter they liberally applied to their shoulders, necks, and faces. Their sparkly bodies looked pretty in their sundresses. I looked down at my t-shirt and shorts and shrugged. Chris was wearing similar clothes, but Alex was dressed differently in his chewed tweed hat and suspenders over a button-up short-sleeve shirt and jeans. I guess I was okay. I wasn't used to considering clothes as I spent most of my life in collared shirts, ties, and khakis – the dress code at St. Philips. I'm glad I remembered to bring my red hunting hat, I thought, as I pulled it on my head, deciding it was costume enough.

Chris took some time moving his stuff from the backpack he would leave behind to Claire's mesh bag. He handed me a glass pipe. "Here, stash this somewhere. We'll get patted down, but not everywhere."

I put the pipe into the pocket of my shorts. Meanwhile, Alex called for a Lyft to drive us to the venue.

"Tickets?" Chris asked as he handed each of us a ticket.

"Seriously," Alex said. "This is going to be a ritual. Before we leave for any show, Captain needs to call for tickets. That way, we'll be extra sure."

Once we piled into the Lyft, I asked Claire, "How did you know about the mesh bags?"

"Phish chicks," she said.

"Chicks?" I asked, to clarify.

"Yes. A Facebook group of women who are avid Phish phans. They know everything," she said.

"Considering the ratio of men to women," Taylor interjected, "It's good to know that there is a community."

"Ratio?" I asked.

"Ha, yes," Claire explained. "Phish is a boy band. There aren't as many women as men in their fan base. So, what women there are at the shows need to stick together."

"But, it's not like that for the Grateful Dead," I insisted, thinking about Aunt Karen and her friends.

"Totally different scene, man," Alex said from the front seat. "I've been to both. Well, at least what they call Grateful Dead now. But you know what I mean. Bobby's band with John Mayer and Oteil. Dead and Company."

The first thing we saw when we piled out of the Lyft was a Ben and Jerry's truck. We were amazed to learn the scoops were free. Chris and I chose *Phish Food.* Claire and Taylor chose *Cherry Garcia,* and Alex was thrilled because they had a coconut vegan ice cream. He and a woman wearing a red-spangled headband clinked cones like one would with wine glasses.

"Where is the lot?" Alex asked her, looking around.

"You need to walk past the baseball fields and through campus," she explained. "It's almost like they said okay, you can have Shakedown, but only up here." She gestured with her arm. "It might be because it's a college campus? But watch out. The nitrous mafia set up. Seriously, it's the craziest thing. There are kids playing baseball and families walking, and meanwhile, there is more nitrous than I have ever seen."

"Wow," Alex said. "Thanks for the heads up. Have a good show."

"You, too, kids. Enjoy," she said, as we walked where she directed in search of Shakedown.

"We are not going to blow all our money on nitrous the first minute," Chris said.

"Not even one tiny little balloon," Claire mock-whined, wringing her hands together dramatically with a charming smile in place.

"Not even one," Chris said.

"You're so bossy, Captain," Claire said, but she wasn't mad. Nobody was mad. It was a summer afternoon at a Phish show.

Shakedown, Phish lot, or whatever you want to call it, consisted of two rows in the parking lot where vendors set up their tables. They sold everything from grilled cheese sandwiches, pizzas, stir-fry, burritos, and cold beers; to glass pipes, t-shirts, hand-sewn skirts, glow sticks, and that's just naming a few of the wares available. You could come to a Phish show with nothing but a pocket of cash and find everything you need to succeed, at least according to Cosmic Charlie, this old guy we met when Alex stopped to examine his djembe drums. Cosmic Charlie asked me, "Is this your first show?"

When I said yes, he cautioned me. "Don't let the hatas ask you if you've read the fucking book. Just tell them you have. And watch your money. Don't leave it in your back pocket if you're gonna walk Shakedown. There's a reason it's called that, ya know. What I suggest is you carry your cash in your sock, like me. It may be smelly money, but at least you'll have it when ya need it. Also, stay close to your tribe. Watch out for each other. It's not like the good old days of The Grateful Dead, that's for sure. There are too many kids on the lot. You be careful, hear?"

Claire kissed him on the cheek and reassured him we would be just fine while I listened to the old man and moved my wallet from my back pocket into my sock. Good thing I had paid attention to Alex, who advised me to wear socks and sneakers. We began our walk down the lot, stopping to examine wares when we were interested. Everywhere we stopped, we met new people who became our friends of sorts for the next two days. Whenever we hit the lot from then on, people would yell out greetings to us, and we hug them like it had been days, not hours since we last saw them. I couldn't decide if it was the fakest or most authentic experience of my life.

We stopped at the end of an aisle to watch one of those parachutes we used in gym class in elementary school. The circle of people held their edges and waved the parachute up and down until someone signaled, and they all sat down under the dome until it deflated. Then, they started again. Other guys were throwing Frisbees, and some were playing hacky sack. Girls with big bubble rings were creating huge bubbles that floated overhead—grown adults playing like children. We approached a group of people under a rainbow canopy because the girls were offering henna and make-up. Claire and Taylor wanted to play with the sparkles, and by the time we left, their whole faces decorated with stars and swirls. We walked back through campus to the baseball field park and sat on the grass. We watched kids dressed in their little league uniforms walk with their parents to and from the baseball field. At the same time, groups of other people clustered, smoking joints, laughing, enjoying the summer day, the pop of balloons interrupting. The sun began its descent to the west. Claire pulled clover and wove rings she put on both of our heads. Any other time I would have felt stupid, here I just left it.

Finally, it was time for the show to start, so we began our trek to join the crowd to line up to enter the venue. Security patted down the men, and every bag was opened and searched by the security team who did not look happy to greet the phans. I was just grateful I remembered to move the pipe Chris gave me from my pocket to the waistband of my boxers.

We snaked our way through the crowd to the section of our seats just as the crowd roared. I looked up to see Phish take the stage. Trey picked up his guitar and launched the first song, *Cool Amber and Mercury*. The crowd started freaking out when Page repeated the *Faceplant Into Rock* sample. They closed first set with *Drift While You're Sleeping*, a song I was already learning by heart. In between, I danced as I had never moved before. It was like I suddenly forgot to be self-conscious, and what helped is that everywhere I turned, people were grooving. Nobody sat down, and everywhere I looked, people were grinning. I can't say I had completely surrendered to the flow, whatever that was. But I felt freer than I ever had before, and it wasn't hard to let everything else leave my head with how consuming the music was.

At set break, we made our way to the lobby in search of restrooms. A woman tapped me on the shoulder and handed me an Uno card. "For great dancing," she said.

"Perfect," Chris said as I showed it to him while we waited in line to use the restrooms. "Now, you can start your collection."

"Collection?" I asked, turning the card over. It was a green number one card with the word cactus as well as a drawing of a cactus on it.

"The goal is to collect a complete deck while on tour," he explained.

"I got a red four," Claire showed me after we all reconnected and waited in yet another line to get waters. "If we can even collect a deck from all of us together, I think that might be cool. We can decorate a deck to have ready for Blossom. I brought a deck with us just for this reason. We can start working tomorrow on our deck to pass out."

"That might be cool," I said, thinking about Ali's baseball mitt in *The Catcher of the Rye.* He had written lines of poetry all over the glove, something that Holden cherished. I wondered if you could only decorate Uno cards with Phish references or if it didn't matter if we used lines of poetry. I would especially like to use the lines of that Larkin poem Taylor read. There wasn't time to ask more questions before second set launched. The first hour of music was rocking until they launched into a song called *Joy* I had never heard before. By the end of it, I was almost in tears. My mother's name wasn't Joy, but they could have been singing to her. *Come step outside your room/ We want you to be happy/ 'Cause this is your song, too* just broke me up. I had to take a few deep breaths just to stop the tears that were threatening to well up. I did not expect to be thinking about my mother. She was the last person on my mind all day. I wasn't sure what to do with my feelings. I felt stripped raw. I followed the music through *Limb by Limb* and *Slave to the Traffic Light*, feeling waves of grief mingled with awe at the beauty of the show. It was a weird experience. I think I may have heard Trey tease that *Off to See the Wizard* song from *The Wizard of Oz*, but I couldn't be completely sure since it was so bizarre in this context. Before I could process it all, the crowd was chanting "Let's Go, Blues," and the show was over. I filed out of the stadium, holding tightly to Claire's hand as she weaved behind Alex, Chris, and Taylor. We had managed to stay together for the entire show, something that would not always happen for the rest of tour.

The first thing we all wanted as soon as we got back to *Suby* was food. Alex took control, organizing us to assemble cheese sandwiches he sprinkled with garlic salt before cooking on a skillet on the mini burner. Taylor tore open a bag of chips as Chris passed around the dab cart and cued up Grateful Dead on the stereo.

"Time for tequila!" Claire declared, holding up a bottle. She took a long pull, grimaced, and passed the bottle around. When it was my turn, I was a bit more hesitant, but then drank a small sip. It burned my throat and tasted a bit like dirt to me, like how I would imagine actual soil would taste.

"Too bad we don't have any limes," Taylor said.

"Or salt," Claire agreed.

"I'll take it how I can get it," Chris said, drinking.

While everyone was busy with the bottle, I dug in my duffle bag for my copies of *Growing Up Dead* and *The Catcher in the Rye*.

Because I annotate my text, I immediately found the passage on page forty-nine:

> *As the crowd filtered out of Kingswood, I looked around and understood that I had just partaken in something very special. A ceremony that I had entered almost unwittingly but had nonetheless yearned for. Although it was only my first show, I already felt a part of the scene, one of the family among the grinning Deadheads filtering out into the parking lot. I knew I would be back again. And again.*
>
> .

Conners was right. I had just partaken in something special. I was hooked and ready to continue on this path.

I then skimmed through chapter twenty-three of *Catcher* and wondering if I should look up the Robert Burns poem. I kept thinking about Holden wanting to stand at a cliff to catch the thousands of kids. How he misunderstood the line *if a body meet a body coming through the rye* as *if a body catch a body*. I wondered why Holden was so intent in catching the kids. I mean, I understood it was a metaphor, duh. But what was so special about childhood anyway? Everyone I knew was pretty much in a hurry to survive adolescence and to move on with our lives. I mean, I guess my early childhood was happy when Mom was alive, but for the past three years, I felt like I'd been biding my time, studying only to get into college to escape boarding school. This summer was the first time I'd felt light-hearted like I guess Holden believed children were, but also, more mature than I'd ever been.

"What are you doing?" Claire asked as she handed me a grilled cheese. I bit in and was grateful for the hot sandwich, as we hadn't eaten anything since the ice cream before the show.

"What if we decorated our Uno deck with lines of poetry?" I asked. "Or does it have to be Phish related only?"

"It can be whatever we want it to be," Claire said. "We could even decorate a deck with lines from your books if you like." Claire unearthed the Uno deck she brought along with a collection of Sharpies.

"I don't have any magazines or anything to use to collage," she said. "But if we start with the words, we can do the collage part when we get back home. Or we can just draw on them with these Sharpies. However, it evolves, I guess. I'll start with the Larkin poem, and you start with lines from your books, and let's see where it leads."

I smiled that she instinctively knew what I was thinking. "Yes, I think we should use the Larkin poem."

We sat at the table together, each of us leaned over the cards until the door opened and Chris crashed in.

"This sucks!" he yelled. "This is no scene at all. What the fuck anyway?"

Taylor followed him in, pushing him a little to get through the door. "You're drunk, Chris. You need just to lie down."

Claire opened her arms and said, "Come here, Christopher. Sit with me and tell me what's going on."

Chris slumped next to Claire. "We're in trouble," he slurred. "Curfew."

Claire looked at Taylor for clarification. "What is he talking about?"

"This dude came by and told us to quiet down. I guess there is a ten o'clock curfew here, and we were making too much noise," Taylor explained.

"It's a Phish show," Chris grumbled. "And it's not even midnight."

Claire laughed. "It's well after midnight, and we've had a long day driving here and getting settled and going to the first show. I think you should sleep it off, Chris. We still have tomorrow."

Taylor pulled Chris up and helped him to the bed in the back. She lay down next to him, and after a few minutes, we could hear Chris snoring. Claire giggled, and I just raised my eyebrows in response. Alex opened the door and stepped in. I had almost forgotten he was still out there.

"Did he pass out?" Alex asked. Chris's snoring was response enough.

"What happened?" Claire asked.

"It's just been a long day," Alex said. "The tequila went straight to his head, I guess."

"Are we really in trouble?" Claire asked.

"No," Alex said. "The guy was nice. He was just telling us to quiet down. No big deal. It is late."

"We're sitting on his bed," Claire said to me, so we gathered up the Uno cards, markers, and books from the table so Alex could pull the sofa into his bed. I climbed up to crash on the overhead bunk. Claire followed me.

"Is this okay?" she asked. "Chris is sprawled out on the bed. I don't think there's any room for me there."

"It's more than okay," I said, wrapping my arms around her before we fell asleep.

JUNE 12, 2019

CHAIFETZ ARENA, SAINT LOUIS UNIVERSITY
St. Louis, MO

SET 1: Chalk Dust Torture, The Moma Dance, Waves > Bouncing Around the Room, Undermind, Heavy Things, Roggae, We Are Come to Outlive Our Brains, Funky Bitch, Set Your Soul Free, Run Like an Antelope

SET 2: Gloria, Loving Cup > Twist > About to Run, Mr. Completely > Light > Waste, Suzy Greenberg

ENCORE: Farmhouse, First Tube

15

The next day, the sound of rain overhead woke us, its patter steady on *Suby's* roof. Cuddling Claire's back, I just dug back into our bed. It felt like a nest. I must have fallen back to sleep because when I woke again, I was alone in the bunk and could smell pot smoke mingled with the scent of coffee.

"Wake and bake," Chris said, holding up the bong. "Come on, man. It's the afternoon already. We should call you Rip Van Winkle or something."

I climbed down but shook my head to decline the offered bong. Instead, I accepted the cup of coffee Taylor offered.

"Thank you," I mumbled, taking the first sip. It was strong. "Where is Claire?"

"She went to take a shower," Taylor said. "I'm on my way there now, too."

I sat down next to Alex at the table. "What are you into?" I asked, glancing at the notebook he had in front of him.

"I'm looking up the distances of each venue on tour. It seems manageable except at the end. I don't think we will be able to make a sixteen-hour drive from Mohegan to Alpine. That worries me a bit. I mean, the rest of the tour is broken into manageable legs, see?"

I looked at the flowchart he had written in blue ink on the notebook page. Eight hours, six hours, ten hours. Next to the diagram, he had written the list of venues and dates.

"Would we go back to Maywood in between any shows?" I asked.

"Not if we want to catch them all," he said. "It's tricky, though. I'm looking at that now. If we cut Bangor because it's ten hours from Maryland to Maine and just did Camden, SPAC, Fenway, Mohegan, that might work."

"Seems like a lot of work," I said, frowning at the myriad of notes.

"I don't mind," he said. "I like logistics. It's what I'm studying in college. My goal is to expand my family's restaurant into a national chain."

"Where do you go?" I asked.

"I just attend the community branch of Ohio State near Maywood right now," he said. "My grades sucked in high school, so this is my best chance of being able to transfer to the main campus after this next year. Two years of good grades at this branch, and I'm in."

"So, you'll be at Ohio State after this next year?" I asked.

"That's the plan," Alex replied with a smile before he put his head back down.

When he turned back to his notes, I pulled the Uno deck back out. Usually, I write in my journal first thing in the morning, but I didn't feel like writing at the table with Alex working and Chris banging around the RV. Good thing, as Claire and Taylor returned a few moments later.

"Give me that, Chris," Claire said, grabbing for the carton of eggs Aunt Karen sent with us. "You can't cook to save your life, and we need to eat."

"Fine with me," he said. "Have at it. I'll just sit here and watch the women cook."

"You are such a—" Claire began before Taylor cut her off.

"He's just kidding," Taylor said. "Relax. I swear, sometimes I think you two need to be put into time-out."

After we ate, it was still raining, and since we had all gotten high, it seemed a good idea to crash again until it was time to leave for the show. Claire and I climbed into the bunk. Alex settled on the sofa, and Chris and Taylor returned to the main bed. Claire and I were quiet, but we made out more than we slept. It felt protected up here in the bunk, private almost.

Leaving for the show was different than yesterday; we were all more subdued. Maybe it was because of the rain or because we felt more settled in. Whatever the reason, it seemed jarring once we got into the venue. The crowd was the exact opposite. Because the St. Louis Blues were playing in the Stanley Cup, people gathered around the televisions in the main lobbies, and the energy was intense. Claire and I lost Taylor, Alex, and Chris before the show started. We wove our way back to the same space we were the night before, but we didn't find them before the first note, so we just accepted that we'd be on our own. All through the first set, the crowd would cheer at what seemed like incongruent times, but we quickly figured out the cheers weren't about the music. The cheers were for every goal the St. Louis

Blues scored. Chris Kuroda, the lighting guy, got into it by flashing blue and gold lights on the stage. It was at set break when they won the game. Claire and I texted and received the text back: *On the rail. Come down.*

"Do you want to push your way down and ride the rail?" Claire asked.

"Down there?" I asked, shaking my head. "No. I'd rather stay here where we can move."

Phish came out and played this old disco song, *Gloria,* before launching into a Rolling Stones cover, *Loving Cup.* I wasn't a hockey fan, but the energy of the crowd lifted me for sure. I had never experienced anything as wild as this. It was crazy. After we all filed out of the venue, Chris, Alex, and Taylor met us outside, finding each other through a flurry of texts.

We were all so pumped up after the show; we decided to walk back to Shakedown before returning to the RV park. Sheer exuberance replaced the subdued feeling from before the show. Everyone was reveling, music playing, balloons popping. We bought beers and smoked joints, talked with every person we encountered, accepted Uno cards, and antelope stickers. Alex and I purchased incredible tie-dye t-shirts. Claire and Taylor found the round sunglasses they were seeking, something called Baba Cool shades. They had the phrases, *You Enjoy Myself,* and *Funky Bitch* spelled out in beads adhered to the frames. Chris focused on buying shots and White Claws, an alcoholic seltzer everyone on the lot was drinking.

"This was the best party I've ever attended," Claire said on our Lyft ride back. She, Taylor, Alex, and I squeezed in the back seat while Chris sat upfront, which was a big mistake. First, Chris tried to change the radio station, much to the dismay of the driver. Then, he kept hitting the driver with his arms, wildly gesturing as he slurred his insights of the show, reaching around to talk to us in the back seat. The driver was more than mildly irritated. I was afraid we were going to be kicked out of the car if Chris kept it up.

"Phish knows how to throw a party," Alex agreed. "Phish lot is the best. Next to the actual shows, of course."

I thought about this. Phish lot. Shakedown. Grateful Dead. Phish. Get on the bus. Back on the train, although I knew the song refers to that phrase. Read the fucking book. I still haven't read the book. I needed to ask Claire about it already or use my phone to research instead of acting like I knew what everyone was talking about. What book?

"Stop!" Chris yelled.

The driver slammed on the breaks and pulled over just in time for Chris to open the door and to vomit. Luckily, we pulled over close enough to walk the short distance to the entrance of the RV park because the driver was furious.

"Fucking Phish!" he yelled as he drove off. We all burst out laughing, except Chris, of course. After he had thoroughly expelled, Alex and I pulled him from under his armpits and half-dragged him back to *Suby Greenberg* so he could sleep it off. Again.

We didn't sleep, however. We cracked open the White Claws Chris had bought, cranked up Joe Russo's Almost Dead, and passed around the cart. It was our last night in St. Louis, their fans were reveling, and we embraced the celebratory mood. I lead the first toast, "Next stop, Blossom!"

"Blossom," they chimed back. Claire beamed up at me and kissed me.

JUNE 19, 2019

BLOSSOM MUSIC CENTER

Cuyahoga Falls, Ohio

SET 1: Soul Planet > The Moma Dance, Kill Devil Falls, Your Pet Cat > Back on the Train, Everything is Hollow, About to Run, Divided Sky, I Didn't Know, Walls of the Cave

SET 2: Stealing Time From the Faulty Plan > Birds of a Feather > Crazy Sometimes, Miss You, Everything's Right > Chalk Dust Torture > Slave to the Traffic Light

ENCORE: Split Open and Melt, A Life Beyond The Dream

16

Divided sky, the wind blows high

"Divided Sky"
Anastasio

Since Blossom Music Center was less than a three-hour drive from Maywood, we were able to park *Suby* and be on Phish lot early on the warm summer day. I pulled my red hunting hat on my head and grabbed Claire's hand, feeling excited knowing what to expect on the lot. Claire and I had worked at Aunt Karen's kitchen table to complete our Uno deck during the days between St. Louis and Blossom. Then, we discussed our criteria for handing out cards on the drive to Cleveland.

"I think we should do what the St. Louis woman did," Claire said. "We should dole them out to the best dancers."

"I don't want to be responsible for paying attention to dancers," I said.

"You're funny," she said, laughing. "You don't have to be responsible, per se. But, if you see someone getting down, you can give them a card."

"Just not while they're dancing," Alex interjected.

"Yeah, see?" I said. "I'm not going to interrupt somebody's flow. I don't want to have to remember them for the end of the set. That's just too much to do at once. I think we should decide to give everyone who is wearing red a card."

"Red?" Claire asked. "Why red?"

"It doesn't matter the color. Red, blue, green, purple. I just picked red randomly," I said. "You don't like red?"

"No," she said. "I mean, yes. I like red. Okay, red. Everyone who matches your hunting hat gets a card."

As was accustomed, Chris, acting as captain, called for a ticket check before we hit the lot. Rituals and traditions bonded our family, and checking for tickets was just practical, especially when dealing with Chris, who seemed to be as disoriented as ever.

"Has anybody seen my charm?" Chris asked as he rifled through his backpack. "I'm not going until I find it."

Because we knew better than to argue, we filed back into *Suby* to look.

"Found it," Alex said. "It is hanging from the rearview mirror, man. Right where you left it."

Chris pulled the hemp necklace over his head and tightened it until the glass charm rested centered around his neck. "Okay, fam. I'm ready now."

The lot was much bigger than at St. Louis, and the celebratory mood was contagious. It was a hot, sunny, summer day in Ohio. The kind of day that makes you feel anything is possible. Before we entered the venue, Alex pulled out a square of acid from his pocket and doled out tiny bits to each of us. I felt nervous since I had never taken psychedelics before, but I figured this would be the right time if I ever were going to, and since everyone else did, I thought it would be best to stay attuned with them. I remembered what Peter Conners wrote. It was essential to stay on top of the trip, whatever that meant. I was going to try.

Although we had seats down front, we chose to walk the lawn first. There was a fantastic tree up the hill we decided would be our meet-up location in case we got separated during the show. I looked around, surprised by the number of parents with small children in strollers and these sling things on their bodies. Families were claiming their own little space on the lawn by laying down blankets and tarps. Not that babies were predominate, it threw me that they were even at the show, I guess. I couldn't imagine having to carry a baby and all that gear with us to a show, especially in this heat. The parents looked dazed, and the kids' hair was all matted with sweat and clung around their flushed faces. But then I remembered Aunt Karen telling me how she and my mom were kids at Grateful Dead shows.

Claire explained these were *Little Ragers*. They had their own social media group and organized this safe space for their families. At least the parents didn't have to miss shows, I guess. They just take their kids with them. I smiled, trying to picture my father at a Phish show. No way. He'd have a nervous breakdown. Definitely not his scene. I don't ever once remember my mom mentioning her childhood on tour. It's like she abandoned this life entirely except for the music she played while cooking. I would never have known if it were not for Aunt Karen. It seemed to me like a massive part of life to leave behind. I wonder if that contributed to my mother's depression. What if she hadn't completely disconnected from this world? Would she still be alive? Too many questions crowded my head to be at a Phish show. I wondered if the acid was taking effect.

Before the first note, we made our way down to our seats to secure what Claire called our designated dance area. Just before Phish launched into *Divided Sky*, Taylor told Claire she was feeling strange and needed to sit down. She grabbed Chris to go up to the tree. Alex followed them out of the pavilion, but Claire and I stayed where we were. We promised to catch up with them later. I was grateful because the acid had taken effect, and there was no way I wanted to leave our little universe we created in this vast crowd. I couldn't imagine doing anything else but move my body, seemingly of its own accord, following the music as it dipped and soared, entering my ears and rolling down my spine. I could feel it in my toes. Everything seemed wildly funny, absurd, and profound within the same space. I couldn't stop the train of thoughts roaring in my mind long enough to be able to verbalize them, even if I could talk over the music. And I didn't want to talk. I just wanted to hold on.

At set break, Claire and I shuffled our way out of the pavilion to find the long lines to use the restrooms. Dusk was descending, and people were wearing glow sticks in their hair and around their necks. The line for the men's room was much shorter than the line for the women's room, so we strategized to meet back in front of the water fountains situated between the two. I thought I got there first, so I stood to wait for Claire, only she never came back out. I realized I had no sense of time, so instead of relying upon my watch because I was too far gone to remember actual numbers, I decided to track a girl in a pink sundress who stood in line. I figured by the time she got into the facility, used it, and returned, surely Claire would find me. And then, I lost the girl. She never came out. Was this restroom a vacuum of sorts? Where did the girls go? Was there a different exit from the entrance?

And then, this weird thing happened. I stood away from the lines of the restroom, but still parallel to the water fountains to keep watch. What I didn't notice at first was a line forming behind me. Like, three guys seemed to stand behind me, which I thought was weird until that line grew to ten people. I kept turning around to see the line grow, but nobody seemed to be fazed by the fact that we weren't in line for anything. I looked at the restroom lines. Looked to my right to see lines formed at the concession stands selling beer, water, and food. Then, I'd turn around to look at the line behind me. It was very confusing. I wanted to tell the guy standing right behind me that we weren't waiting for anything, but he was involved in a conversation with his friend. The more I concentrated, the more I began to realize everyone in line was chatting with a person or with a small group, content to be waiting. Or perhaps they weren't waiting. Maybe if I moved to the right a few steps?

The moment I walked away, I got lost. A cheer rose suddenly, signaling the beginning of second set. Suddenly, everyone began making their way back to the lawn or the pavilion. Where was Claire already? Where were the restrooms? I looked behind me and was relieved to see there was no longer a line behind me. I guess I had imagined that part. Maybe those people were just waiting for their friends like me and not waiting in an imaginary line with me. It was all very confusing. However, by the time I had figured that all out, I had walked to the edge of the lawn. Did I see a blue scarf? I almost yelled out, "Mom," but stopped myself in time. Instead, I tried to follow the blue scarf, but then, it disappeared, and I was alone. Everyone around me was dancing to the show, so I decided to retrace my steps back to the restrooms. I just had to think for a moment. The toilets had to be just outside the pavilion. Claire would be standing there if I could only find my way back. I walked against the flow of the crowd and finally found the clearing. Yep, there were the restrooms, the water fountain, but no Claire. I sat on a bench and waited. I even thought to check my phone for texts, but there weren't any.

A girl with blonde braids smelling strongly of patchouli sat down next to me. I looked at her, and when she asked if I was having a good show, I tried to explain my situation. I'm not sure if I spoke the words correctly because everything seemed very disorienting to me, even forming simple sentences. But I guess she understood because she offered to go into the women's room to look for Claire. At least, that's what I thought we had discussed, but then she never came back out from the vacuum either. I'm not sure how much time had passed, but I decided to go back to the pavilion to look for Claire. I showed my ticket to the security guys and made my way down. It seemed like even more people were down there than before. I jostled my way back to where we danced first set, a difficult task as people seemed very territorial about their groove space.

Suddenly, I felt disconnected and wondered if the acid had finally worn off. How long did this drug last? Since I felt sober, I walked back out of the pavilion and found the restroom area immediately. Hopefully, I would locate Claire this time. Perhaps we had crossed paths, which is why we lost each other. I rechecked my phone. Nothing. I texted her, "Where r u?" Then, I sat down on a bench and waited. At this rate, I worried I would miss the rest of the show, but I needed to find Claire. Before I made the trek up to the tree to look for everyone, I realized I was parched, so I got in line to buy a bottle of water, and as soon as I paid for it, I chugged it.

"Hey, man," I heard and turned to see that Cosmic Charlie guy we met in the lot in St. Louis. "Your aura has changed. Oh, I see. You've lost your lady and ate something psychedelic, right?"

"Right," I sat down next to him. "But I think it's worn off or something."

"Nah, it hasn't worn off. It's all about set and setting. Haven't you ever read Timothy Leary or heard of Ram Dass?" He laughed. "You kids. I swear. Okay, listen to me. You are safe. You will find your lady, but until then, go enjoy the show."

"Are you sure?" It didn't seem the best advice.

"Yes, I'm sure. This is all an illusion—a small venue in the middle of nowhere in a small state. There is nowhere you can get lost and nothing to harm you. Go dance. Connect to the music, and everything is gonna be alright. Trust me. You're here for the show. Don't regret missing that."

So, I did what he said. Instead of walking up to the tree, I returned to the pavilion and decided I might as well pay attention to the music and reconnect with my family afterward. I was sure we would laugh about this later. Just making this decision and not wasting any more time in limbo felt reassuring. I wound my way through the crowd and settled back to our seats. The light show was astonishing. I felt the high of love and well-being flood through my body again. The acid had not worn off, or maybe it came in waves. The band was on fire, and each one of the musicians appeared to be wearing a halo, even the Fishman who was wearing his signature circle-printed housedress, a fact that was so absurd, I kept laughing.

Everyone seemed to be grinning at each other or blissed out with their eyes closed. I had never seen such uninhibited dancing. Different from the St. Louis shows, maybe because that was an indoor venue, and this was out. Perhaps because no one was distracted watching the game on their phones. I don't know. It was more like what I would imagine a tribal ritual around a fire than a supposed rock and roll concert. As if on cue, the crowd threw up their glow sticks at different intervals. Before I could figure out how they choreographed that, Claire emerged from the crowd and appeared before my eyes. I reached out to touch her, just to make sure she really existed or if the acid was making me hallucinate even more.

"Where were you?" she yelled into my ear to be heard over the crowd.

"Where was I? Where were you?"

Claire reached into her bag and retrieved a bottle of water, took a long pull and handed it off to me, then began dancing like a maniac. The bass resonated from the bottom of my soles through my fingertips, where the keyboards landed. Some of the music made perfect sense, and some of it was disjointed and raggedy. As I concentrated on Kuroda's magic and followed Trey's guitar, I imagined hippies dancing so hard; they began to float right to the top of the pavilion.

17

Claire and I found Alex, Chris, and Taylor under the tree before encore so we could close out the show as a family. Taylor was sitting with her back, supported by the base of the tree, writing frantically.

"She says she needs to get this poem down," Chris explained. "I'm so far gone, I couldn't even hold a pencil if I had to, but she's been writing ever since we got up here."

"That's wild," I said. I hoped Taylor was okay. She looked happy, head concentrated over her page, writing.

Claire grabbed my hand a few minutes into *Split Open and Melt*, the first encore song.

"Let's go have some fun!" she said. "Let's hand out some cards."

She split the deck, and we took off, half-dancing, half-walking through the lawn. At first, I kept to my rule of red: only handing cards out to people wearing red. Then, I just started giving anybody I wanted to give a card. It was fun. Nobody seemed irritated because we didn't interrupt or stop to talk. We just danced over, handed a card, and danced away. We only traveled around until the second and last encore song of the evening, *A Life Beyond The Dream*. Swaying, holding hands with Claire, Alex and Chris on one side, Taylor, who had abandoned her writing to join us on the other, was the most profound moment of my life.

On our way out of the venue, I spotted Cosmic Charlie. I grabbed Claire's hand, pulled her over to him, and said, "I found her. Look. I found her."

He smiled and said, "I knew you would. Hey, kid. I've got something for you." He reached into his bag, pulled out a book, and handed it to me. "Read this. It's the name of the game."

I looked down at the black and red cover illustration depicting a VW bus driving on a plume of red smoke from a dragon. The title read *Divine Right's Trip* by Gurney Norman.

I looked up to ask Cosmic Charlie if this was the fucking book, but he was gone.

I turned to ask Claire, "Where did he go?" but she had already taken off, so I just hurried to catch up with her, shaking my head and the weirdness of it all.

Later, in *Suby Greenberg*, I tried unsuccessfully to explain it all to Claire. We were still tripping, but it had worn off enough, we had danced hard enough, and smoked enough weed to lie next to each other in the bunk to talk.

"So, you don't know what the fucking book is either?" I asked, flipping open the book Cosmic Charlie gave me.

"There is no book; I don't think. It's called *The Helping Friendly Book*, but it's just a myth from Gamehendge, which was part of *The Man Who Stepped into Yesterday*, Trey's senior project in college," Claire said. "I know C.S. Lewis inspired him. You know the song, *Prince Caspian*. It reminds me of my mom. She read me *The Lion, the Witch, and the Wardrobe* when I was little."

"I love those books. I've read them all," I said. "That's a nice memory of your mom."

"I haven't seen her since I was seven," Claire said.

"That's sad," I said. "Why not?"

"She lives in France," Claire said. "She was an exchange student when she and my dad met at Ohio State. We lived in Columbus until they broke up, and she went back to Europe."

"And you've never gone to visit her?" I asked.

"I've never even spoken with her. She's just gone. And then, Dad took the position at the hospital and moved us to Maywood, where he met Boots, and then they got married. So, it was like my life was entirely different suddenly. Different city. Different house, school, friends. Different mother cooking, not that Boots is that big of a cook, but you get what I mean."

"How old were you then?" I asked.

"I think ten? Fifth grade," she said. "I know it was fifth grade because Taylor and I had become best friends as soon as we moved in, and that was first grade. She and I were junior bridesmaids and loved wearing matching dresses, so that part wasn't bad."

"I don't have any friends I've known that long," I said. "Well, except Joel. He was my best friend in New York, but I haven't kept up with him since I started at St. Philips."

"Do you like boarding school?" Claire asked.

"I like it, and I don't," I said. "Like how you said your life was just radically different suddenly? That's exactly how it is with my life before and after."

"Before and after?" Claire said.

"Before my mother died," I said. "And after. Before she died, we were a typical New York family, living together. My dad worked a ton while I went to school. I wouldn't say all the memories were happy, but we were a family. After she died, my dad and I rattled around like zombies for the first summer, and then I was shipped off to school."

"Would you have gone to boarding school if your mother hadn't died?" Claire said.

"No, I don't think so. I mean, we never discussed it, and I just always assumed I would go to the same school as Joel. It's a private school, but it's where most kids we went to middle school with go, you know. Only I didn't. At the end of the summer after Mom's funeral, Dad just casually mentioned I would be starting St. Philips in the fall. It's where he went to boarding school. And when I do come home for summers, most of the kids I know aren't in the city. They're at summer camp or their family's summer homes or traveling abroad," I said.

"What did you do?" she asked.

"Mostly just walk the city, hang out in Central Park or stay home and read and play video games. Dad and I play tennis, so we try to get in a few games a week when I'm home. We order in food. Go to the movies. Just regular stuff, I guess."

"Regular for a New Yorker," Claire said.

"I thought I saw my mom at the show," I said. "I know that sounds weird, but she was wearing a blue scarf, and I followed her for a moment."

"Psychedelics are weird," Claire said. "May I ask? I mean, may I ask how she died? Was she sick or—"

"She took her own life," I said. It was the first time I'd told anybody. Spoken the words aloud. Guys at school knew my mom had died, but I never talked about the details.

"That's so sad, Sam. I'm sorry," Claire said. When I didn't answer, she asked, "Are you tired yet?"

"My body is," I admitted. "But my mind is still racing. You?"

"Same," she said. "Why don't we just listen to some music until we can fall asleep."

That sounded like a good idea, and it was. I don't think I fell completely to sleep, but I know I drifted off at some point.

When we got back to Maywood, I lugged my stuff to the porch and walked into the house with my backpack slung over my shoulder. Aunt Karen wasn't home, or maybe she was in her studio, which was good as I didn't feel like talking. Even though I felt worn out, I needed to think, so I made my way down to the elm tree. I hadn't thought about Mom in a long time, and Claire brought up all sorts of feelings I needed to sort out by myself. When I first went to St. Philips, they sent me to the school counselor, but I didn't talk much. Because my grades were excellent, and I never got into any kind of trouble, the school left me be. Of course, Dad and I never talked about Mom. We never talked about anything substantial.

During the last two summers, he worked all day while I lounged around the apartment. A few nights a week, after work, we'd play tennis. The rest of the time, we skimmed the surface and just kind of co-existed. Without Mom as a buffer, we didn't have much to say to each other. Of course, he still worked all the time. Maybe even more now that she was gone. It's not that I don't love my dad, I do. I just don't feel like I know him as a person. If he was the "figure" of Dad before Mom died, he was even more so after. I could always count on him. I just didn't know him.

I missed my mom, of course. For all her faults, at least she was an authentic person to me. She was my primovant. I orbited her sun. I missed having a direction in which to operate. There was something about Claire that reminded me of her. Mom had a flair for the dramatic, and when I was little, she was the mom who always let us make forts and bake cookies and host dance parties. Those were the good years, the years I like to remember. Even though she would fly off the handle about the littlest things, like a burned pot roast, which caused her to smash the ceramic pan into a million shards on the kitchen floor, she was alive.

Then, suddenly, she wasn't. There were no more days where Mom was fun and no more days when Mom was mad. She was like a balloon that had deflated. I don't know what exactly happened that caused the depression, though. By the time I was in middle school, I would come home to a dark apartment. Mom sat at the window, smoking cigarettes and not reading anymore, or she would hole up in her bedroom for days. I thought if I stayed as quiet as possible, she would be happy. But I was wrong. Nothing I did made her happy. Not that I think it was my fault, per se. But I was the one who found her, and that memory was just too painful. Maybe it was inevitable that all this stuff was going to surface while I stayed at the Calico House. Aunt Karen still had pictures of Mom all around the house, whereas I just kept that one photo in my sock drawer at school. Too many memories were flooding, and I know that I saw a blue scarf last night, even though that doesn't exactly make sense.

The day of the memorial service was sunny but brisk, much like spring is in New York, but the tulips had bloomed, which would have made Mom happy. I wasn't focused on the red tulips or on the small altar Aunt Karen had assembled around a framed picture of Mom, using flowers, Mom's favorite books, and candles at the base of the Hamlet statue where our small group stood. Instead, I stared at the birdhouse with the pineapple top. Since Mom chose cremation, Dad decided to hold the short memorial service in Gramercy Park so everyone could just walk back up to our house for the reception after. Also, because Gramercy Park was Mom's special place. Dad bought our apartment because the park so enchanted her. She loved her key.

Mom's two musician friends from the New York Symphony played Bach, and then the Beatles and Mom's poet friend read the beginning of Walt Whitman's *Song of Myself* from *Leaves of Grass*. Grandma and Grandpa, Aunt Karen, Dad, our closest neighbors, and a few school friends and their parents were in attendance. Dad had gotten special permission to allow more than five guests to enter the park for the hour the memorial service lasted. I focused on the birdhouse, mentally reciting Paul Laurence Dunbar's poem, *Sympathy*. I had just memorized it to recite for English class and the lines *When the sun is bright on the upland slopes;/ When the wind stirs soft through the springing grass,/ And the river flows like a stream of glass;* were repeating on a loop in my head I couldn't shake. Before we filed out of the park, I mentally finished the poem as my prayer to Mom. *But a prayer that he sends from his heart's deep core,/ But a plea, that upward to Heaven he flings—/ I know why the caged bird sings!*

She loved helping me memorize this poem. Helping me brought out an enthusiasm I hadn't seen in her in a long time. It made me want to work more just to keep the momentum. But in the afternoon when I raced home to tell her how well I did in my recitation, her bedroom door was closed. I knew that if I opened it, I would find her in bed, sleeping with the curtains drawn, so I just did what I always did. I retreated to my room to read and to play video games until Dad got home from work, and we would order in dinner. Sometimes, Mom would come out and join us, although she mainly only picked at the food. She wasn't always like this, though. She used to be a lot like Aunt Karen dancing to music barefoot while she cooked in the kitchen. Mom played all the same music Aunt Karen plays, which is how I know most of the songs of those old bands like the Grateful Dead, Allman Brothers, and the Beatles. She even rolled out pasta and would shop for fresh herbs, like basil, to blend into pesto sauce.

The night of my poetry recitation, she didn't even come out to eat the pizza Dad had ordered. Mom loved pizza. She said it was her one junk food indulgence. Dad helped himself to a slice before excusing himself to retreat to his study to work, and I just took the box into the living room to eat while streaming random movies on the television. I must have fallen asleep on the sofa because the next thing I knew, Mom was whispering in my ear. She sat next to me and pulled my head into her lap, pushing back my hair from my forehead in small strokes and softly singing her baby songs to me. I didn't know then it would be the last time she cuddled me, the final real moments of my childhood. I didn't know then she was saying good-bye.

Not even a week later, I would find myself concentrating on the pagoda birdhouse with the pineapple top in Gramercy Park to distract myself from the quiet weeping of the guests gathered to pay their respects. It was awkward. I didn't know what to say to the comments, "I'm sorry for your loss" and "My sympathies." I mean, of course, I'd mumble "thank you" in response, but it all seemed so hollow. Meaningless. My insides felt scooped out, and I couldn't escape the panic settling in. I didn't want to meet anyone's eyes to see their pity and sorrow. It was too much. Instead, I allowed my mind to run poetry while I stared at the birdhouse and wondered what birds fed from them.

I don't think I ever remembered seeing any actual birds landing there and that fact concerned me so much, I returned to the park every morning that summer just to see if I could see a bird until Dad packed me up and sent me away to St. Philips. I guess I had forgotten about that because I didn't return the next two summers to check. It never occurred to me. And now, this summer, I had been focusing on the ducks. Strange how the subconscious operates. I would have to write about this in my journal tomorrow. Right now, I felt exhausted and starving, empty and sad.

When I crouched down to stand up, I must have hit my phone in a way to access the LivePhish app Claire downloaded on my phone because music spilled out. I pulled my earbuds from my back pocket and plugged in. I leaned against the tree as the sun fully set over the pond, Trey's voice reminding me *everything's right; just hold tight.* I smiled, and began to walk back to the house when I had to just stop in my tracks once more to listen:

> *Focus on the past and that's what will last*
> *Nothing that is real and nothing you can feel*
> *Focus on tomorrow you'll have to borrow*
> *Images and mind and friends you left behind*
> *Focus on today, you'll find a way*
> *Happiness is how rooting in the now*
> *Because everything's right, so just hold tight.*

Man, I certainly hope so.

18

And the days turn to years
And it hasn't stopped yet
The memories we shared
I will never forget
No, I will never forget

"Miss You"
Anastasio

It was well past dusk by the time I returned to the house. Candlelight flickered from lanterns lining the steps to the front porch, welcoming me home. My soul felt soothed when I smelled the aroma of Aunt Karen cooking in the kitchen. I found her singing along with The Beatles. She turned from the stove when I entered. "Hey, Sam, honey. Are you hungry? I cooked dinner, see?"

Aunt Karen had set the table. She heaped fried chicken, mashed potatoes, gravy, and green beans on our plates. When I frowned at the chicken, she clarified, "Not one of mine. I bought this chicken from the market."

"I want to talk about Mom." I sat at the table but didn't pick up my fork.

"Cleared some cobwebs at the shows, huh?" Aunt Karen asked, as she tasted the potatoes, and reached for the salt.

"What does that mean?"

"It's what we used to call our hallucinogenic experiences, 'clearing the cobwebs.' Sometimes it's necessary," she said. "Your mother is always with you."

"I know that." Tears pricked the corners of my eyes, but I held them back.

"Well, especially now. All the time you spend at the elm tree?" she said.

"What does that mean?" I asked.

Aunt Karen put her fork down and wiped her mouth with a napkin. "It's where I scattered her ashes, honey. Around the elm tree. It's what she wanted. I thought you knew that."

"How would I know that?" I said.

"The elm tree was your mom's favorite place. It's where she would go to think. It's where she would go to read. It's where she instructed to spread her ashes in the note she left. So, that's what I did. I guess I just assumed that's why you were so drawn to the tree this summer so that you could feel close to her. I thought you knew all of this already. Your dad never mentioned it?"

"Dad and I don't talk about anything. Especially about Mom." I felt like crying. "There was a note?"

"Yes, I still have it, tucked in our family picture album. I'll get it for you in a moment. Of course, I don't think she ever intended for you to find her. I know she didn't. I mean, I didn't know ahead of time that she was going to kill herself, but I do know how much she loved you. It was all a colossal mistake. She would never have wanted to hurt you, let alone traumatize you. That much, I know. I knew my sister. Maggie fought against her depression so hard for your benefit. The first years of your life were her best years. The happiest I had ever seen her. But she was ill, Sam. Mentally ill. I don't know if she was labeled bi-polar or what her specific diagnosis was, exactly. It began when she was a teenager. Of course, I am three years younger than her, so I wasn't completely aware of everything Maggie suffered, but she started having bouts of depression when she was in high school. Grandma and Grandpa did their best, of course. When Maggie went to college and met your dad, she seemed to have outgrown her problems, but I guess one never outgrows mental illness. Obviously, or your mom would still be alive."

"Can I see the note? Does it explain?" I asked.

"Explain what?" Aunt Karen frowned.

"Why. The *why*," I said.

"I will get you the note right now, but I'm not sure it has the answers to the questions you are asking." She stood up from the table. "It doesn't matter, though. You have the right to read it, and I believe you're old enough now, too. I'll be right back."

I picked up my fork and started to eat while I waited. I couldn't help it. I was hungry, and Aunt Karen was a great cook. The chicken was tender, and the potatoes were so good, I helped myself to a second scoop, dousing it with even more gravy. I hadn't eaten this well since Mom stopped cooking, and that was years ago. The food at St. Philips was bland and boring, and, in the summers, Dad and I ordered in every night. I didn't even remember how much I missed home cooking until this summer. Aunt Karen returned, holding an old burgundy leather photo album. I leaned over the table to get a better look, but Aunt Karen didn't spend any time leafing through the old pictures from their childhood. Instead, she turned the album on its side to shake it. Mom's letter fell to the table. It should have had a big thud to mimic my heart, but it was just paper, of course. It made no sound as it fluttered on the surface of the kitchen table. I picked it up, pulled it out of its stamped envelope. You could tell it had been handled many times from the creases of the folds of the letter. My breath caught to see Mom's backward scrawl, but I didn't want to read it there. I wanted to be alone, so I excused myself and went up to my room. It was too dark to read at the elm tree, which I would no longer call *my* tree; apparently, it was my mom's.

Immediately, I understood this note was postal mailed to Aunt Karen. It wasn't left behind like you'd expect a suicide note to be. Maybe that's why I never knew she had written it. I recognized the blue parchment stationery right away. Mom was a stickler for good paper and ordered this particular stationery by the pound, practically. Although the folds were permanently creased, I could read the letter.

> *Dear Karen, my lil bit,*
>
> *It breaks my heart to think of you at the Calico House reading this letter, so I want you to go down to the elm tree now. Are you there? Don't read another word until you can promise you are there. I feel you; I know. I want you to spread my ashes, around and around the base of this tree, my childhood friend. The*

place I go in my mind when I can't seem to cope. The place where you can go and know I am with you. Will always be with you.

I need you to promise you will take care of Sam. Andrew will send him away to school. I know he will. It's the school he attended. But take him for the summers. Take him to this tree. Take him to the trestle, too. Let him know how much I love him. When I first had him, I knew my life was complete. Like, I finally had a reason to exist. And I do, but I don't. I'm not a good mother, Karen. I tried so hard, but I'm not like Mom. I don't sew. I hate gardening. Staying alive will hurt him. He's getting old enough- he's aware. There are days when I can't stand to see the disappointment in his eyes when I can't lift my head a minute longer. He will hate me. I can't stand the idea he will hate me. He is my end-all, be-all. The love of my life, the dream of my dreams. It will be better for him when I am gone.

Tell him the good things, please. Know how much I have always loved him. Next to him, I love you best. My little sister, my lil bit. It's too dark now. I can't see beyond. I'm sorry. For every little thing and more... I am so sorry.

Mags

I let the letter drop to my lap and just sat still. I didn't want to talk with Aunt Karen right now, nor did I want to reach out to Claire. I just wanted to be left alone. I didn't even realize I was crying until one tear landed on the letter. I was careful to dab the spot, so it didn't smear the ink, but I don't think my one tear was the only tear dried on the stationary.

19

Aunt Karen was painting her Chagall piece by the pond when I went to look for her the following afternoon. I was surprised, as I know that paining was not planned to be included in the show, and lately, the only work Aunt Karen did was to prepare for her show in Chicago. Curiosity, more than anything else, inspired me to approach her. I still wasn't exactly ready to talk about Mom, though, so I was surprised at what popped out of my mouth. "There was no *why*, then."

She kept her back to me but froze her paintbrush mid-air. "No."

"Why are you working on *that* painting?"

"It's for you. I need to take a break from my collection, let it breathe a bit, so I thought I would finish this for you," Aunt Karen said.

"What does that mean, let it breathe?"

"Sometimes, when you are working on one long piece, your brain gets fuzzy, and you lose perspective. At least, I do. I feel like a hack, and I lose sight of the reason, and that's when it's time to switch gears. Paint something else or garden or clean shit out of the chicken coops, and today, I just don't feel much like cleaning shit, you know. It's good to have more than one painting going at a time or several poems if you are a writer or different songs if you are a musician. It keeps the work fresh."

"I get that, the fuzzy brain thing. It's how I feel right now," I said.

She resumed painting. "You have gone through a life experience most adults, let alone kids have never gone through. I mean, I was an adult when my parents died, and they both went peacefully. Nothing like what you experienced, Sam. It's a lot. Even for the strongest of men and trust me, you are becoming a powerful person. This summer, you have opened yourself to new experiences, and you're in the process of sorting out your life. I am right here if you have any questions or want to know more about your mom when we were kids, but honey, I can't answer the why. It's the question that keeps me up nights, too. I wish I could have done more for her, but I honestly didn't know how bad it had gotten for her. I mean, I was busy for years caring for Grandma and Grandpa, but still. I wish she would have called me. Come home for a visit. Something. I would have done anything to have prevented her from taking her own life, and I regret more than anything that you were the one to find her."

"It's because we had half-day," I said.

"Half what?" She turned from her painting to give me her full attention.

"I don't think she remembered our school let out at noon that day. Otherwise, I wouldn't have been the one to find her. Usually, I had chess club after school on Fridays, so I didn't even get home until even later, but that day was a half-day, so..."

"Oh, my God." She clasped her hand across her mouth. "That makes so much sense. Oh, Sam. You have no idea. I knew Maggie would never have intended for you to be the one to find her. She had to have had some other plan and you finding her was just one big stupid accident. Oh, honey. I am so so sorry. I am heartbroken. But this just makes so much more sense now. And you must know, none of this, in any way, was your fault. Not in any way."

I nodded in agreement. "It wasn't my fault. I know that. But I feel responsible, too. I knew she was depressed. I've been thinking about it so much lately. How dynamic her personality was. How one day, she'd be so on, and the next, off. How I didn't even know what to expect from day to day, that it was almost a relief when she just stopped. I didn't mean to say that. That was a terrible thing to say. I didn't mean to stop living. I meant..." I was having a hard time explaining. "I meant, the year before she killed herself, she went into a deep depression, and her quietness was a relief. I'm ashamed."

"Okay, kid. First of all, you were her son, not her husband. You were not responsible for her depression. Of course, you felt relieved when her manic phases ended. I'm sure your childhood was a bit of a rollercoaster, knowing what I know about my sister. But Sam, you were and still are, a kid. She was the mother. She was an adult, responsible for her own life, and your dad is the only one of us who can feel ashamed that he wasn't around enough to notice."

"I don't think much keeps Dad up at night," I said bitterly.

"I can't reply to that, Sam. I'm not going to bad-mouth your dad, but he's never been my favorite person in the world. I mean, when he and your mom first met, I worried. Your dad has always been a bit narrow-minded, which is why they didn't come here very often. But love is inexplicable. You can't always choose who you love. And, the fact is, he's the only dad you have, so you owe it to yourself to give it a chance. I mean, you spend your vacations with him when you're not in school, and it's been okay, right?"

"It's been fine. It's fine. We're just not very close, and he never wants to talk about Mom, so we don't. Mostly, he's busy with work," I said.

"Do you like school?"

"Not really," I admitted. "Boarding school sucks, but I hope when I go to college, it will get better. It's only one more year."

"Do you know where you are applying for college?"

"Not yet. I'm not sure what I even want to study, to be honest," I said.

"Well, you know I've always thought you'd end up a writer, like your mom always wanted. That's what I think," she said.

"I don't know. You're probably right. All I seem to like to do is write in my journal. And I've always been in AP English. I like to read. But you know what I'm thinking?" I said.

"What's that, honey?" Aunt Karen asked.

"I think I should go to the rest of the shows. I've found my tribe if that isn't too cheesy to say."

"It's not cheesy at all. I'm grateful you've found friends. I adore Claire and think your relationship with her is lovely. It's your summer. Your last summer before you launch into college and things start to get more serious, in terms of life. I think you said you'd be back by mid-July, and that leaves the rest of the month before we leave for Chicago. The opening of my art show is Saturday, August tenth. From there, you'll go back to school. But in the meanwhile, there is plenty of time. You are young. You need to make the best of your time, and if going to more Phish shows makes you happy, then you should go."

I nodded but didn't speak. I still had a lot to consider. I looked over at the elm tree, and even though I now know it is technically *my mom's* tree, I decided to go down there. I kissed Aunt Karen on the cheek, which made her smile and grabbing my journal and my books, I found my nook at the root base, sat down, and looked out at the pond. Ducks again, which made me feel a narrow sense of comfort. I think Mom would like to know I found Holden's ducks on the pond sitting at her elm.

20

Saturday night was Holler, the poetry series Taylor attended. I spent the day reading at my usual spot under the elm tree. After finishing *Growing Up Dead*, I also finally finished reading *The Catcher in the Rye*. The carousel scene was a metaphor for my life. We kids went round and round, like Phoebe, with no regard to the actual mechanics of life. And I loved the last lines of the book. So true. *Don't ever tell anybody anything. If you do, you start missing everybody.*

I didn't know where to begin with my essay, though. I mean, if I started writing about my mom and Claire's mom, I wouldn't know where to stop. I couldn't believe that Castle guy jumped out of the window. No wonder Holden flipped out after he saw the guy dead on the sidewalk, still wearing the turtleneck Holden lent him. I mean, it was crazy, really. I completely identified with Holden from the moment I began the book but didn't understand that he and I both witnessed suicides. It was goddamn eerie. I sat there a minute, just thinking. Then I decided.

I wrote the bullshit teachers like to read in our summer reading assignment essays. I analyzed the book in a purely academic style, not writing anything personal at all. It's best that way sometimes. Best to keep teachers out of my business. I did not want to return to the school counselor. Especially now that I had friends to talk to. After I finished the essay, I took out my journal and wrote what I really thought. I decided to start the day Dad took me out of school and work backward from there. By the time I got up from the elm tree to stretch, I had filled almost my entire journal, and it was time to get ready for the poetry reading.

Claire looked pretty when she picked me up. She wore a simple t-shirt dress, sandals, and had piled her hair on top of her head in a bun. I'm glad I had thought to wear a collared shirt, the most formal clothes I'd worn all summer. It was a simple polo I wore with khaki shorts. It was our first official date if you didn't count Phish shows.

"You don't drive at all?" Claire asked as we pulled out of the driveway.

"Not at all," I said. "I'm a New Yorker. Nobody I know drives. Although I will admit, I wish I did drive so I could take a turn when we continue on tour."

"You're going with us?" Claire said. "Fantastic! When did you decide?"

"I don't know what you're asking. Decide? I never didn't decide," I said. "I guess I just assumed from the start I'd stay on tour with you as long as I could."

"Well, I'm delighted," Claire said. "I wasn't sure if Chris turned you off with his drunken craziness."

"I love the captain," I said. "I'm not turned off. I think you're all a bunch of nuts, and I am happy to call you my family."

Claire pulled into the parking lot of Mellow Mushroom, the pizza restaurant Aunt Karen, Luke, and I ate a few weeks earlier. When I raised an eyebrow, Claire explained. "There are only two places in Maywood that serve alcohol: Mellow Mushroom and Joe's Bar. But, since Joe's doesn't serve food, minors aren't allowed in. So, Eric hosts Holler here every month so we teenagers can attend as well as the older poets, who I promise, will not get up to read at the mic until they've had something to drink. So, it works for everyone."

When we walked in, Claire lead me to the bar section of the restaurant. There was a small plastic portable stage with a microphone on a stand at one end and the bar at the other. Taylor and Chris hadn't arrived yet, so Claire and I found a booth big enough for us all and sat down. I pulled my journal and the copy of *Divine Right's Trip* from my backpack and put them on the table.

"How is it?" Claire asked, looking at the book.

"Weird," I admitted. "It starts with the bus narrating the story, which confused me, of course. But, as it turns out, the bus doesn't narrate the whole story. It is about a dude named D.R., which is short for Divine Right or David Ray, which is his 'real' name who has adventures back in the olden days, like the '60s. They even used payphones. I mean, I've seen public phones in New York, of course, but nobody uses them anymore. They do a lot of psychedelics, and they throw this thing called the I-Ching that I completely don't understand."

We ordered pretzel bites and sodas from a server wearing more piercings on her face that I'd ever seen before. Hoops sprouted from her ears, eyebrow, nose, and even her lip. Claire and I looked at each other and cracked up. I loved that we didn't always need actually to say anything to communicate.

"How is your art coming along?" I asked.

"Good," Claire said. "I've decided to create just two parts of the series, and install them in stages—each of the two nights at SPAC. I mean, I don't want the entire tour devoted to worrying about setting everything up, getting the right photographs, and then deconstructing it. I want these pictures for my portfolio, so they need to be right."

"I'll help you," I offered.

She smiled. "I was counting on that."

Taylor and Chris arrived just as our pretzel bites arrived at the table. Taylor also wore a dress. Her hair was pulled back into a ponytail at the nape of her neck. She carried her journal and walked away from our table. Chris sat down with us to explain Taylor had to find Eric, the host of Holler, to sign up for the open mic.

"I got one of the last spots," Taylor said when she slid into the booth with us. "Did you order me water?"

"No," Chris said. "I'll go up to the bar and get it for you now."

Meanwhile, Claire had unearthed her flask and was pouring into our sodas. "Rum," she explained. I smiled. It wouldn't be Claire without her trusty flask.

I offered Taylor a pizza bite, but she declined. "I don't like to eat anything before I read," she said. "I might throw up."

She did look nervous, but when she saw the copy of the book, she smiled. "You brought the book to be signed? That's great. How did you know? I wish I had a copy."

"To be signed?" I was confused.

"Yes," she said. "The feature readers tonight are Gurney Norman and some dude named Ed McClanahan. They're from Kentucky."

Chris returned with two glasses of water.

"Wait," I said. "Ed was mentioned in *Growing Up Dead*. I'm going to find the passage. I swear, I remember reading his name." I dug back into my backpack for the book. "Here it is. Page119. He was a Merry Prankster. Palo Alto. Friends with Ken Kesey."

"Hold on," Chris said, picking up the book. "You brought this book but didn't know the author was reading tonight? How weird is that."

"Very," I said. I looked around, trying to find Ed and Gurney, but I didn't see any hippies. "I'm going outside to get some air."

I stood up abruptly and stumbled to the door. Since it was only seven o'clock, it was still light outside. I leaned against the building and took a few deep breaths. Claire followed me.

"What is it, Sam?" she asked.

"This is too big of a coincidence," I said. "I mean, if we were in New York, that would be one thing, but we're not. We're in this tiny town at this poetry reading. What are the chances?"

"I'm not sure I understand," she said.

"Okay, first, I run into the Cosmic Charlie dude twice. In two different cities," I began to explain.

"That's not so weird, though," Claire said. "He's following Phish. We were following Phish. We'll probably see more of the same people at Camden, right?"

"Right," I said. "But did *you* get a book? He gave me this book. He doesn't know where we're from. He doesn't know the author would be here tonight. Yet..."

"Here we are," she finished.

"Here we are," I repeated. "Too big of a coincidence."

Claire laughed. "Okay, well, if Peter Conners walks in right now, it would be too big of a coincidence."

"That's for sure," I said.

"But, Sam, listen. Writers are people. Just people. And we *are* at a poetry reading, somewhere you'd expect writers to gather, right?" she said. "They're going to start the open mic in a minute, and we don't want to miss Taylor. She may read that poem she wrote at Blossom. Let's go back in now. Do you feel better?" she asked.

"No, but let's go in. I don't want to miss Taylor," I said, and followed Claire back to our booth. She slid my soda to me, and I took a sip. Lethal. I wouldn't expect anything less from Claire. I took another healthy slug as Eric took the stage, welcomed everyone, explained the rules of the open mic, and got the crowd applauding.

Claire was right. The writers were just regular people who happened to be writers. First at the mic was a woman dressed in a leopard-printed mumu and matching turban who ranted feminism in a comedic manner.

"Huh," Chris said. "It's not often that feminists are funny."

"Shut up, Christopher," Claire said, swatting at him. He just turned and drank straight from the flask, not bothering to conceal it.

A tiny, fierce, self-proclaimed lesbian in high heels read a poem as short as her stature. A dreamer whose hands shook so much, a podium placed as service. A bard whose brilliance compensated his slur stumbled through a profound poem.

"He's drunk," Claire said. "I think I know him, though."

"That's because you do," Chris said. "He's a surgeon. He works with Dad."

The irritable host still managed to be charming even as he loudly hushed the crowd around the corner. A man wept while reading a mountain mastectomy poem. One person read about transitions as *she* moved from *he* to *they* in one line. My favorite was a poet whose Spanish wove without interpretation, its beauty enough. Porch sitting, mason jars, canned peaches, the Elkhorn River, and Serpentine Mound intertwined with balconies in Bulgaria, plums in Hungarian grandmother's kitchens, mountains in Costa Rica, and Ganymede on the Olentangy. The images floated around in my mind, hard to catch and consider since each speaker could only read one poem, and Eric kept the pace brisk.

Finally, Eric called Taylor's name to a good round of applause as she made her way to the stage. Although she had seemed nervous the entire time waiting, once she grabbed the microphone, she was as confident as I had ever seen her.

> *I met god at the Speedway today.*
> *She spoke to me. Energy into*
> *the universe caught in ink—*
> *chance opportunity for dreams*
> *I have forgotten ignited in pages*
> *of text. My heart leaps*

because when you do
what you are meant, god
speaks through you.
I'm proud to remember
second-person, reminded
by those who dare to howl.
When I am not silent, not
in mourning, breathe
the present and don't worry
your memory taxed by useless
words because poems
are not designed to preach
but to find truth I seek
as I listen to music and sigh.
The happily-ever-after
found in the space between
breath. Everyone thinks
but only poets write down
ideas caught as if pages
were butterfly catchers.

We applauded Taylor loudly as she returned to our table with a shy, proud smile. Before we could congratulate her more, Eric was introducing Ed McClanahan. I was stunned when this old, grandpa-looking guy pulled himself up from a table and made his way to the stage. This is a Merry Prankster? He wore jeans, a vest, and a tie-dye, but nothing else about his appearance would have placed him in the Beat culture in my imagination until he opened his mouth to speak. He was hilarious. Told stories about Wavy Gravy. Read a little bit and then talked about *Divine Right's Trip*, indicating to where Gurney was seated, but all I could see was the back of some white-haired guy's head until it was his turn to take the stage. Gurney sported a sweater, button-up shirt, and khakis. How could these two guys be so old? My mind was blown.

After Gurney cracked the crowd up, reading a story about when he was an undergrad and met Robert Frost. Apparently, Robert Frost and a guy named Mr. Crowley misunderstood each other in a conversation. Frost thought they were talking about Henry Miller, yet Crowley though they were talking about Arthur Miller, the playwright who married Marilyn Monroe. What's even funnier is that Robert Frost didn't even know who Marilyn Monroe was. I sat there imagining how amazing it would be to have met the great Robert Frost.

"Let's meet them and get your book signed," Claire said once the readings ended.

"I'm not sure," I wavered.

"We have to," Claire said. "He'll be thrilled you have his book. Come on," she said, pulling me up by the hand.

We had to wait a while, as a crowd had formed around the men. Everyone was eager to shake hands and ask for their books to be signed. When it was our turn, Gurney asked for my name.

"Sam," I said. "It's nice to meet you, Mr. Norman. So, I need to ask. Do you know Cosmic Charlie?"

"Cosmic Charlie?" he repeated, frowning to remember. "I don't think so. Ed? Do you know a Cosmic Charlie?"

"No, can't say I do," Ed replied. "Sounds familiar, but at this age, it's hard to remember everyone you meet, you know?"

"He is this guy I met in St. Louis," I explained. "He's the one who gave me this book. Would you please sign it to him?"

"So, not, Sam?" Gurney asked.

"No, please. Write it to Cosmic Charlie," I said.

"Okay, here you are," Gurney said. "Thanks for coming out tonight."

Chris and Taylor seemed to be arguing when we returned to the table. Claire picked up the flask lying open on the table and slipped it into her bag just before the pierced server came over to drop off our check. It was apparent Chris had too much to drink again, so I dropped some bills on the table, and we ushered him out the door.

"Where's your car?" Claire asked Chris.

"I didn't drive," he said. "We were dropped off. Alex gave us a ride on his way into work."

"Good thing," Claire said. "Because you are in no shape to drive."

"I'm in some shape to do some nitrous," Chris said as we settled into Claire's car.

"Forget it, Chris," Taylor said. "I told you no, and I mean it."

"What's he talking about?" Claire asked as she pulled out of the parking lot.

"He wants to break into my dad's office and steal his nitrous," Taylor explained.

"Not steal. We won't steal. We will borrow. Yeah, that's it. Borrow," Chris said.

"How are you going to borrow nitrous, Christopher? You're not making any sense," Claire said. "You're upsetting Taylor. Enough."

"Upsetting Taylor? Nah, she's always upset. Who cares if she's upset?" Chris said.

"That's not fair," Taylor said. "You know what, Chris? You're an asshole."

"Fine, I'm an asshole," Chris said as Claire drove into their neighborhood. She pulled into a driveway of a house a few doors from their own.

As Taylor exited the car, she leaned down and said, "You're spoiled, Chris, and I'm sick of it. You run over all of us without caring about anything but yourself. I'm done. Do whatever you like, but don't include me in your plans."

She slammed the car door, walked up to the front door, opened it, and turned off the porch light from inside. Claire didn't say a word as she backed up the car and pulled into their driveway. Then, she leaned over and said, "Get out."

"See you," Chris said as he stumbled out of the car. He walked to the garage where *Suby Greenberg* was parked.

Claire sighed. "Let's go to the Calico House," she said. "I need to get away from here."

21

Aunt Karen and Luke were still up when Claire and I walked into the house. They were sitting in the living room, drinking wine and listening to music.

"How was the reading?" Luke asked.

"Good," I said. "But, they were old."

"Old?" Aunt Karen looked startled. "Who was old?"

"We met Gurney Norman and Ed McClanahan tonight," Claire explained. "Sam is tripping on how old they were."

Aunt Karen laughed. "What did you expect, Sam? We Woodstock folks are grandparents now." She turned to Claire and asked, "Would you like some tea, honey?"

Claire laughed, said yes, and followed Aunt Karen into the kitchen. I sat down across from Luke and retrieved *Divine Right's Trip* from my backpack. "How do you know these guys?" I yelled to Aunt Karen.

"Oh, I've met them," she said, popping her head back into the living room, holding a box of tea in her hands. "They're friends of Wavy Gravy, who was a dear friend of your grandparents. I think the last time I saw him was at your grandmother's funeral."

"Your aunt knows a lot of characters," Luke said. "It's one of the things I love most about her. She has this way of drawing people out. Keeps life interesting, that's for sure."

"You are hippie royalty, Sam, and you don't even know it," Claire said.

"I don't know about royalty, exactly," Aunt Karen said, returning to the living room with the mugs of tea. "But you do come from a family who went to Woodstock in '69 and then followed the Grateful Dead through the '70s and '80s. I was twenty-seven when Jerry died, and it devasted me for a bit, I must admit."

"How old were you at Woodstock?" Claire asked.

"Oh," Aunt Karen answered. "I was only one year old. Maggie was four. Then we spent our elementary school years on tour and staying at various friends' farms and communes with Grandma and Grandpa. We didn't truly settle in here until Maggie was almost ready for high school, and I entered middle school. It was a different era to be sure. A different way of living. I told you a lot of this already, Sam."

"I know," I said, opening the family album from that era again. "We just like to hear the stories."

"We do," Claire chimed in.

"I still have some of those dresses and skirts if you want to see them," Aunt Karen said. "I'll let you borrow if you like."

"I would love that," Claire said.

"Okay, we'll go up into the attic tomorrow, then. I assume you'll be here in the morning?" Aunt Karen asked as she and Luke retreated for the evening.

"Yes. Good night," Claire said.

"Good night, you two," Aunt Karen said. "Be sure to blow out all the candles before you go to bed."

"We will," Claire said, pulling the family album on her lap. "I just love these pictures."

"I thought you were obsessed with all-things-eighties," I teased.

"What?" She looked startled. "Oh, yes. Well, some of these pictures at the end are from the eighties."

I laughed. It was good being alone with Claire.

"I wish we could just stay here until we leave for Camden Thursday," Claire said.

"Why can't we?" I said. "Aunt Karen doesn't seem to mind. She seemed to take it for granted you are staying tonight."

"I know. I thought that was cool," Claire said. "Okay, listen, though. I do want to stop by the library tomorrow. The book I reserved is ready to be picked up. You'll like our library. There's something I want to show you."

"At the library?" I said.

"Yes," she smiled. "I'm glad we went to the reading. For Taylor. Her poetry is good, isn't it?"

"Was that the poem she wrote at Blossom?" I asked.

"I don't think so. Maybe. She was laughing at the notes she took. Some of it made sense. I don't know. I guess she pulls things, strands or whatever, and then uses them in her writing later," Claire said. She set the photo album down and was scanning Aunt Karen's books on the shelves.

"Sounds like you know a little something about writing," I said.

"I write a little. Not like you and Taylor. But I write. I just like to read more," she said. She pulled out a book and turned the cover to face me. "Do you like Neruda? Let's take our books upstairs and read together in bed."

It was the most intimate suggestion I had ever received from a girl. I held out my hand in response. We blew out the candles, turned out the lights, and quietly retreated to my bedroom, where we lay side-by-side reading until we fell asleep. "Like an old married couple," Claire said.

The next morning, Claire and Aunt Karen rooted around the attic for her old show clothes for Claire to borrow. Then, Claire and I drove to the library. She was grinning when she parked in front of Maywood's small library, a red brick building in the center of town between the post office, a law firm, and a dental office. Inscribed in marble above the double doors was the phrase, *in omnia paratus.*

"That's where you got it," I said.

"Yep," she grinned. "We started chanted that as our motto when we were in pre-school, and Taylor's mom would bring us here for story hour."

"Pretty sophisticated motto for a preschooler," I said.

"Ha! Yes. We definitely were not ready for all things then," she said.

"But you are now?" I said.

"I certainly hope so," she said.

"Okay, but what about *Gilmore Girls?*" I asked.

"*Gilmore Girls* is the television show Taylor, and I are obsessed with. Especially when Rory joins the Life and Death Brigade and jumps with Logan. Their motto is in omni paratus. I don't know.

It just seemed like fate or whatever that this was me and Taylor's slogan and is also from *Gilmore's*. See?"

"Sure," I replied as we entered the library.

While she went to the front desk to retrieve her reserved book, I scanned the shelves looking for a new book to take with us for the next two weeks we'd be on tour. I hadn't finished *Divine Right's Trip*, but I wanted to have another book with me as a back-up. I like having a book going at all times. Several books. I picked up *The Goldfinch*. It was heavy, but that assured me it would last the next few weeks. I knew it won the Pulitzer, and I liked that the protagonist's name was Theo. My name was going to be Theo if it wasn't Sam. My mom told me that. I brought it to Claire and asked her to check it out for me, as I didn't have a Maywood library card.

Once we checked our books out, Claire suggested we return to the Calico House to swim in the pond. It was already a hot and humid day. It was nice to set a blanket under the elm tree with our books and a small cooler of drinks. We spent the day swimming, lounging under the tree, reading, and when we got hungry, we meandered into the house for snacks.

"Listen to this," Claire said, reciting from the Neruda book.

I love you without knowing how, or when, or from where,
I love you directly without problems or pride:
I love you like this because I don't know any other way
to love, except in this form in which I am not nor are you,
so close that your hand upon my chest is mine,
so close that your eyes close with my dreams.

"That's a sonnet," I said.

"Yes. It's called *One Hundred Love Sonnets: XVII.* How did you know?" Claire said.

"Because I had to memorize a Shakespeare sonnet in sixth grade," I said.

"And you still remember it?" she asked.

"Yes. I'm cursed with a phenomenal memory." I said. "Like an elephant."

"Recite it for me," Claire said.

"Okay," I said. "*Shall I compare thee to a summer's day—*"

"*Thou art more lovely and more temperate,*" Claire interrupted.

"Wait," I said. "You know it, too?"

"Yes," she said. "Ninth grade Drama class. We were required to recite a Shakespeare sonnet, and this was the one I memorized."

Together, we recited the rest, smiling at each other.

"I like Neruda's sonnet better," I said.

"I like anything better than early modern English," Claire said. "Don't get me wrong; I love Shakespeare plays. When I see them, not to read. It's just too tedious to have to translate every word practically. But, when they're acted out, I seem to understand the plays better. Does that make sense?"

"Well, he was a playwright," I said. "What I mean is that I don't think he ever expected classes of kids studying every little word, searching for meaning. He wrote plays to be performed. So, they make sense when they are acted out versus just read."

Claire leaned over and kissed me. She whispered, "You're just so damn smart."

"As are you," I responded. "I've been thinking about what you said at Holler. About writers just being people. My entire life, I have looked to authors as gods almost. You know, like these elevated beings who divine the truth of the universe through their books. I've learned most of everything I need from fiction. Not studying textbooks, but stories. Writers are like the ultimate authority to me. I never actually think of them being people who run errands or eat dinner or—"

"Go to the bathroom," Claire interrupted. "I know what you mean. But they are. Just people. Like us. Like you. Someday, I'm going to show up to your book release and wait in line to get my copy of your best-selling book signed."

I was startled. "Why?" I asked.

"What do you mean, why? Because you're going to write a book," she said.

"I mean, why would you wait in line?" I clarified. "Aren't you going to be with me still?"

Claire smiled. "You're such a romantic. But now it's time to pick up our stuff and head back in. What should we do for dinner? Are you hungry? I'm hungry."

"Sure," I said. "I could eat."

We folded up the blanket and gathered our things and walked to the house. Aunt Karen met us on the porch, having just finished working in the studio for the day. She suggested we order Chinese as she was expecting a group of women to attend a Red Tent party.

"Although the moon is waxing, I missed the Strawberry Moon ceremony, so I'm calling a Red Tent tonight," Aunt Karen said. "You are welcome to join us, Claire."

Claire's eyes lit up. "I'd love to."

"I guess that leaves me to my reading," I said.

"Are you sure?" Claire asked. "I mean, I don't have to participate."

"No," I said. "Do. It's cool. Maybe I'll hit up Chris and check in with him. We've got shit to do to be ready to roll Thursday."

After we ate, Chris knocked on the kitchen door. He wanted to go back to his house for a while and then meet Drake at the trestle later.

"We're good on tickets," Chris said as we settled in *Suby Greenberg* to roll a joint. "At least for Camden, Fenway and Mohegan. We still need SPAC, but we have extras of every other show, so I know we can trade. I'm not worried about tickets. And I spoke with Tippy this afternoon, and his parents said we could park there. They have this huge house with plenty of room on their driveway for *Suby*. He and Chad or maybe Plums will hop on with us to SPAC."

"How do you know Tippy?" I figured this was the easiest place to start.

"Camp Fitch," Chris said. "Come on. Let's spark this outside."

"We met Tippy at camp years ago," Chris said as we leaned against the garage to smoke. "We've all gone to the same camp because our dads went to that camp. It's on Lake Erie. Tippy's parents drove him from New Jersey, and George drove us from Ohio. Every. Single. Year. It's like a religion to them—some kind of cult or something. I'm kidding, of course. Anyway, it is a cool camp. Last year, Claire and I went back to Camden with Tippy for the shows. We finished camp and drove back to Camden with Tippy. It was me and Claire's first two shows. Epic. What's best is that Cherry Hill, Tippy's neighborhood, is two seconds from Camden. It's his home venue, so he knows everybody. It's like a family reunion."

"That's cool," I said. "So, Plums and Chad are Tippy's friends? They've sure got some weird names. How did you get tickets? Tippy?"

"No," Chris said. "Cash or trade. It's this site where you can buy or trade tickets but not at a profit, like scalper scum. It's cool. Closely monitored. The only way to go other than knowing someone or being miracled."

"Does that still happen?" I asked. "I know it happened during the Grateful Dead, but..."

"I don't know," Chris said. "I've only been to those two Camden shows, the two St. Louis and Blossom with you and we had tickets. I guess we'll find out if it comes down to that."

We returned to *Suby Greenberg* to listen to Merriweather, last night's show. Chris pulled the sheets from the bed to launder, and I decided to make myself useful and collect stray trash, straighten up, and survey the refrigerator and cabinets. We sat down at the table to write a list.

"Tomorrow, we'll shop for supplies," Chris said. "And tonight, we'll meet Drake for weed. So, I need to ask you for money."

"Of course," I said, a bit startled. I reached into my pocket for my wallet.

He pointed to his notes. "This is what I think you owe for tickets, weed, food."

"I'm going to need to find an ATM," I said, looking at the total.

"No problem," Chris said. "We can stop tomorrow morning when we go to the store. But now it's time to meet Drake at the trestle. Ready?"

When we arrived at the trestle, only a few kids were there. Chris and I stayed in the parked car, finishing out the first set.

"*Silent in the Morning, David Bowie, Squirming Coil,*" Chris sighed with satisfaction. "I can't wait for Camden."

Drake pulled up a minute later and jumped into the backseat.

"I can't stay for long," he said. He pulled out the bag of weed and several dab carts and handed it to Chris. "I'm not going with you guys. I'm not going anywhere this summer. And I've even gotta get back home in a minute because I lied and said I just needed fucking toothpaste so I could borrow the car. It can't go on forever, but I can't take it much longer."

"What's going on with your 'rents?" Chris asked. "I mean, I know they were strict, but man, this is like a whole new level or something. What the fuck? I'm sorry, man."

"It's just because my mom lost her job. She's insane. She's so used to managing work shit that she just turns around and micro-manages the shit out of my sisters and me. They're flipping out, too. Once she gets a job, she'll go back to being too distracted to worry about us, but until then..."

"And it couldn't happen at a worse time," Chris said. "Summer, I mean. Couldn't she have lost her job in January or February when we're all in school and not trying to hit shows?"

"Tell me about it," Drake grumbled. "Alright, man. I'm out."

"Bet," Chris said, bumping.

"See you, man," I said. I felt terrible for Drake. He looked pitiful as he climbed into his car and pulled away.

Chris pulled his car out and said, "I'm not entirely bummed Drake can't go. I've got enough to worry about making up with Taylor to have him further messing things up."

"Have you two talked?" I asked.

"We've texted," Chris said. "But I'm not worried. I've got ten solid days of Phish to woo that woman back into my arms."

I laughed. "You may need more game than that."

"Fuck!" Chris groaned. "*What's the Use.* Not good, man. Not good at all."

"Why? Claire loves this song," I said.

"Exactly," Chris said. "There's no way they're going to play this at Camden. No way. Not when they busted this out last night. I'll leave you to break it to her."

He pulled into the driveway of the Calico House.

"Shopping tomorrow?" I said as I climbed out of the car.

"See you then," he said as he waved good-bye.

I stood under the paper lanterns that lined the roof of the front porch and listened to the drums around the bonfire. I didn't dare approach. I'm not exactly sure what a Red Tent is, but I'm pretty sure I wouldn't be welcome in that circle of women. I retrieved my copy of *The Goldfinch* and fell asleep reading. I vaguely heard Claire slip into bed and put her head on my back, between my shoulder blades.

"Did you have a good time?" I murmured.

"Yes," she replied. "Good night, love."

"Good-night," I said and drifted back to sleep.

22

Can't I live while I'm young

"Chalkdust Torture"
Anastasio & Marshall

Chris, Alex, and Claire arrived before noon Thursday to leave for the shows. It was an eight-hour drive to Tippy's house in Cherry Hill. Red hunting hat firmly placed on my head, I grabbed my duffle, a cooler, and Aunt Karen's eggs from the porch and loaded into *Suby Greenberg.*

"All aboard, Captain!" I yelled. I don't know the last time I'd been this excited. Even going shopping yesterday was an adventure. The process itself was the end result. Or the journey is the destination. Whatever the cliché, each step of the process contained me with delightful anticipation for what lay ahead when the band launched the first note. It was better than Christmas when I was a kid, and that was a magical time in New York, for sure. Nine shows in two weeks on the road in this RV with this tribe was more than I could ask for. I don't think my father could have ever expected this is what I'd be spending my time doing when he arranged for me to stay the summer with Aunt Karen, but since she was cool with it, I wasn't going to worry. He and I had only spoken twice on the phone, briefly. For once, I wasn't lonely after I hung up. I had a family now. I felt like my life had a purpose for the first time. I'm not quite sure what that purpose was exactly other than traveling around, following Phish, but I was sure it would lead somewhere if nothing else but then to expand my life. But something was fundamentally shifting inside me. The boulder of grief I concealed in sullen silence for the past three years was no longer a burden. My dreams were clear. I no longer felt haunted by guilt. My grief was more a dull ache and lingering bruise. Something I knew I would carry for the rest of my life. However, I no longer throbbed with the shock of trauma. The loss was now wedged deeply within my heart like a truth you just accept as a fact of life. If anything, I felt confident my mom would want me to echo her childhood footsteps. It was almost a quest of sorts. If I followed Phish now, would it lead me back into a deeper understanding of her past rooted deeply in this carried tradition? We weren't on a bus following the Dead. We were a new generation of seekers, intent in preserving the beauty of freedom from that culture into a new evolution. Where it would lead was yet to be found, which incited pure adrenaline; anticipation to join in what would be a remarkable slice of reality shaped between a guitar, bass, keys, and drums performed by four ordinary dudes with extraordinary ideas. The fact that this tribe had found me and dragged me into this journey seemed destined. I couldn't wait to swim among the sea of thousands of other like-minded people. I was ready for all things.

The fam met my exuberance with smiles, and we were all in high spirits the entire drive to New Jersey. We listened to the Merriweather shows, ate snacks, and tumbled around *Suby* as Alex and Chris took turns driving to Cherry Hill. Tippy's house, a beautiful Tudor-style mansion, was tucked into a wooded front lot. We followed the driveway to the back where Tippy told us to park *Suby* in front of what he called the carriage house. It looked like a separate garage, but above it was a full apartment, including a bathroom Tippy invited us to use for the weekend. The backyard was beautiful, like something out of *Better Home and Gardens,* including an organic-shaped pool and a hot tub. Blooming landscaping edged the large stone patio where clusters of furniture surrounded an outdoor fireplace that even had a television above it. Blooming wisteria wound around a wood pergola that covered a bar and outdoor kitchen area. I was thrilled we were going to spend the weekend here.

Tippy, a teddy bear of a guy with a full head of brown curly hair, came out to greet us, pulling first Chris and then Claire into a hug.

"Greetings," he said as we shook hands. "You made it."

"Yes," I said. "Thank you. It's great to meet you finally."

"Of course," he said. "Let me show you guys the carriage house so you can get settled."

"We'll stay in *Suby*," Chris insisted.

"Whatever you want," Tippy said. "But this is here if you need it. I'm sorry my parents aren't here to greet you. They had to go into the city this weekend, but they said to say hello. Well, at least to Chris and Claire. But their hospitality extends to everyone, of course."

"It's cool, your parents letting us park here," Chris said.

"Of course," Tippy said. "You're Camp Fitch family, and you know how sentimental our dads are about that."

"Camp Fitch forever," Claire said in a withering tone that cracked Tippy up.

Tippy opened the garage door and said, "Claire, this is where you can spread out your art to work."

"This is perfect," Claire said. "Thank you, Tippy."

The apartment in the carriage house revealed a living room, a small kitchenette, two bedrooms, and a full bathroom all beautifully decorated and fully outfitted.

"This is really nice," Alex said. "Who lives here?"

"Nobody," Tippy said. "Not anymore. My nanny lived here when I was growing up, but unlike Peter Pan—"

"You grew up," Claire concluded.

"Exactly," Tippy said. "Now, it's just here for guests like you, so welcome."

We trekked back downstairs just as Tippy's friend Plums showed up, holding paper bags of food.

"Cheesesteaks from Chick's Deli," Plums said as greeting. He was a short guy who wore glasses. "Best cheesesteaks on the planet."

We climbed back into *Suby*. Plums doled out the sandwiches while Claire and I passed around bottles of water. He was right. They were the best cheesesteaks I had ever tasted, perhaps because it was the first solid food I had eaten all day. While we ate, Tippy caught Claire and Chris up on the gossip about people they knew at Camp Fitch. Plums excused himself back to his car to retrieve the t-shirts he created to sell on the lot. They were amazing.

Plums explained, "The key is not to violate any copyright laws. There are actual copyright cops who walk the lot, looking for infringement issues. So, we create our t's with that in mind—no Phish logos. Only snatches of song lyrics and other innuendos only phans will understand. It helps that we have this amazing artist. This dude I know from school. See?" There were about a half dozen different designs in vibrant colors.

"If you want to help sell," Plums continued, "I'll give you a free t-shirt to wear. You'll carry them in a backpack, and we'll keep the surplus in our car to reload when you need."

This was not something I wanted to do at all. I didn't want to be responsible for selling and handling money. I was here to play. I wasn't the only one; nobody else jumped in either.

Plums laughed. "That's okay, too," he said. "I've got a crew ready to make some cash. No worries."

Alex said what I was thinking. "Sorry, man. It's not that they're not cool. I just don't want to hassle with money if I don't have to."

Plums rose to leave. "Okay, I'll plan to catch you on the lot tomorrow. I've gotta meet with my sales team. See you guys," he said as he gathered his bag of t-shirts and departed.

Alex had pulled out the bong and was packing hits. He asked Tippy, "What time do you want to leave for the lot tomorrow?"

Tippy took a deep pull from the bong and answered as he exhaled, "We should plan to take off before three or so. The venue is only five minutes away, but there will be traffic. Do you guys want to watch the Bonnaroo sets? Did you see the picture of Trey watching Cardi B on stage? It was hilarious."

"Periodt," Claire said. When we laughed, she said, "What? I like Cardi B. She's tough."

"I heard she had a wardrobe malfunction," Taylor said. "She had to finish her set in a bathrobe. Is that the picture?"

"No," Tippy said. "She was in costume, but the look on Trey's face is priceless. See?" He held out his phone for us to see. We followed Tippy back to the carriage house where there was a television in the living room and two large sofas for lounging. Tippy cued up the Bonnaroo sets, and we spent the evening watching. Taylor decided she was chasing a *Strawberry Letter.* Claire said *What's the Use.* Chris and I avoided each other's eyes when she said that. I didn't have the heart to tell her that it was a longshot.

Alex said, "I'm just happy to see whatever they pull out. I'm just glad to be here."

Around midnight, Tippy rose and said, "Alright. I'm going to get some serious sleep. We'll take my mom's minivan. It may not be cool, but it will fit all of us."

We all thanked Tippy and retreated to *Suby* to settle in, even though he had offered for any of us to sleep in the carriage house. I thought we were content to spend the night together until Taylor suddenly declared she was going back to the carriage house to sleep.

"I don't want to share a bed with Chris tonight," she said.

"Do you want me to come with you?" Claire asked, even though we were tucked into our bunk.

"No," Taylor said. "Stay here with Sam. I'll be fine. See you in the morning."

"I guess they're not made up yet," I asked Claire.

"Apparently not," Claire said. "But I don't want Taylor to be alone. I'm going up."

"I'll come with you," I said. We climbed down the bunk and walked back up to the carriage house where Taylor was sitting on one of the sofas, crying. Claire and I flanked her. Claire put her arms around her friend.

"I just wish I had what you and Sam have," Taylor sniffled. "Something real."

"Real?" Claire said. "This isn't real."

My heart stood still. What did she mean, this wasn't real? I couldn't even meet Claire's eyes. I just sat, looking down.

Claire continued, "What I mean is that Sam and I have a summer romance, but you and Chris have known each other for years. Have you not talked yet? Is that it?"

"No," Taylor said. "We haven't talked anything out. That's what's killing me. I don't know where we stand. I certainly did not want just to sleep next to him like nothing is wrong when everything is wrong. I kept waiting the entire drive to see if he would at least try to be with me a little and nothing."

I was stuck on the phrase, summer romance. Was that all this was? Maybe I was an idiot, though. I hadn't thought about it like that, but Claire was right. I mean, I had to go back to school in August, and it was almost July. What did I think was going to happen anyway? Still, it made my heart ache a little, I confess.

Claire led Taylor to one of the bedrooms once she had calmed down a bit.

"She's going to sleep in there," Claire said when she returned to the living room. "I think I'll stay here with her."

"Do you want me to go back to *Suby* or...?" I asked.

"That might be best," Claire said. She leaned down and kissed me. "I'll see you in the morning, okay?"

"Okay," I grumbled. I stood up and felt utterly down until Claire leaned over and whispered, "But thy eternal summer shall not fade," a quote from *our* Shakespeare sonnet that reassured me we were fine, so I retreated to *Suby* feeling a little less let down. I was grateful it was dark and quiet, so I could climb into the bunk alone and lose myself to sleep.

JUNE 28, 2019

BB&T PAVILLION
Camden, NJ

SET 1: Set Your Soul Free, Strawberry Letter 23 > My Friend, My Friend, Halfway to the Moon, The Old Home Place, Train Song > Horn, Birds of a Feather, Wolfman's Brother, Wombat > Timber (Jerry The Mule), Drift While You're Sleeping

SET 2: Mercury > No Men In No Man's Land > We Are Come to Outlive Our Brains, About to Run, Light- > Run Like an Antelope

ENCORE: Sleeping Monkey > Quinn the Eskimo

23

The next morning, Claire climbed into the bunk and woke me with a kiss. "Now it's my turn to say I'm sorry," she whispered.

"It's Phish Day," I said in response. "Better than Christmas. Phishmas. We should call it Phishmas."

"I just wanted to start the day off on the right note," Claire said. "See what I did there? *Note?* As in, *note-for-note.* Musical *note.*"

"Yes," I laughed, then asked, "How's Taylor?"

"Better," Claire said. Then, she kissed me again, only this time more seriously. We made out for a bit until everyone started to stir, and the day launched with a good start. Alex began to mixing pancake batter with the blueberries Aunt Karen picked for us as Chris brewed coffee. Claire and Taylor headed back to the carriage house to shower and dress for the day, which gave me time to pull out my journal and write. When they returned, we sat down and ate.

As Claire and I cleared the table, Taylor and Chris excused themselves to the carriage house to talk privately. Alex rolled joints while I sifted through Uno cards. It was almost noon, and I wanted to take a shower before we left the show, so I gathered my things and headed to the carriage house. I opened the door quietly, but Chris and Taylor weren't in the living room, so I just made my way to the bathroom. When I got out, the living room was still empty. Maybe I had misunderstood, and Chris and Taylor were in Tippy's parent's house because they weren't in *Suby* when I opened the door. Claire and Alex were lounging on the sofa, Uno cards spread out on the table and a cloud of pot smoke surrounding their heads. It was becoming a familiar enough of scene to feel like home to me.

Tippy knocked and opened the door, introducing a guy standing behind him as his friend, Chad.

"Ready?" he asked. "Let's roll."

"I think I've got everything," I said. I wasn't carrying my journal or books or anything but the wallet in my front pocket tonight.

"Tickets," I said just as Claire asked, "Where are Chris and Taylor?"

"I don't know," Tippy said. "Carriage house?"

"They weren't up there when I took a shower," I said.

"What do you mean, they weren't up there?" Claire asked frowning. "I thought that's where they said they were going."

Before we could ponder any further, Chris opened the door, holding Taylor's hand.

"Is it time to go?" he asked. "Tickets!"

Alex opened the glove box to retrieve our tickets, and we filed out of *Suby* to drive to the show.

Chad loaded three backpacks presumably full of t-shirts in the cab before pushing in the middle backseat next to me. "I hope they don't let Trey play too many old man dad songs tonight," he said to no one in particular.

Alex said from the second back seat, "Old man dad songs?"

"Yeah, man," Chad said. "The whole *Ghosts of the Forest* thing and talking about death and living in the moment and all that other bullshit in Trey's new songs." Then he turned to me and asked, "How many shows have you seen, dude?"

"This will be my fourth," I said.

"This tour or, like all together?" he said with a bit of a sneer.

"All together," I said. "St. Louis were my first two shows. Blossom was my third. And now I'm here." I wasn't going to take the bait even as he chuckled sardonically. I took a good look at the guy. He couldn't be much older than me and certainly not older than Alex, yet he was acting like a douche.

"That's cool. I can hang with tourists," he said. Then, he leaned up to the driver seat. "Tippy, do you think Jeff and Mike hit the lot early or lagged?"

While they talked about their friends, I turned to Claire, who was sitting on my other side and squeezed her hand. Not the most fun drive to a show, but certainly the shortest. It was only a forty-minute drive from Tippy's house to the venue.

I smiled at Claire as we stepped into the sunshine. "Not a moment too soon."

"How many shows have *you* been to?" Claire mocked, giggling.

"Hey," Chris said, facing us. "I'm going to hang with Tippy and Chad for a while. I'll hit you up later, okay?" He had one of the backpacks slung over his arm. I looked at Taylor, who was busy adjusting things in her bag.

Alex said, "See you later, man." We watched Tippy, Chad, and Chris take off and looked at each other and shrugged.

"It's fine," Taylor said, looking up from her bag. "We talked and decided it would be best to kind of do our own things for these three shows, especially since he's got Tippy here. He can hang with Tippy's crew, and I've got you. That's what we decided. Let's go."

Alex reached into his back pocket. "Before we go, let's microdose," he said.

"I don't know," I said, thinking about Blossom. He must have read my mind because he said, "It's not going to spin your head like last time. I promise. It's just going to heighten your senses and give you a small boost, so to speak."

I was grateful we only microdosed when the monster storm blew in out of nowhere. I felt the effects of the acid as we walked the lot, but I wasn't disoriented going through security or finding our seats in the pavilion when the skies were still clear. Once the storm hit, they announced on the speaker for us to take cover, and even though we were under the pavilion, everyone in the pit was soaked. It was torrential, causing flooding and only lasted half an hour, delaying the start of the show.

Claire's eyes were glowing, her hair plastered to her head. "That was epic," she declared. I laughed and couldn't stop. Taylor and Alex laughed, too; all of us relieved the storm had abated. Alex doled out a second microdose each as the band hit the stage. We didn't think it could get any better than them busting out with *Set Your Soul Free* to start the show until Taylor got her wish with *Strawberry Letter 23*. She had been chasing it, but it was one of those old songs I swear my mother used to play because it was oddly familiar to me. They played *Drift While You're Sleeping* as the closer of first set, and I felt that an incredible sense of joy and well-being flood through my veins.

> *So I guess that the good times turned out to be*
> *Just the temporary reprieve of gravity*
> *The nights drip over the falls in a barrel with me*
> *We'll do it again when we meet on the other side*

The lines set me on a train of thoughts. I lost track of the second set until they closed with *Run Like an Antelope*. It's weird. When I eat psychedelics, my mind races too quickly to verbalize, which is humorous and causes me to laugh endlessly. Maybe it's the way for everybody. I'd have to ask Alex tomorrow if I remember. I would like to be like Taylor and write when I'm tripping, but I don't think my pen could hold my thoughts still. I would like a way to remember all these fantastic thoughts, which seemed so implausible, I started laughing again. Just following Kuroda's light took me on endless journeys. Then I would zone in on Mike's bass, understanding what I consider the root of the music or I follow Page's keys before Trey pulls me back with his commanding tones that I instinctually hum deep inside my chest.

I was still flying when the show ended, and we tromped our way through puddles and mud back to Tippy's minivan. We stopped for waters, then leaned against the van, drinking and being quiet together until Chris and Tippy ambled our way, thankfully without anyone else in tow. I don't think I could deal with that Chad guy in my state. I felt like Alex, I guess. Content to be quiet. He was like a silent, older brother I instinctually knew to trust from the moment he cautioned me about the tea. We had traveled together for four shows, and I still didn't feel like I knew him but, at the same time, felt completely comfortable just being with him. He was magical during shows, though. He danced with his hands, not his body. He carried glowsticks, and when he spun his hands to the music, the glowsticks trailed lights, creating their own mini magical light show. Alex would tilt his head back, delighted grin in place, eyes half-closed in bliss as his arms did all the dancing. I was more comfortable swinging my arms just watching him, although not as uninhibited as Claire, who thought nothing of throwing both her arms up, hands above her head as she spun around and around and cheered when the music delighted her. She and Taylor danced like I imagined fairy sprites to dance. My dance moves left something to be desired as Claire and Taylor have started teasing me by calling me Fozzy Bear, the Muppets character. That was fine with me. I did have an ambling manner when I dance, like how I would imagine a bear would. The shows inspired all of our energy and depleted us by the end. I felt empty in a good way. Scooped out and left cleansed. I was happy listening as everyone rehashed the details of the show. Even when Claire leaned over and asked if I was okay, I just smiled and nodded. I was beyond words for once and at peace.

JUNE 29, 2019
BB&T PAVILION
Camden, NJ

SET 1: Mike's Song > I Am Hydrogen > Weekapaug
Groove, Divided Sky, Everything's Right > Guelah
Papyrus > Sparkle > Roggae > 46 Days

SET 2: Blaze On > NICU > Golden Age > Ruby Waves > Death
Don't Hurt Very Long > Rift > Beneath a Sea of Stars Part
1 > Waiting All Night > Ghost > Say It To Me S.A.N.T.O.S.

ENCORE: You Enjoy Myself, Grind

JUNE 30, 2019

BB&T PAVILION
Camden, NJ

SET 1: The Curtain With > Fast Enough for You > Buried Alive > Camel Walk, Reba > Sample in a Jar, Pebbles and Marbles, Tela > The Mango Song > Driver > David Bowie

SET 2: Mr. Completely > Twenty Years Later > Big Black Furry Creature from Mars > Tweezer > Shade > Most Events Aren't Planned, Makisupa Policeman > Chalk Dust Torture > Suzy Greenberg

ENCORE: Punch You in the Eye > What's the Use? > Julius

24

Since not all Tippy's friends turned out to be as rude as Chad and the weather stayed clear, the weekend was incredible. With Tippy's parents gone for the weekend, we had full reign of the backyard pool and hot tub. He blasted music from outdoor speakers, and when we weren't at shows, we were out there. Chad was a regular but was easily avoidable, and at least a dozen other friends, as well as Plums, wandered in and out who were perfectly friendly and even kind. We slept in snatches and ate microdoses at intervals. One moment bled into the next, yet each adventure was its universe. Working on her art in the garage consumed Claire, so we never got to the lot early. We danced in the moat after the first night because the energy there was incredible. You couldn't see the band very well, but there was so much space for dancing, we stayed there. There were fireworks at the end of Saturday's show, and for whatever reason, they banned glowsticks for Sunday's show, which didn't bother me too much, but I'll bet the Little Ragers weren't too happy. Those kids like their glow sticks. As did Alex. He couldn't dance without them, but luckily Taylor had a few at the bottom of her bag. There wasn't even an announcement of the ban. Security just started confiscating the sticks as we went through.

By the end of the third night, I was starting to feel like I was coming down with a cold. "The wook flu," Chris declared when I sneezed. "It's inevitable when we run as hard as we have this weekend.

It's worth it, though. You can sleep all day tomorrow and on our drive to SPAC Tuesday."

"We're staying here until Tuesday?" I asked Chris as we lounged in Tippy's hot tub after the show Sunday night. We were alone as Claire and Taylor were off listening to a podcast called Phemale-Centrics in *Suby* because they heard one of the broadcasts was an interview with Bella, Trey's daughter. Claire and Taylor were obsessed with all things, Bella. Alex was swimming laps, something he had done every night after the shows. I don't know where the guy gets the energy after dancing as hard as we do, even though his hands do most of the dancing, especially in the moat of Camden. Magical, like a church but with no pews, so there was plenty of room for dancing. Tippy and his buddies were somewhere in the house, so Chris and I had a somewhat quiet moment.

"That's the plan," Chris said. "Tippy's folks won't be back until tomorrow, and he needs to stick around to see them before he leaves with us for SPAC. And it gives Claire one last day on her work in the garage before she loads it up."

"She seems happy with the progress," I said.

"Claire is always working on some project," he said. "It's all working out. We can get to SPAC early so she can install her work, and I can search for tickets."

"Nobody has tickets yet?" I asked.

"Tippy might," Chris said. "But we still need ours. He said he'd ask around, though. We'll just see what happens."

I smiled at Chris and said, "I guess we suck at calling songs. They played *What's the Use* for Claire."

"And *Strawberry Letter* for Taylor," Chris said. "So, they're happy."

"Is Taylor happy? Are you just taking a break from each other, or have you broken up?" I asked.

"I'm not sure what we're doing," Chris said. "Saturday, we had sex before the show, so I assumed we were making up, but then Taylor said she wanted to do the rest of the shows and that I should go off with Tippy and his crew."

"Are you serious?" I said. "She made it sound like it was your idea to go on your own."

"I'll be honest," Chris shook his head. "I will never understand. I mean, I've lived with Claire since we were ten years old, and Taylor and I have been going out for at least two years, and I still don't know shit about women."

I laughed and said, "Wait. You had sex before Saturday's show? In the carriage house? I wondered where you were when I went up there to shower. It was quiet."

"We heard you," Chris said. "We were in one of the bedrooms, dude, waiting for you to get done."

I laughed. "Sorry." Then I asked, "How far of a drive is it to SPAC?"

"Only four hours," he said. "We'll leave in the morning so we can get into the lot and help Claire set up. Then we'll do what we do. Like always."

I liked *always*. Liked that I knew what to expect when we drove. How to find Mama Vo's for chicken tofu Banh Mi, where to find incredible posters for *Suby,* which vendors were on the take, who was raising their family on tour, how much I should pay for a White Claw, what to take with me, and what to leave behind, both literally and metaphorically.

"After SPAC, it's only another four-hour drive to get to Boston," Chris continued. "We have reservations at an RV park. We'll be able to walk to the train station to take into Fenway for the shows."

"And we'll be in Boston for the Fourth of July," I said.

Alex finished his laps and draped a towel around his neck before he approached us in the hot tub. "I'm going to sleep now. I think I'll go up to the carriage house tonight."

We said our goodnights as Chris, and I got out of the hot tub and cracked open beers. We sat on the patio, looking out over the back yard as Tippy, Plums, and Chad opened the glass doors and walked outside.

"He's spun," Tippy said. "The kind of guy who took a thousand hits of acid spun."

"Who are you talking about?" Chris asked.

"This dude we know from school," Plums said. "He fucking took off with a backpack of t's and thinks we don't know how to track his ass down. We took the fucking yellow bus together in middle school. I mean, where does he think he can hide?"

"Fucking wook," Chad said. "If he's not at SPAC, we'll find him later."

"Later? Fuck later. I'm going to his house now," Plums said. He turned to us. "Are you still searching for tickets? I think I know someone."

"Yes, cool," I said. I stood up. "I'm going to look for the girls."

"I'll come with you," Chris said. We nodded to the guys and walked back to *Suby*. Claire and Taylor were finishing their podcast. Claire and I decided to take the other bedroom in the carriage house to give Chris and Taylor *Suby* for the night. I wanted a night alone with Claire, but she was too keyed up to sleep, so I offered to trek back down to the garage to look at her pieces.

"I will never again in my entire life work with fibers," Claire said as she flicked on the light. "Too tedious. I don't like to sew. Guess that rules out fashion design for a major. But I'm pleased with how this turned out. At least, on the ground. But, if we can install it, I hope it works. It has to work. It just has to."

Spread on the garage floor was black fabric drop cloths. On top of the fabric lay five large hoops.

"I bought the black fabric so I could see all the detail as I worked, but of course, these hoops will stand vertically, picking up the light," Claire explained. "I used hula hoops and PVC for the poles, and I bought these five ground spikes that have this special tool if you and Chris can help me screw them in. Each hoop will stand on its pole that will be drilled into the ground, making it structurally strong to withstand the collaboration component."

Inside each of the hoops was an elaborately constructed spider web. Claire turned up all the lights as we walked closer to the circles so I could inspect each one. Shiny white fabric wound around the surface of the hoops. Woven into the gossamer-looking strands that made up the web were shimmering beads and metal charms. When I looked closer, I could make out the quotes.

"I used craft wire to shape each letter of the word," Claire said. "Then, and this is what took the longest. I wrapped this super tiny thin gossamer thread around each letter. Finally, I had to string each letter together to make the words. String the words to become quotes and finally adhere the quotes to the web. I knotted each matching point of the web, see? You could, but please don't, but you could grab the webs from the center and pull, and it will bounce back to its shape," Claire said. "That will be important for when people add the tags."

"Tags?" I asked.

She held up a box decoupaged with images from "Charlotte's Web" illustrations. Inside were round shiny paper tags with a slit in each. The top of the box stood open, where she had scribbled instructions. "People will read the web and then write the name of their childhood best friend and then use the slit to attach to the webs. By the end of the day, it should look like drops of dew shimmering on the webs. If I get enough people to participate."

"Incredible," I said. "I guarantee you are going to have people. Don't worry about that."

"I will give you a minute to read it now," Claire said. She pulled me to the end of the garage. "Start here. This will be the first web. What people see first."

Inside the first web read:

You have been my friend. That in itself is a tremendous thing.

Woven inside the next three webs were further quotes, like:

With the right words, you can change the world.

I stopped to think about that quote for a moment. I think that is probably my life's belief. I thought about my journal and Taylor's poetry and the books I read. It's true. Writing can change the world, but apparently, so can art if Claire's work was any indication.

The next quotes read:

A spider's web is stronger than it looks.
Although it is made of thin, delicate strands,
the web is not easily broken.

That quote seemed to be symbolic of Claire herself. I laughed when I read:

People are very gullible. They'll believe anything they see in print.

And I thought of Taylor with:

It is not often that someone comes
along who is
a true friend and a good writer.

Some of the quotes were small. Some were bigger.

Trust me, Wilbur.
You've got a new friend, all right. But what a gamble
friendship is!

The quote that best-fit summer tour read:

*Never hurry and never worry! Children
almost always hang onto things tighter
than their parents think they will.*

The quote that made me catch my breath, remembering the scene
from the book was:

We take to the breeze, we go as we please.

The last web read:

*What do you mean less than nothing? I
don't think there is any such thing as
less than nothing. Nothing is absolutely
the limit of nothingness. It's the lowest
you can go. It's the end of the line.
How can something be less than
nothing? If there were something that
was less than nothing, then nothing
would not be nothing, it would be
something - even though it's just a very
little bit of something. But if nothing is
nothing, then nothing has nothing that
is less than it is.*

"I've always loved this book," Claire said. "And I don't know.
It just makes sense to me, you know. Phish is about friendship.
Community. Bringing people together as family. At least, that's what
this experience has been for me. Especially this summer. So, these
webs just made sense in my mind. Interconnected webs of us all. To
each other. To the universe. And I thought people would enjoy
thinking about their childhood friends while they're at a show with
their current friends. And, after the Barbie doll show, I wanted to
create something with a positive message. Work that strives to build

community, not just make scathing commentary about the problems with society. I mean, that's important, too. I guess the Barbie doll exhibit was my feminist homage to Judy Chicago, and this is my tribute to E.B. White, two artists I admire. I don't know if I'm explaining this well enough."

"You are," I said. "I completely understand. I think it's incredible. Not to mention, the webs are aesthetically beautiful on their own. It must have taken hours and hours."

"Yes," she turned to kiss me. "Good thing I started these months before you moved here. You have been quite the distraction."

I took her back upstairs and showed her how distracting I could be.

JULY 2, 2019

SARATOGA PERFORMING ARTS CENTER
Saratoga Springs, NY

SET 1: Cathy's Clown, Tweezer Reprise > Carini > AC/DC Bag > The Moma Dance > Theme From the Bottom, Meat, Home > Bathtub Gin > Walls of the Cave

SET 2: Cool Amber and Mercury > Down with Disease > Scents and Subtle Sounds > Twist > Wilson > Scent of a Mule, Fuck Your Face > Halley's Comet > Harry Hood

ENCORE: Fee, A Life Beyond The Dream, First Tube

25

Now I see that webs were woven

"Devotion to a Dream"
Anastasio & Marshall

To leave early Tuesday, we tackled more tasks than we anticipated on Monday. While Claire and Taylor worked to gather the art materials and load the webs into *Suby,* Alex and Chris did a grocery run. I stayed behind to help Tippy clean the backyard and the carriage house before his parents returned home later that afternoon. They were as kind and welcoming as their son when we met them for on the patio for dinner. Cooling off in the pool after eating was the perfect ending to a hot and sweaty day of work in the July heat. The next morning, the four-hour drive to the venue was easily manageable, even with Claire's hoops stacked in their fabric bags standing vertically and not stored under the bed horizontally like they were the first leg of the journey.

"I can't trust laying them on top of each other," Claire said when Chris protested. I don't know why he'd be bothered. He and Alex always took the front seats as they took turns driving. Typical sibling bickering. Even with the addition of Tippy, it still wasn't crowded, though. It was worth the hassle once we had installed the webs. Claire spotted what she called the perfect small grassy knoll near between two rows of the vending lot after walking around to determine easy access for the maximum amount of people and for what she considered to be the most magical spot destined for alchemy. The process took Claire over an hour, walking around contemplating the lot, which was huge with vending. It was clear the day was going to be epic, even if it was a sticky, sweaty July day. I could feel the energy building as I met smile after smile.

Although the ground spike bases appeared to be simply screwed into the ground, as they came with individual wrenches. Chris, Alex, and I sweated it out, taking multiple turns forcing the spikes into the dirt. Tippy had taken off to find his crew and to start the search for tickets.

"Did you know this venue was so green?" I asked Claire, looking around at all the trees. "And did you anticipate the lot to be this big?"

"Yes, I have maps, and I researched aerial views before we got here," Claire said. "But I didn't know the exact spot until I knew where we'd park and until I could feel the space. It's not just about the physical location. It's spiritual."

It was the perfect setting for this installment. The webs appeared to glow, sunlight glinting from the beads and metallic charms. The webs stood tall on their poles firmly anchored into the ground against a backdrop of verdant trees that provided enough shade for us to set up an area with chairs and a blanket close to the installment. We hadn't finished before people began crowding, asking Claire questions, and picking up tags from the box. Alex busied himself, taking pictures from every angle, and Taylor opened her journal, ready to take notes on people's conversations and reactions.

Chris and I walked back to where we had parked *Suby* to retrieve a small cooler of ice and waters. Chris grabbed four camping chairs, and I reached for a bottle of rum, a portable speaker, and a blanket. He and I lugged everything back and set up.

"Claire couldn't have chosen to install her work next to *Suby*?" Chris grumbled.

"I guess not," I said. "She was pretty particular about the location, that's for sure. But for the hours of work she put into this project, I wasn't about to argue."

"But I want to raise the flag and set up the canopy for once," Chris said.

"It is convenient to have *Suby* in the lot," I said.

Chris made me laugh when he said, "I know. I don't think Lyft drivers appreciate me. But I'll be okay to drive after the show. I don't know if you've noticed, but I'm not drinking these days."

"What's up with that?" I asked, thinking of the bottle of rum I grabbed.

"Taylor," Chris said. "It's her one major request. And I know I was getting out of hand, so okay. I won't drink. She didn't say I couldn't smoke, though." He held up his cart.

"Sounds reasonable," I said. Chris not smoking would probably be entirely unrealistic and unnecessary if you asked me. He seemed to be high twenty-four-seven, but only acted like a dick when he drank. Smart move, Taylor, I thought.

Tippy returned with his crew for Chris, who took off promising to come back with tickets. Alex wandered off, so that left me with Taylor and Claire. It was the best afternoon. We sat in the shade, sipping rum, listening to Moe. and hitting the cart. We greeted folks who wandered to the webs. We met a couple from New York who was currently homeschooling their three kids in Kentucky. She made jewelry and charms from natural crystals and stones she sold on Etsy. He had a grown-up job but liked to talk about frisbee golf and these obscure weird punk bands from the '90s. They were both super nice and friendly. She opened her bag and offered us band-aids, Advil, tissues, water, and snacks.

Another woman who owned a restaurant called Minglewood came by with a group of sparkly-clad women she called her dance team. She raved over the webs and offered to show Claire's work if she was ever interested. A trio of older guys who said they'd been going to shows together since college talked to us about traveling around in *Suby*. One guy was a lawyer. The other had flown in from Aspen, Colorado. He liked to hike and ski, and highly recommended we experience natural hot springs if we ever made it out west to Dick's. The third was a teacher who belonged to a social media site called *Chalkdust Torturers*. A few of the kids we met at Blossom and kids we met at Tippy's house came by to see us. What made it feel like a family reunion was when the kind Phish Chick woman we met in line for Ben and Jerry's at St. Louis recognized us and said hello. Claire was right. Summer tour was an inner-connected web of souls who were all connected to their own experiences, history, friends, which then wove all of us together. Some folks were taking their moms or dads to their first show. Others had their kids, which was the best. Seeing their eyes light up when they saw the webs and their parents read the quotes to them was beautiful. The webs were quickly filling up with tags, and it was getting almost time to go in for the show, but Chris was nowhere to be found.

"We still don't have tickets," I said to Claire.

"I know," she said. "And I don't really care. Do you? Should we walk around a bit and look now?"

I could tell she didn't want to leave. I didn't blame her. She was busy taking more pictures now that the webs were full. I walked over to Taylor, who was contentedly sitting under the trees writing in her journal.

"Whatcha got going on?" I asked as I lowered myself into the chair next to her.

"A new one," she said. "Wanna hear?"

"Of course," I said.

She read,

> *We walk where they once tread softly*
> *trampling memories underfoot*
> *in blatant disregard for tradition*
> *more intent in carving our path*
> *stepping on heads in the process*
> *breaking stalks of geraniums*
> *crushing violets underneath*
> *dividing time between roots of trees*
> *and gnarled branches of roses*
> *weighted down by blooms losing*
> *petals when the wind blows*
> *the nature of a thing*
> *cannot be named.*

"You wrote that today?" I asked. I loved it when Taylor read her poems. She sounded sure of herself, more confident, and she had this low, lovely voice.

"It's rough, I know," Taylor said. "It's a first draft."

"It's good," I insisted. Before I could say anything more, Chris, Tippy, and Chad approached, waving tickets in their hands. It couldn't be Plums who I liked. They had to bring fucking Chad, the rudest person I'd met on tour thus far.

"I've got good news and bad," Chris said. "The good news is I got two tickets."

"And the bad?" I asked.

"Yes," he said, cracking Chad up, who slapped Chris on the back like it was the funniest thing he had ever heard. I wondered what drug he had already taken.

Chris continued, "That's the bad. And the good. The good and the bad."

I looked at Taylor. "Go," I said.

"Are you sure?" she said, looking worried. "Let me talk with Claire."

She got up and walked over to Claire to talk. I glanced over just in time to catch Chad, reaching to pull one of the strands of the most significant web.

"Hey," I yelled, standing up so abruptly, I knocked the camping chair over. I stormed over to him. "What the fuck do you think you're doing?"

"Fuck off, man," Chad said. "I was just looking."

Chris pulled my arm. "It's cool," he said. "Come on, Sam. It's fine. Chad wouldn't touch anything, right?"

"I was just fucking looking," Chad said. "But now you've pissed me off, so I'll do whatever I want to do. Who the fuck do you country ass Ohio boys think you are, anyway?"

Tippy put his hand on Chad's chest and pushed him. "Come on, Chad. It's a show. Fuck this. It's time to go in. Let's go to the show," he said, as he coaxed his asshole friend away from Claire's webs. Chris had his hand on my arm, which I jerked away. I was heaving. I was so angry. That guy had pushed me too far. "Fucking wook," I muttered.

Chad turned around abruptly. "What the fuck did you just call me?"

"Wook," I said. "You're a fucking wook. What are you going to do about it anyway? And just for the record, I'm from New York, you asshole. Not Ohio. New York."

Tippy turned around and mouthed, "I'm sorry" as he pulled Chad away. Claire and Taylor hurried over to where Chris and I stood. He and Chad kept walking, which was good.

"What the hell just happened?" Claire asked, concerned. "Are you okay?"

"I'm okay," I said. "That fucking wook was going to destroy your web."

"I don't know if he was going to destroy it," Chris said.

I turned on him furiously. "You're defending him? Exactly what do you think that asshole planned to do? Read it? I guarantee that monkey can't even fucking read. He's an idiot. He's been an idiot all weekend, and I'm done."

"I'm not defending him," Chris said, throwing his hands up in surrender. "I'm your brother. You're right. I'm sorry."

I looked up at him and felt like an asshole. "No, it's cool. I'm sorry. It's cool," I mumbled.

"Wow, man," Chris said. "I'm sorry. I've never seen you like this."

"I don't think I'd ever felt like this before," I huffed.

Claire turned the camping chair right side up and pulled me down. She handed me a bottle of water and then the bottle of rum. I drank accordingly.

"You two should head in," she said to Chris and Taylor. "I've got this."

"Let's take all this stuff back to *Suby* first," Chris said. "Then we'll take off."

We gathered everything and left the installment. I was grateful to step into our home for a minute. It was quiet, serene, and I could finally catch my breath.

Chris looked at me and asked, "Are you going to be alright?"

"Yes," I said. "You and Taylor go in. We'll stay behind." I looked at Claire, who nodded.

Once they left, I looked at Claire and said, "I'm sorry we have to sit tonight out."

"I'm not," she said, sitting on the sofa next to me, putting her feet in my lap. "I'm exhausted. Let's just sit here for a moment and then get something to eat. I'm starving."

"Sounds good," I sighed. "I'm sorry."

"For what?" Claire said. "For defending me? For having my back? For finally having enough of that wook's shit? There's no need for I'm sorry. I would have punched him."

"Punch him in the eye," I joked. Claire laughed. She stood up and reached for my hand.

"Let's go lie down together," she suggested. "I'm completely worn out. I just need to close my eyes for a minute."

I followed her to the big bed and held her in my arms until we both fell asleep. Two hours later, we roused ourselves to find something to eat and to check on the webs. They were full of tags, so Claire snapped more pictures before we decided to eat first, then take the webs down.

"I may want to wait until people let out of the show," Claire said as we shared a French bread pizza and chicken kabobs.

"That's not a good idea," I said. "People are fucked up when they come out. You don't need a bunch of people stumbling around, falling into it. Potentially destroying your work. I mean, you've gotten enough pictures, right?"

"Yes," Claire said. "You may be right."

"I'll help you," I said. "It's quiet now. We'll take everything down and then sit at *Suby* and get fucked up. We need to catch a buzz, don't you think?"

"I think that's a solid plan," Claire said. After we had eaten, it only took an hour to deconstruct the webs carefully, put them into their fabric pouches, and load them into *Suby*. Claire and I pulled the canopy out, hung the flag, cued up Billy Strings, and sat down with the rest of the bottle of rum, counting Uno cards we had collected until the show ended. We checked the setlists as the show unfolded, so we knew what they played, but neither of us felt like we were missing anything even though the setlist was sick. I reminded myself sitting out an occasional show was part of tour when I saw we missed a *Hailey's Comet > Harry Hood*. Before the last encore song popped up on the Phish.net feed, Taylor ran up to us.

"It's gone! It's gone!" she yelled.

"What?" I stood up. "What's gone?"

"The webs," she shrieked. "They're gone! They're missing."

I stopped and took a good look at Taylor. Overreacting like this was not her usual behavior. She was generally so mild-mannered.

Claire stood up and said, "It's okay, Tay. We took them down. They're safe. Thank you, but they're okay."

Taylor burst into hysterical laughter. She said, "That's good. Oh, that's good. I was freaking out."

"We know," I muttered. "Sit down. Do you want some water? Where's Chris?"

"I don't know," Taylor said. "I definitely don't want to sit down. I'm keyed up."

Claire asked, "What did you take?"

"Nothing," Taylor said. "I mean, I smoked. But I didn't take anything."

Claire turned to me and said, "Do you think someone dosed her?"

"Something. I'm not sure what, but something," I replied and then repeated, "Where's Chris?"

Taylor spun around. "I don't know. I lost him at set break."

"You've been alone since set break?" Claire asked.

"Not alone," Taylor said. "I danced with cool people. Everyone was super kind."

"This is not good," Claire murmured to me. We watched as Taylor bounced around like a wind-up toy. First, she opened the door to *Suby*, then closed it without going in. Then, she sat down in the camping chair for a minute before jumping right back up. She walked a few paces away from us and then again. It was bizarre.

"Do you think she'll be okay?" I asked Claire.

"I certainly hope so," Claire said. "Taylor, come back here. When was the last time you've eaten something? Let's go in and get a snack."

Claire lead Taylor into *Suby* to get some food into her system. Hopefully, that would help bring her back down. The problem was that Taylor didn't seem to understand that she was under the influence of something. I wondered where the hell Chris was.

After Taylor picked at a sandwich, Claire suggested we walk the lot for something to do. The show had ended, and the lot was active. "I figured this would deplete some of her energy," Claire said.

"If we can keep track of her on the lot and not lose her," I said, watching Taylor skip ahead. "Do you think Chris knew she was this high when she left her?"

"I'm not even sure Chris left her, per se," Claire said. "It's not unusual to lose each other at shows. We lost each other for a while at Blossom."

"But we found each other again," I pointed out. "And I don't think walking around is helping Taylor. Maybe we should just go back. She is like a planet without an atmosphere."

"A planet without an atmosphere?" Claire repeated back.

"*Goldfinch,*" I said.

"You and your books," Claire smiled at me. "Are you ready to write your own yet?"

"Other than my journal?" I said. "No."

"Maybe when we get back, Chris will be there, and we can clear this whole thing up," she said.

Chris was not there when we got back to *Suby,* but Alex was sitting in one of the camping chairs under the canopy. Next to him was a girl who had long blonde dreads and bare feet.

"Hey, guys," he said as we approached. "This is my friend, Willow. Willow, this is Sam and Claire. So, did you get in?"

"Claire and I didn't," I said. "But Taylor did, and now she's spun."

Claire reached her hand to Willow. "It's nice to meet you."

"Nice to meet you," Willow said, shaking Claire's hand. She nodded at me.

"I love your dreads," Claire said. "How long have you had them?"

"A year," Willow said. "They're a lot of work, but I love them."

I turned to Alex as the girls launched into a conversation about dread maintenance and asked, "Did you? Did you get into the show?"

"We did," Alex said. "I found a ticket just as I gave up. Willow already had a ticket, but she hung with me until the last minute. Is Taylor okay?"

"She will be," I answered. "She will come down eventually. Claire put some music on, hoping she will dance herself out or at least start to come down a bit."

An hour later, Chris arrived back at *Suby*. "Greetings!" he said. "Everybody ready to roll?"

"This is Willow," Alex said. "Okay, if she comes with us tonight?"

"Hi, Willow," Chris said. "Of course. The more, the merrier."

"Where's Tippy?" I asked.

"He's staying with his crew," Chris said. "We'll catch up with him again tomorrow."

Alex pulled the flag and rolled up the canopy as Chris, and I folded the camping chairs. We loaded everything in and left the lot. Taylor had settled down. She sat on the sofa with her journal, yet she tapped her pen on the table with a staccato beat. Claire had pulled Chris aside and whispered furiously with him before we hit the road, but I don't know what was said. It was only an hour before we pulled into the RV park. Nobody talked much as we settled in for the night. I followed Claire and Taylor to the restrooms, took a hot shower to wash off the wook, and then walked back to *Suby* alone. They followed about a half an hour later. Claire climbed into the bunk with me.

"Do you think she'll be able to sleep?" I asked.

"She took a shower," Claire said. "She seemed like she was calming down. That was just weird."

"What did Chris say when you talked with him?" I asked.

"You know Chris," Claire sighed. "He didn't have much to say other than she was fine when they got separated, and he had no idea how she got dosed."

"Do you believe him?" I asked.

"Yes," Claire said. "Chris is a lot of things, but I don't believe he dosed her, and I don't believe he would have left her in that state."

I hoped Claire was right, I thought. The silence was interrupted by the sounds of Alex and Willow. Claire and I started giggling at first, but it wasn't funny twenty minutes later when things began intensifying by the sounds of it.

"Are you kidding me?" I whispered.

"I mean, we're right here," Claire whispered back.

We tossed our pillows over our heads to muffle the sound and somehow fell asleep.

JULY 3, 2019

SARATOGA PERFORMING ARTS CENTER
Saratoga Springs, NY

SET 1: Fluffhead, Guyute, Martian Monster, Llama, Steam > Poor Heart > Crazy Sometimes > The Horse > Silent in the Morning, Sleep, Drift While You're Sleeping

SET 2: No Men In No Man's Land > Dirt > Plasma -> We Are Come to Outlive Our Brains -> Plasma -> Tweezer Reprise > The Wedge > Sneakin' Sally Through the Alley -> Run Like an Antelope, More > Slave to the Traffic Light

ENCORE: Rock and Roll

26

The next day, Claire and I took off to search for tickets as soon as we hit the lot. Taylor was still sound asleep, having not been able to come down until the sun rose, according to Chris, who stayed up with her. He seemed sincere and even apologetic about what had happened last night. I'm not sure if we'll ever know what she had taken exactly, but it was clear to all of us that she had been drugged.

"I'm going to hang around here in case she wakes up," Chris said, opening the canopy and raising the flag. "Look for all of us."

"We will," Claire promised.

Alex and Willow took off in their own direction. I grabbed my backpack, checking to make sure I had a sealed bottle of water, my journal, and my books, which turned out to be serendipitous when we found Cosmic Charlie on the lot. He didn't seem to remember us at all until I pulled out the copy of *Divine Right's Trip* and handed it to him.

"I wanted to return your book," I said. "You're not going to believe this, but I met Gurney Norman. I had him sign it for you. See?"

Cosmic Charlie opened the cover and smiled. "What I see is that you're a good kid."

"Thanks, Charlie," I said. "I liked the book. Do you have another for me?"

"What the hell do you think this is, a library?" he grumbled back. "Now, scram. I've got drums to sell."

Claire laughed, kissed him on the cheek, and said, "See you later, Charlie."

"Later, girlie," he said, and he winked at me before he turned his attention back to his sales.

"Funny," I said. "Anywhere else, I would say it's too much of a coincidence, running into that guy over and over."

"That's summer tour," Claire said. "We're like a traveling town of sorts. The residents are pretty much the same as the tourists come and go."

"Coincidence is God's way of staying anonymous," I quoted.

"What's that?" Claire asked.

"Another line from *The Goldfinch*," I said. She squeezed my hand in response.

That was true when it came to the vendors for the most part. Many of the same people were doing the same leg of tour as we were; however, we didn't find our tickets from them. We bought them from a couple we hadn't met before. They said their friends had to give up the tickets because the wife had gone into labor early. I didn't need to hear all the details about the birth, but Claire seemed interested enough to encourage the whole story. I plastered a polite smile on my face. Part of what you had to do to score good tickets, I guess. They were friendly people, so I gifted them with an Uno card. We walked around another hour, looking for two more tickets to no avail.

"Let's go back to *Suby* to touch base and to get something to eat," Claire suggested. It was another hot July day, and going back to cool off under the canopy was a good idea. Tippy was sitting with Chris when we walked up. They were eating burritos.

"I brought extras for you," Tippy said as greeting, pointing to extra foil-wrapped burritos.

"Thanks, Tippy," Claire said. "Is Taylor awake?"

"Not yet," Chris said. "She's still sound asleep. I just checked on her a minute ago. She's still alive."

"Very funny," Claire said as she walked into *Suby*. I sat down with Chris and Tippy. They were listening to Turkuaz. The burrito I accepted from Tippy was delicious. Claire popped back out with two beers in her hand. She gave me one as she took the last burrito from Tippy.

"I checked on her. She's still breathing," Claire said.

"Very funny," Chris said. "Of course, she's still breathing. She just may not wake up for a long while is all."

"You didn't see her last night when she first got out of the show, Christopher," Claire said. "It was bad. I have never seen her like that, even when she and I stole Boot's diet pills in eighth grade."

"Look, I feel bad," Chris insisted. "I didn't intentionally leave her during the show, and she didn't answer any of my texts when I tried to find her. But I promise I'll stay here and stand guard. I've got this. I will take care of her."

"What do you think she was on?" Tippy asked. "Methamphetamines?"

"I don't know, but I know I'll never smoke anything with anyone at a show," Claire said.

"Sounds unrealistic," Chris said.

"How so?" Claire asked.

"It's just, everyone smokes at shows," Chris said.

"I didn't say I wouldn't smoke," Claire explained. "I meant I won't accept anything from anyone outside of our family is all. I don't want ever to get spun like that."

"I saw a chick hit the ground at Camden," Tippy said. "It was bad. Some guy had to do mouth-to-mouth, and another chick was screaming; she didn't have a pulse. The paramedics came by with Narcan and took her to the hospital. Fucking fentanyl."

"There are a lot of posts on Phish Chicks about Narcan," Claire said. "They take a course or training and then carry it with them in case something like that happens."

"Yeah, but how do you know?" Chris said. "I mean, how do you know if someone is overdosing or faints because they are having a seizure or are diabetic, for example? You need to know before you start wielding a needle of Narcan at someone."

"I've seen people fall over on nitrous," Claire said. "One dude was twitching, and his lips were blue."

"That's because he didn't get enough oxygen," Tippy said. "People are fucked up. They come to see Phish and treat it like it's an orgy. And nitrous is killing the scene. Fucking fentanyl and fucking nitrous."

"How do you really feel?" Claire quipped, cracking us all up.

"I wonder if it's the same as the scene with the Grateful Dead, back in the day," Chris said. "I mean, we've all heard those old stories about the brown acid at Woodstock."

"I don't think so anymore," Tippy said. "The new Dead is old, man. Old. Have you watched any of the shows? The entire audience looks like a GOP convention."

"Mayer and Oteil aren't old," Claire said. "And John Mayer is hot."

"But the tempo is horribly slow. As if their old audience can't move fast anymore or maybe because Weir is ancient. Whatever it may be, I'll stick with Phish," Tippy said. "That fucking *Tweezer* reprise and *First Tube* closer is anything but old man music."

"But Trey's *Ghost of the Forest* is," Chris said. "*Life Beyond A Dream?*"

"Old, how?" I asked. "I mean, what band is still writing and creating good original music after thirty-plus years? And aren't you just echoing what that wook, Chad said at Camden anyway?"

"You're in a mood," Chris said. "Relax, man. Old or not, I'll take Phish; however, I can get them. Last night was crazy, so fucking good."

The afternoon slid by as we sat under the canopy, smoking and laughing at the random bits of conversation we'd catch as people walked by. Comments like, *one day, you're smoking your first joint, the next you're at a Phish show.* No kidding, I thought. That was me exactly. *This is what it feels like if your life takes a bad turn,* one solemn man said to his friend. We all cracked up when a girl called to her friends, *wait up, I'm just trying to get the acid out of my teeth.* A man said to his buddy, *I saw that cop from one thousand miles away,* and another guy said, *he's a wook in sheep's clothing,* reminding me of that fucking Chad. I laughed when I heard one guy say to another, *dude, the brain is the only organ that names itself. Think about it.* Indeed. The best lines used Phish lyrics like; *I swear I both bagged and tagged that man before* and, of course, the all-important phrase, *surrender to the flow.*

Tippy took off to find his crew and sell t-shirts before the show, and Taylor was still sleeping when it was time for me and Claire to go into the show.

"Where's Alex?" I asked Chris as we waited for Claire to get herself ready for the evening.

"With Willow, I assume. He does his own thing," Chris said. "No worries. He likes to carve his own path."

"Carve Willow's path, maybe," I joked.

"I know, right?" Chris said. "They were a little loud last night."

"Are you sure you'll be okay staying behind tonight?" I said.

"Of course," Chris said. "I might lift my alcohol ban, though, and drink a little tequila while I hang out just to pass the time."

"Just not too much," I cautioned.

"Not too much," he promised as Claire stepped out of *Suby* wearing a bikini top, a silky patchwork skirt, and butterfly wings. Every inch of skin glowed from her beloved gold body glitter.

"Aunt Karen's skirt," she said, twirling around. "You like?"

"Very much," I said, leaning to kiss her. She was beautiful. The sun was shining, and it was time to go into the show. The perfect moment in life, to be honest. I'd never been so happy. A surge of adrenaline coursed down my spine in anticipation, even as we walked past a line of police officers holding automatic rifles on our way into the venue. Claire and I paused. We learned there was a shooting a concert a few weeks ago, and they were there to protect us according to one of the Little Rager dads we followed into the venue.

But nothing prepared me for the elation I felt when Phish launched the show with *Fluffhead* followed by *Guyute*. At the end of first set, Claire and I sat together on the lawn.

I said, "I'm grateful we got in tonight and that we're alone. At the risk of sounding embarrassing for the rest of my life, this set will remind me of you. I can't help it. I'm a sentimental guy. I just am."

"I love you for being sentimental," Claire said.

"I love you, too," I said for the first time.

Note for note; it was probably the best show of the tour for me. And then, *Dirt*. That song always gets me. It reminds me of how I felt at St. Philips, grieving, and alone before I found Claire and found Phish and found my family finally. I thought about the passage I had read in *The Goldfinch*:

> *But sometimes, unexpectedly, grief*
> *pounded over me in waves that left me*
> *gasping; and when the waves washed*
> *back, I found myself looking out over a*
> *brackish wreck which was illumined in*
> *a light so lucid, so heartsick and empty,*

that I could hardly remember that the
world had ever been anything but dead.

I had felt that way so many times at school. So many times,
until this summer. I confess, tears were streaming down my face, as I
sang, *I'll never hear your voice again/shout your name into the wind.*
Claire was good, though. She just held my hand and stayed steady
next to me. Luckily, *Plasma* grounded me and then Claire and I sang
on the top of our lungs, *I'm the glue in your magnet* during *We Are
Come To Outlive Our Brains.* Before I could take a breath, they
fucking launched into *Tweezer Reprise* for a minute before cascading
us over *The Wedge.* I could barely hold on, and I hadn't eaten one
dot of acid. By the time we ran like an antelope, I didn't think I could
bear it until Trey pleaded there must be something more than this,
and then, we all became slaves to the traffic light. I have never danced
so hard in my entire life—fucking best show I had ever seen.

"Lone encore," I said to Claire as we shuttled out of the show.

"But it was my anthem," Claire said. "*You know her life was
saved by rock and roll!*"

"I'm so grateful we got this show and not last night," I said. "I
mean, both would have been great, but I don't know, there's some
kind of alchemy I can't explain. Like, we were intended to see this
show together. Not last night's. Tonight. Like, it's our show. I told you
I will forever remember you from this show."

"It's ours," Claire said. "*No one can take that from me.*"

Taylor was sitting with Chris under the canopy when we got
back to *Suby.*

"How was the show?" she asked.

Claire leaned down to kiss Taylor on the cheek and said, "Wonderful, brilliant, perfection. Are you feeling better, love?"

She and Taylor went into the RV as I sat down with Chris under the canopy. He handed me the bottle of tequila.

"Here. Make a dent in this. I didn't drink because as soon as Tippy and Alex get back, we'll head out," Chris said. "I want us to get an early start for Boston tomorrow. It will be cool to see what's going on there for the Fourth."

"Do you know where we are staying?" I asked. Because I was still vibrating from the show, I set the tequila aside. So high, I didn't even want to come down.

"Wompatuck State Park," Chris said. "What's cool is that the train station is three miles from the entrance of the park so that we can ride in and out of Fenway both nights, and no one has to drive anywhere."

"Or take a dreaded Lyft," I joked. "I'm excited. I've only been to Boston a few times and only when I was just a kid. I've never been to Fenway. Have you?"

Chris said, "It's all new territory for me, too."

When Tippy, Alex and Willow arrived back to *Suby*, we were all ready to leave the lot. I guess Willow was now going to be part of the family for however long this romance lasted. Chris and I loaded everything up while Tippy took down the canopy and flag. Next stop, the home of the Red Sox, Harvard, and baked beans.

27

When your reaching just pushes it further away

"Julius"
Anastasio

"I thought I was going to bust out when you called him a wook," Tippy said, laughing. We were about an hour outside of Boston, listening to Tedeschi Trucks Band. I looked up from *The Goldfinch* to answer him.

"Why?" I said. "I'm sorry, man, I know he's your friend, but he is a fucking wook."

"I'm a wook," Willow said.

"How so?" I asked.

"My friends and I call each other wooks," she said. "We're all on tour. We rebel against the establishment. We do our own thing. We wear dreads."

I noticed Taylor roll her eyes at Claire. Then, Tippy pulled out his phone and said, "Look at this." It was a hilarious meme that read: *ain't nobody told you about wooks yet? There are tour wooks, feisty wooks, trustafarian wooks, weekend wooks, 9-5 wooks, pre-wooks, post- wooks, spun wooks, recovering wooks, city wooks, country wooks. I'll tell ya I seen lots a wooks.*

"It can be endearing. A kind, clean wook like a wokewook," Claire said.

"Depends on the usage," Alex said. "I've known a bunch of fucking wooks you wouldn't want to know. Like scary spun-out dudes who would steal your shit, never have a ticket and always be begging for money wooks."

"I guess I've always considered myself more of a hippie than a wook," Claire said.

"So, there's a difference between hippies and wooks?" I asked. "Or is it a never judge a wook by its cover kind of thing?"

"Here, listen to this," Claire said, reading from her phone. "*Hippies will puff lightly on your joint; wooks will borrow your dab rig and never return it. Hippies will bum a ride in your Vanagon; wooks will live in it. Hippies will give you their Phish ticket; wooks will scalp it for three times face value.* That's from a site I just found called "Rooster." There's a whole article about wooks."

"I always like Chewbacca," Taylor said. "I guess I have an affection for wooks then. I'll be a wook."

"As much as we love dancing barefoot?" Claire joked. "We've all got wook foot! Although some of those wooks are sepia-toned."

"Sepia-toned?" Taylor asked, frowning at Claire.

"I mean they're kinda dirty and covered from head-to-toe in dust," Claire said, leaning over to grab Taylor's hand. "What else did you think I meant? You know I speak like a painter."

Taylor smiled at Claire and opened her mouth to speak, but Willow cut her off. "I think we've been hit with some shade."

Both Taylor and Claire whipped their heads at her. "Exactly what are you implying?" Claire snarled.

"Just because you have dreads does not entitle you to the use of *we*," Taylor said, clasping her hand tighter with Claire's. "Claire

213

and I are *we*. You and I are not *we*. I barely know you. What Claire meant was her way of expressing herself, which is as a painter, not as a racist."

"I wasn't referring to race," Willow said. "I just explained I considered myself a wook. Her comment felt like a double threat. My dreads are not a comment on your race."

"Not a comment on my race?" Taylor said. "I'm sorry, but have you ever heard of the term *cultural appropriation,* or did you not get that far in school?"

"Cultural appropriation?" Willow said. "I could dread your hair if you'd like."

"Oh my God," Taylor fumed. "Would somebody please—"

"Okay, okay," Chris interjected, his hands up in surrender. "But to change topics, I want to see the Boston Pops play. It says they go on at eight at the Hatch Shell."

"Hatch shell?" Taylor said. "What is the Hatch Shell?" Chris knew he could distract her with mention of the Boston Pops. I was grateful everyone was willing to switch subjects. We still had time before we arrived in Boston, and *Suby* was starting to feel a bit cramped.

"The Hatch Memorial Shell is the downtown Boston amphitheater where they have an outdoor concert before the fireworks. Sounds fun," Claire said. "We'll go to an actual restaurant and eat and then go to the concert and stay for the fireworks."

"Yes," Taylor said. "A restaurant sounds perfect. I'm a little tired of lot food."

"As long as it's vegan," Willow said. Alex nodded his agreement. Whenever I looked at them, they were holding hands or kissing or touching each other.

"Okay," Claire said. "I'll find a restaurant that serves vegan, too. Now let's talk songs. What's everybody chasing these last four shows?"

"Last four shows," I said. "Can't we just keep going?"

"I wish," Chris said. "But Alpine is sixteen hours from Connecticut, and we said we'd be back to Maywood by Thursday the eleventh, and it's a twelve-hour drive from Mohegan to home."

"I'm chasing *Petrichor*," Alex said. "I have never seen that performed live."

" *Winterqueen* for me," Claire said.

"I think I've heard all my songs," Taylor said. "I need to think."

"I need *Squirming Coil*," Chris said. "We've heard *Slave* how many times? Not that I don't love that song, but I'd love a *Squirming Coil*. Am I the only one who kind of groups those two songs in my mind?"

"No," Alex said. "I do, too. Like how I put *My Friend, My Friend,* and *Guyute* together or confuse the beginning of *Slave* with *Fluffhead*."

Willow said, "The songs I screw up are *Maze* and *David Bowie*."

" *Punch You in the Eye* and *First Tube*," Taylor said.

"Those are your calls?" Alex asked.

"No," she said. "Those are songs I put together in my mind. I confuse which song is which at the beginning of those two pair of songs. I'm not chasing any song actually, now that I got my *Strawberry Letter.* I'm just along for the ride. What about you, Sam?"

"Me?" I asked. "I'm too new to know any of this. I'm still trying to figure out how *Reba* is one song. It feels like three songs to me."

"The whistling of *Reba* and the whistling of *Guyute*," Alex said. "There's another connection." He started whistling, and we joined in, laughing and starting and stopping until we were whistled out.

An hour later, we arrived at Wompatuck State Park and settled into our camping site. We had no trouble finding the train station that was within walking distance. However, stepping off the train was disorienting. The city was teeming with tourists celebrating the holiday. We ducked into a busy bistro to eat and to ask around where the best place to see the fireworks would be. The crowds were overwhelming after swimming in the Phish lot for so long. Entirely different species of humans, for sure.

"There's no way we are going to get a table," Chris complained, gesturing to the bustling restaurant. Every table was full, and people were clustered around the entrance waiting to be seated.

Claire marched ahead to the hostess stand, and ten minutes later, we were seated.

"You are magical," I whispered to her, reaching for her hand under the table.

"I used *open table*," Claire confessed, showing me the app on her phone.

"They have meatloaf," Chris said. "Or mac and cheese."

"Let's order both and share," Taylor suggested, as she reached for the breadbasket.

"They have vegan food, too," I pointed out to Willow, who was seated between Alex and me. She smiled in return and took a sip from her water. She and Alex ordered salads that included strange ingredients like melon, cashews, and figs. I chose pasta with roasted red pepper sauce, pine nuts, fresh basil, and chicken. Chris ordered a steak with bearnaise sauce after Claire agreed to share the truffle mac and cheese and meatloaf prepared with three types of meat topped with a sundried tomato sauce with Taylor.

After we had ordered desserts that we shared around the table, we left the restaurant to follow the flow of foot traffic toward the Hatch Shell only to see lines of what had to be at least twenty military vehicles lined up. There were security entrances to get into the amphitheater, and armed guards stood at attention with their dogs.

"How badly did you want to hear the Pops?" Chris asked Claire.

"Not this badly," Claire said. "It's like a military zone or something. Let's get out of here."

We walked along the Charles River until we found a bridge to cross to the Cambridge side. It was much less crowded, and our pace slowed as dusk descended.

"We need to find somewhere to hang out if we're going to stay for the fireworks," Claire said. Although there were still a lot of people, we found a spot on the esplanade to sit. The fireworks show was spectacular. They set them off from barges in the middle of the river, which allowed both sides to see everything. However, it didn't seem worth it trying to find our way back to the MGS train stop to get back to Wompatuck. We got lost several times and had to wind our way through crowds of tourists. It was well after midnight before we climbed back into *Suby*.

"That was intense," Claire said as we climbed into our bunk to sleep.

"Worse than Times Square on New Year's Eve," I said. "Not that I would know. I've never gone anywhere near Times Square on New Year's Eve. I watch it on TV with the rest of the country."

"That's funny," Claire said. "Why would you never go actually to experience it when it's in your city?"

"It was never my parents' thing, I guess," I said. "We always had a party or went to a party or something. I don't know a lot of New Yorkers who go to Times Square. It's more of a tourist thing."

"I've got it," Claire said. "I've got the greatest idea. Why don't we plan to meet up again in New York for New Year's at Madison Square Garden? Phish usually plays more than just one show. This way, we can count on exactly when we can see each other again."

"Sounds good," I agreed, but my heart was sinking. I didn't want to think about summer ending, let alone consider New Year's Eve. We still had four shows left—no need to get ahead of ourselves. I wanted to focus on the moment. Still, I could feel something shifting even as I was anxious to slow the flow.

JULY 5, 2019

FENWAY PARK
Boston, MA

SET 1: Free > Blaze On, 555, Tube, Brian and Robert, Halfway to the Moon > Ocelot > Rift, Everything's Right > Runaway Jim

SET 2: Sand > Axilla, Mercury > Wading in the Velvet Sea > Fuego -> Say It To Me S.A.N.T.O.S. > Character Zero

ENCORE: Bug > The Squirming Coil

28

Arriving in front of the Green Monster from the train was not as easy as we expected. Of course, we got turned around exiting the station and had to circle, until we found our way. It didn't help matters that Chris was irritated with Claire for taking so long to get ready for the shows.

"We're late, Claire," Chris grumbled on the train.

"Late for what exactly?" Claire replied. "We're not going to miss the show. There's still plenty of time. Relax."

They bickered the entire ride and argued when we lost our way to Fenway until Taylor finally erupted. "Enough," she said. "We know you're siblings but stop already. I don't know how much more I can take. It's too hot for this nonsense."

Ironically, because we were cutting it close to the show, the hustle to get to our seats was enough to quell their squabbling. We naturally separated them between Alex, Willow, and Tippy. As soon as the band took the stage, the sweaty irritation we all suffered melted away as we entered back into Phish's dreamscape. I marveled at how no matter what city or venue, once the music started, we were all transported into the same universe. I wondered how different it would be to see Phish at Dick's in Colorado or at the Gorge in Washington from seeing these shows on the east coast this summer. Of course, St. Louis wasn't the east coast, and because it was the only indoor venue, it did feel different in that there was no rhythm to the show starting just before dusk and then continuing into the night. Before I could consider how interesting it would be to close our leg of the tour back at an indoor venue like I knew Mohegan to be, Chris seemed to be arguing with the guys standing in the row in front of us.

"What's going on?" I asked Claire.

"I think he's pissed those guys keep talking," Claire said. "I don't know. I can't hear very well. You're closer. What do you think is up?"

I watched as Tippy put his arm around Chris and guided him past us, out of the row. Taylor followed to stand next to Claire as the guys walked up the aisle.

"Those guys just wouldn't shut up, but Chris has lost his mind," Taylor said. "Hopefully, Tippy will calm him down."

"I'm glad he got Chris out of here," Claire said.

I reached into my bag for Uno cards I handed to everyone around us to mollify any other disruptions and to soothe ruffled feathers. At least, I hoped it helped. Meanwhile, Claire and Taylor grinned at each other wearing their Baba Cool shades, singing along to *Blaze On*. Chris and Tippy stayed gone until the refrain of *Everything's Right,* and our group seemed to hit their stride until the last note of *Runaway Jim*, the first set closer. Drenched in sweat from dancing in the sweltering humid evening, we wound our way to the lines for bottles of water and to use the restrooms. Alex and Willow wandered away during set break in search of her friends. Tippy invited us to go with him to meet Plums, but fearing Chad in their midst, we opted not, so Tippy took off alone.

"I wish they let you keep the bottle caps," Claire said. "It's a stupid rule. What do they think we're going to do? Pelt the band with bottle caps?"

"Here, sister," a woman in a red sequined hat said, handing Claire a bottle cap. "I came prepared. Take what you need." She reached into her bag and unearthed a few more.

"Thanks," Claire said, accepting the caps. "That was smart."

"That's what you learn from twenty years on tour," the woman said. "Enjoy your show."

"Twenty years," Taylor repeated after we walked away. "Can you imagine? We'll be almost forty."

"Look around," Claire said. "There are lots of people in their forties here."

It's true. At every show, we had met people from all ages and life stages from parents to wooks to grandparent-aged people to seeing Little Rager babies with their parents loaded down like Sherpas with diaper bags and totes full of snacks and band-aids. We had chatted with lawyers and teachers, artists and business owners, college students, and parents. Some people were there for one show and others were traveling a leg like us. The guy from Colorado we met at SPAC had flown to his friend's house in Pittsburg. They drove to SPAC then planned to go to a day of moe.down before driving to Boston for tonight's show (which was entirely out of the way and didn't make any sense, his words; not mine) before he flew back home to see the band again at Dick's in August. The teacher we met at Blossom was celebrating his tenure at his one show before he taught summer school. Some of the parents homeschooled their kids so they could do so on tour. I had a feeling once you saw your first Phish show, you learned to weave them into your life however you could. At least, that's how I felt about the band now. I couldn't imagine a day going by without listening to their music, and I knew I'd be planning as many shows as my school schedule would allow from now on.

"That is one of the most meaningful songs ever," Claire said about *Sand* before they launched into *Axilla,* and there was no space to talk or think. The hilarity of the entire crowd screaming, *heigh-ho, heigh-ho, heigh-ho* with *S.A.N.T.O.S.* is absurdly compelling. Still, nothing could match the spirituality of McConnell alone on the stage, offering the last notes of *Squirming Coil* to close the show. I felt wrung dry, both from sweating in the intense heat of the day and from the music that fulfilled its promise in lifting me out of myself and dropping me back to the earth transformed. Even Chris and Claire seemed finally subdued, their early tension dissipated. They were quiet on the train back to the park. Alex had texted for us not to wait for him. He and Willow had met up with her friends, and he didn't know when he'd be back. Tippy texted he was staying with his Cherry Hill gang, so that left the four of us back at *Suby.* I rummaged in the fridge and pulled out a tub of hummus, some carrots, and a wedge of cheese. Chris unearthed a box of crackers, a bag of tortillas, and a jar of nuts. We arranged the snacks on the table and cued up Grateful Dead as the girls were at the public restrooms showering.

"I'm wiped out, man," Chris said, handing me a White Claw. "Are you tired?"

"It's the heat. The humidity drains you, I think. That and dancing like we do."

Chris laughed. "We do throw down. It's the best part of Phish shows. Nobody tells you to sit down, that's for sure." He handed me the cart, and we got high, listening to Jerry.

Claire and Taylor smelled so good when they returned, Chris and I decided to follow suit and found our way to the showers. I felt peaceful, hollowed out, and cleansed when I returned to *Suby* to sit next to Claire and eat. Chris walked in a few moments later, and we ate, the Grateful Dead soothing as we ended the evening.

JULY 6, 2019

FENWAY PARK
Boston, MA

SET 1: Carini > Possum, Set Your Soul Free > Thread, Wolfman's Brother, Reba, Back on the Train, Mound, About to Run, Down with Disease > Simple > Backwards Down the Number Line > Death Don't Hurt Very Long > 46 Days > What's the Use? > Mexican Cousin > Also Sprach Zarathustra > Split Open and Melt, Suzy Greenberg

ENCORE: Rise/Come Together > Wilson

29

The weather was like hot soup, the air so dense you could swim in the humidity. We barely left *Suby* all day, choosing instead to stay inside, napping and lounging. I read and wrote while Claire worked on the next collaboration art piece she planned to install. I dreaded anticipating the moment we would have to rouse ourselves and walk the three miles to the train station, endure the forty-minute ride and then push our way back into Fenway for night two, but it was Saturday night. We had an entire free day Monday after we arrive in Connecticut, and because we had tickets, we were going to summon our energy to go into the show.

"Has anybody seen my glass pendant?" Chris asked.

"Uh-oh," I said to Claire. "We better help, or we're never going to get to the show. You know he won't leave unless he's wearing his necklace."

"It's not just a necklace," Chris yelled. "It's a charm. It's my charm. I need it." He was frantically opening every cabinet and drawer, searching.

"Chill out," Claire said. "When was the last time you wore it? Think."

"I had it at SPAC," Chris said. "The whole time. I know that."

"You didn't wear it last night?" Claire said. "Are you sure?"

"Of course, I'm sure," Chris insisted. He had moved to the back where the bed was, lifting the pillows and shaking out the blankets.

"Exactly how lucky is it if you didn't even think to wear it last night?" Claire mumbled but started turning pillows over on the sofa, reaching between the seat cushions. Taylor got down on her knees to peer under the table and in the corners of *Suby's* floor.

I went to the front, opening the glove box and center console to no avail. We continued to search in earnest for another ten minutes. Claire even opened the refrigerator. When I raised my eyebrows, she shrugged. "I can think of weirder places," she said.

"What do you want to do, Chris? It's time to go. We need to leave if we're going to make the show," Taylor said.

"Maybe I won't even go," Chris said. "Maybe it's an omen."

"I would tell you you're ridiculous, but I won't. I get it, actually," Claire said, being uncharacteristically empathetic when it came to Chris.

"Do you want us to stay behind with you?" I asked half-heartedly. Even though it had been a low-key day and I still felt tired, I did want to go to the show.

"No," Chris said. "We'll go. I mean, I'll go. I don't like it, but I wasn't wearing it last night, so maybe that means some reverse mojo or logic or something. Fuck it. I'm not going to miss the show over a pendant. Let's go."

Even though we grabbed our rain ponchos and Claire packed her things into a plastic tote, nothing prepared us for the torrential storm and dramatic lightning that hit the venue about an hour before the show. The stampede to enter the venue was chaotic; I held Claire's hand tightly as we found our seats.

"Do you think they'll cancel the show?" Claire asked.

"I have no idea," I said. "This storm is intense."

"There's no way they'd let us in the venue if they were planning to cancel," Chris said. "They will come on. Once the rain subsides a bit, they'll play. They have to. They're Phish."

His logic may have been flawed, but he was right. About ninety minutes after they started the night before, the band took the stage. They played one long monster set instead of their traditional two. Maybe because I'm not a huge fan of *Carini* or maybe because I was exhausted to start, the show didn't lift me the way I expected it to. The *Wilson* closer was the best part of the show for me. One, because I'd never heard a *Wilson* live. Two, because it meant the show had ended, and no matter how driving Trey's guitar, I looked forward to the last note in anticipation of a warm sleeping bag in my bunk with my arms around Claire. The relief I felt as we meandered our way out of the venue and back to the train station allowed my spirits to lift in response, making me smile inside at my disappointment. It seems not all shows are equal. Not every show was going to magically transport me to a different spiritual realm, which made the experience at SPAC even more significant in my memory.

"Maybe because we didn't eat psychedelics?" Claire said to me on the train.

"Meaning what?" I asked.

"The show didn't seem to resonate with me tonight," Claire said. "Maybe you need to be tripping to connect with the show."

"I don't think that's true," Chris said. "Tripping can enhance the experience, but it's not necessary to the experience. I think it was because I didn't have my glass pendant. That's what I think."

"If that was true, why was last night's show better?" Claire teased him.

"I don't know," Chris said. "But what I do know is that I think Willow had something to do with it."

"Wait a minute," Taylor said. "What are you saying? You shouldn't just randomly accuse people, Chris. That's wrong."

"What's wrong is that Willow is the only new person in *Suby*," Chris said. "I'm serious. What do we know about her anyway? She could have pocketed it, and nobody would be the wiser. She is a self-proclaimed wook. She said so herself."

"I'm sure we'll find your pendant," Claire said. "I think it's an issue of psychedelics. The difference in your perspective of shows that is."

"Psychedelics can make you miss the show altogether," Taylor said. "Like me at Blossom. I mean, I got some great writing out of the experience, but if you asked me to name a single song that was played, I wouldn't be able to tell you now without looking up the setlist."

"Have you heard of this dude named Ram Dass?" I said. "After Cosmic Charlie mentioned him to me, I looked him up. He talks about his spiritual enlightenment stemming from the dread of coming down from psychedelic experiences. Meaning, he never wanted to come down, which he called a huge red wave and a heavy burden. I feel that right now. I feel incredibly down."

Claire slipped her hand in mine and squeezed. She whispered, "I love you."

That lifted my spirits, as did grilling cheese sandwiches back at *Suby* feeling comfortable in warm, dry clothes listening to Widespread Panic while passing the cart around. Claire heated bean dip in the microwave while Taylor sliced tomatoes and cucumbers. As we sat down to eat, Alex and Willow arrived back. Claire jumped up to grill a few more sandwiches, and I moved over to give them room to sit down.

"That *Carini* was sick," Alex said. "I don't even care that it was a repeat. That was what the show needed to get us going."

"How funny," I said. "I thought the exact opposite. Maybe I just don't understand the song. It seems stupid to me."

"Absurd, maybe," Alex said. "But stupid? Really?"

Before I could respond, Willow launched into a complicated story of the history of the song. Something about a dude who worked for Phish named Carini and a show in Amsterdam and a rich girl's parents and the story of how it evolved to be played in rotation.

Chris interrupted her. "Hey, did you notice? We jinxed the whistling in *Reba*."

"Jinxed, how?" Taylor asked.

"By whistling on our drive down here, remember? We whistled, and then when they played the song tonight, no whistling. It's because of us," Chris said. "We jinxed it."

"Better watch what we whistle and sing," Claire said. "We only have two more shows."

"You're not going to Alpine?" Willow asked. "That's crazy. You have to go to Alpine. The entire tour isn't worth it if you don't go to Alpine."

"We've been on tour since St. Louis, for the most part," Chris said. "We have to head back home, regrettably."

"You could come with us," Willow offered Alex. "You don't have to go back home."

"I do, though," Alex said. "I have to work."

"Fuck work," Willow said. "Quit. That's what I did. I quit."

"I don't have that luxury," Alex said.

"What luxury?" Willow said. "Just do it. It will be fine. We always find a way."

Alex stood up, his face red. "You have no idea what I'm talking about. I don't just work *some job*. It's is my family's business. My family," he said.

He pulled his tweed cap down further over his eyes and muttered, "Pinche gringa," as he stepped out of *Suby*.

Willow jumped up and followed him. We didn't know what to say, so Claire just got up and starting clearing plates. Chris handed me the cart.

"See what I mean?" Chris said. "She's a wook. This just proves it."

"Remember that dude Ram Dass I told you about on the train?" I said. "He also said to treat every person you meet as if he or she is God in drag."

Chris laughed. "God in drag," he repeated. "That's hilarious."

Taylor picked up my copy of *The Goldfinch* and started leafing through, stopping to read my notes.

"I usually write notes in the margins," I explained. "Maybe it's a bad habit, but it's what I've always done. I have a shelf of the books I've annotated I like to keep. Makes it easier to go back to find quotes or favorite passages. But, since this book is a library book, I had to use post-its and paper clips."

"I do the same," Taylor said. "You went to the library? Our library?"

"Yes," Claire answered. "Before we left, we stopped there. So, I could show Sam—"

"In omnia paratus," I recited.

Taylor laughed. "You should have seen the look on your face that night at the trestle after you jumped. It was priceless."

"I still can't believe I did that. Just followed Claire off a bridge. What was I thinking?" I said.

"You were thinking that you'd fallen madly in love with me and would follow me wherever I go," Claire said, reaching to kiss my cheek.

"No kidding," I said. "Look where it landed me."

As we started getting settled into sleep, I asked Claire, "Is Alex going to be okay?"

"Yes. He'll be fine. I guess it's just not something we talk about much, but Alex has to work to pay for school. His family doesn't have money like ours. I mean, I never think about it, really, but Willow pushed too far. He got this time off to come with us, but he must return to the restaurant. It belongs to his family, so it's not an option for him. It's his whole life. He's going to college to learn how to expand his father's little restaurant into a national chain. Like a big corporation. It's cool. And his family is lovely. I've known them forever," Claire said.

She adjusted her pillow and continued. "I don't know. Some people see Phish for fun, and others adopt it as a lifestyle. I've loved this, of course, but I know I still need to graduate and go to college. I'm not willing to chuck it all to go on tour, slinging whatever on the lot to make money for the next show. I hope to find a balance between life and Phish. Not life as Phish. I think there's a difference. Most of the people we've met have real lives. They vacation at Phish. Does that make them not real phans?"

"Of course not," I said. "I just think Willow... Well, I don't know anything about Willow, so I'm not going to assume anything, unlike some people we know who will go nameless. There is a bigger issue at hand. Alex is over eighteen. We're not. We don't have a choice. We're still minors."

"Only until next week, though," Claire said. "Isn't your birthday next week?"

"You're right. I'll be eighteen. Still, as much as I love the band, I know I have responsibilities. Even Peter Conners went to college. He didn't just tour with the Grateful Dead. And I think he has a real job and a family and everything."

"Chris is already eighteen," Claire said. "He's a year older than Taylor and me even though we'll all just be seniors this year and graduate together."

"I like our idea to meet up at Madison Square Garden for New Year's Eve. I'm always home for winter break anyway. You can see where I live and see some museums or shows." I pulled Claire into my arms.

"Sounds like a plan," Claire said. "In the meanwhile, I'll be in New York this fall for college tours and hopefully, interviews."

"But I'll be back in New Hampshire then. One last year of St. Philips. One more year."

"And then we can be in college together," Claire sighed, cuddling under my arm. I never heard Alex and Willow return to *Suby* before we fell asleep, content together in our bunk.

30

The moment ends though I feel winds

"Moma Dance"
Anastasio & Marshall

It was only a two-hour drive from Boston to Connecticut. Chris pulled into the Seaport RV Resort and Campground, located in a town called Mystic, Connecticut.

"No way!" Claire declared. "We have to find Mystic Pizza. Do you think it's a real pizzeria?"

"What are you talking about?" Chris asked.

"The movie. The Julia Roberts movie, *Mystic Pizza*. It was our favorite. Remember, Taylor?"

"Of course, I remember," Taylor said. "I think we've seen every movie Julia Roberts was ever in during our all-things-80's phase."

"What phase?" Claire said, looking up from her phone. "I still love everything about the '80s. And it does exist. It's not just a movie prop. We can go there and eat a slice of heaven."

"Perfect," Taylor said. "Wait, though. Alex, where's Willow?"

Chris looked back at Taylor and asked, "You're just now noticing Willow's gone?"

"It's alright," Alex said. "Willow left. She couldn't understand that I have real responsibilities which pissed me off, but whatever. She took off to find her people because I wouldn't agree to go on to Alpine with her. She wanted to leave at midnight, but I convinced her to wait until at least until the sun rose this morning. I walked her to the train station, and that's it, I guess. It was a fucking long night."

"I'm sorry, Alex," Taylor said.

"Well, I'm not," Claire said. "She did not have your best intentions at heart, Alex dear. But we do. I can promise you that."

"It is what it is," Alex said as we pulled into the RV park. There was a pool again, a fact that cheered Alex, who liked to swim after every show if he could. After we had hooked up, opened the canopy, and raised the flag, we decided to find this famous Mystic Pizza.

"At least call for uber and not Lyft," Chris said. "I think we're permanently banned from all things Lyft."

"You may be blacklisted, but I'm not," Claire said. "But, okay. I'll call for an uber. It's only a five-mile drive there. Did you know there's an actual Weekapaug? It's in Rhode Island. Listen to this." She launched into reading the history of the song from Phish.net that detailed how the band members derived the song from misunderstanding and creating their own lyrics to a Frankie Valli song, *Oh What A Night,* so Claire cued that up to listen to on our uber ride to Mystic Pizza that turned out to have the most heavenly slices, true to their reputation. After we had eaten, we wandered the docks.

"Where the earth meets the water," Claire whispered to me as watched the sunset on the Atlantic before we returned to *Suby* for the night.

The next day, we had space and time to enjoy the RV park for once, as we weren't there to drop our stuff and rush off to the next show. Alex wasn't the only one to use the pool. We splashed around, retreated to *Suby* to listen to music under the canopy, ate when we wanted, and treated the day like any other camper on vacation at the park. Claire and I spent some time organizing our Uno decks, the cards we had collected, and the few we still had to give away. From her backpack, she unearthed a velvet drawstring bag to carry the cards we planned to bring with us to the show. She reached in and pulled out Chris's glass pendant.

"Ha!" She exclaimed. "Found it."

"What in hell was it doing in there?" I asked, holding my hand out for the charm.

"I have no idea, but I told Chris we would find it," Claire said. "I knew that Willow didn't steal. She was a piece of work, and I hate her for breaking Alex's heart, but she isn't a thief."

"I'm just a little freaked out how fast he was to accuse her," I said. "That was bad."

"What was bad?" Taylor asked as she entered *Suby*. Chris was right behind her, so I just held out the necklace in response.

Chris grabbed it and asked, "Where did you find it?"

"In this bag," Claire said, holding up the velvet bag. "Inside my backpack. Care to explain?"

Chris hit his hand on his forehead and groaned. "Fuck." He sat down next to me and said, "I fucking remember now. Oh, man. I feel bad. I put it in the bag and stashed it inside your backpack for safekeeping when we left SPAC. I don't even remember why I did it because it was after a show, and I was seriously spun. Something about knowing I had to take off the charm to retain its power."

"Well," Taylor said, putting her hand on his arm. "It's not like you accused Willow to her face. Or even to Alex. We're the only ones who know, and we won't say anything. Right?"

"I won't say anything," I promised. Claire just clamped her lips.

"I still feel awful," Chris said, his head in his hands.

Claire stood up, looked at me, and said, "I'm going swimming. Are you coming?"

"Yes," I said, following her to the pool.

"I just hate when Christopher does shit like this," Claire said as we bobbed in the water, not really swimming, just standing in the shallow end. "This is not the first time he's falsely accused, someone. He just jumps to conclusions about people and thinks the worst of people for no reason at all. It's infuriating."

"I hope he doesn't do that with me," I said, feeling a little worried.

"Don't worry," Claire said. "I won't let that happen. Someday, though, Chris is going to have to take personal responsibility and not be so quick to blame others."

"I didn't think you liked Willow that much," I said.

"I don't," Claire said. "This doesn't have anything to do with Willow. It's more about Chris and his behavior patterns."

She smiled when I said, "Are you sure you are going to study art and not psychology in college?"

"I'd make a great therapist," Claire said. "But, I still like making art more."

We stayed in the pool while she launched into explaining her idea for her next art project. The more she talked, the more animated she became. I loved how seriously she took her work and how important she felt the impact her work could make on society. Perhaps she was a psychological artist of sorts if there is such a thing. Social activism through art is how she described it. When she talked, it felt like that phrase, *poetry in motion.* Her eyes lit, hands gesturing to explain the details of her work, face flushed, eyebrows furrowed, and then raised in expression—all poetry to me.

That evening, we made a fire in the designated pit and settled in to listen to Phish. We chose shows from the '90s, focusing on the Island Tour, which was the shows at Long Island and Rhode Island in 1998. Claire read to us *10 Little Known Facts About Phish's Island Tour* from Jambase. It was fun to listen to Phish. Almost the entire tour, we had heard to other jam bands, never Phish. I asked Chris why that was.

"It's a rule," Chris said. "Like you don't listen to whatever band it is you are going to see before you see them. I don't know why it's like that. Do you, Alex?"

"I'm not quite sure why, it's what I've always done, but people do play Phish in the lot before shows," Alex said. "So maybe it's not so much of a rule."

"The rule is there is no rule," Claire declared. "Pay attention when we hit the lot tomorrow. Some people blast rap. Others like to play Phish. You'll almost always hear some Grateful Dead, and there are a lot of other bands in between."

"If there is a lot," Alex said. "Mohegan is going to be weird. It's not like the other venues. Security is going to be tight. We'd be best served just going in and out of the shows and not lingering."

"Because it's a casino?" I asked.

"Yes," Alex said. "It's owned by a Native American reservation, the Mohegans."

"It's going to be a full-circle moment for us," Chris said. "Indoor venue like St. Louis."

"There will be a PhanArt show," Claire said, consulting her phone. "We can walk that before the show even if there's not much of a lot at this venue. Wait, though. It's only Wednesday, not tomorrow. Looks like there won't be a vending lot, just this show. I definitely want to walk through. It's at the Earth Expo Center, which is right next to Mohegan Sun. Wonder what you need to do to participate in this? I mean, for MSG at New Year's maybe?"

"I guess we'll have to go to find out," I said.

JULY 9, 2019

MOHEGAN SUN ARENA

Uncasville, CT

SET 1: Energy -> Weekapaug Groove, The Moma Dance > Maze -> Lengthwise -> Maze, Petrichor, Things People Do > Sample in a Jar, Bathtub Gin

SET 2: Soul Planet -> Wider -> Undermind, The Final Hurrah, Beneath a Sea of Stars Part 1, Ghost -> Birds of a Feather, Waste > Golgi Apparatus

ENCORE: Foam, Contact, More

31

It seemed almost ironic the weather was so perfect for an outdoor show and even more perfect for a lot scene, yet Mohegan Sun was an indoor venue, and there was no vending on the lot. Instead, we decided to continue our vacation vibe at the RV park by sleeping in late and swimming most of the day before we loaded up *Suby* late afternoon to drive to the show. Claire debated resurrecting her web installment, but I talked her out of it.

"If it's a Native American reservation, we don't even want to screw into the ground with the poles and attract attention to ourselves. Better to stay on the down-low," I said. "Regardless of whether the venue is actually on their reservation, we do not want to mess with that."

"I guess you're right," Claire sighed. "And maybe the magic at SPAC can't be recreated anywhere else anyway."

Maybe it was because these were our last two shows, or perhaps it was because we were seasoned phans at this point, but when we hit the lot, we hit it in style. Claire and Taylor were entirely made-up with their beloved glitter, Baba Cool shades, and the butterfly wings Claire liked to wear. Alex wore his signature chewed up tweed cap, and I even pulled on my red hunting hat for nostalgia's sake. Chris donned his favorite bright tie-dye, and we called for tickets to the captain before we walked in.

"Pretty tickets," Claire cooed, holding up her ticket.

"Our only mail-order," Chris said. "These are keepers."

"Sam," Claire said. "Do we have our Uno cards? How many do we still have to hand out?"

I held up the thin stack in response as we gathered our tribe to walk the lot.

The first people we ran into were the Cherry Hill gang: Tippy, Plums, Chad, and a few other people we met in Tippy's backyard. Chad and I avoided each other altogether, which suited me just fine. The last thing I needed in the previous two shows was any conflict. My fatigue in Boston had worn off, or the days between were so restful, I felt my regular energetic self again. The last place I wanted to waste a good mood was on a wook who felt entitled to piss on other people. We ran into that couple who were homeschooling their kids in Kentucky, gave them Uno cards to share with their children, and stopped to chat for a bit with the men who drove from SPAC to moe.down to Fenway.

"I decided to stay on tour," the man from Colorado, whose name was Steve, told us. "Just these two shows, and then, I'll have to fly back."

"Unless we go to Alpine," his lawyer friend named Joe said.

Even as Steve protested, I had a feeling if we went to Alpine, we'd see him on the lot.

"Goals," I whispered to Claire as we walked on. "Those guys have real jobs and real lives and families and still seem to be able to catch shows."

"I wonder if the Kentucky couple ever brings their kids to shows," Claire said.

"Like Little Ragers?" I said. "I don't think so. Those families seem to be a tribe all their own."

Before we headed in for the show, we ran into Willow and her friends. Of course, we did. We only stopped briefly to greet her before we continued in our direction, and she took off on hers. Alex barely mumbled, keeping his eyes downcast under his tweed cap, and Chris reached up to handle his charm back in place around his neck, so I know he felt terrible about falsely accusing her. There was no time to consider regret in our rush to make it into the venue and to find our seats before the show started.

First set launched me thinking how incredible no two Phish shows were ever the same. I had seen ten shows, and this eleventh show included songs I didn't even vaguely know like the opener, *Energy,* and that other song, *Things People Do.* When they launched into *Weekapaug Groove,* again, the understanding of the alchemy of Phish hit me. Of course, they'd play that song here, but of course, we had just discussed it and therefore had conjured it, especially when Alex got his *Petrichor.* Tonight and tomorrow were the last two opportunities for Alex to fulfill his chase, and he got it. Alchemy. As Kuroda flashed his magic, I appreciated the aesthetics of an indoor show. There was less of a division than outdoor shows, in that there was no sunset to demark time. Instead, the invention of the artistry of the lighting rig that operated as a fifth member of the band, Kuroda, in synch note for note, defined reality. What I learned to count on was the rhythm of first set into intermission where we would traipse back into whatever lobby to procure waters to hydrate, find restrooms and then head back to launch second set followed by an encore. It was a rule or pattern or rhythm I could count on. Until storms blew that away and they pummel us with one long set like at Fenway. Almost like the exception to the rule emphasized the structure.

Claire and I kissed during *Waste,* and the highlight of the show for me was *Golgi Apparatus.* The lyrics, *I saw you with a ticket stub in your hand* was further evidence of alchemy. These mail-order tickets were the best tickets we had the entire run. I wondered if everyone felt like they had a personal connection to the band and that the shows deeply connected to the energy of their own private lives. They had to if it was true about the connection of every person at the show. Like Claire's webs, actually. We were all intertwined, deciding to commit our time, energy, and money to come together to sing and dance with this band at this exact moment. I knew I could not be the only one who felt like they conjured up a song or just had a deep understanding that certain songs would speak directly to your personal experience. We were not tourists here to see a band on display. We were participants in the dynamic, not just spectators. I was rational enough to know we didn't influence them as much as we look to find strands in the songs we experience. But it did seem a mystical process. I wondered what it was like at Big Cypress with the band as the sun rose on a new year or what it would be like to dance in the sand in Mexico under the moon. Just this run, I had experienced indoor shows and pastoral outdoor shows. We sat under gorgeous trees and navigated our way through downtowns that were sketchy. We danced in the rain on the Red Sox's sacred field and even celebrated hockey triumphs in our pursuit to follow four guys on stage who could spin such magic in four hours, you felt like it was all of space and time.

JULY 10, 2019

MOHEGAN SUN ARENA

Uncasville, CT

SET 1: Buried Alive, Cavern > Dogs Stole Things, Sugar Shack, Stash, Wingsuit, Limb By Limb > Gumbo, Stray Dog, Steam > David Bowie

SET 2: Party Time, Chalk Dust Torture > Ruby Waves > Seven Below, Stealing Time From the Faulty Plan > Piper -> Ruby Waves > I Always Wanted It This Way > Drift While You're Sleeping

ENCORE: Bouncing Around the Room > Saw It Again -> Kung -> Saw It Again > Slave to the Traffic Light

32

Bittersweet the only word to describe the entire day and then the last show. Not that we would never see Phish again, but this was the last show of this particular run, an experience that will never repeat. My first Phish shows and this last proved to far surpass my wildest expectations. It was that good. The twelfth show. The perfect ending to an incredible day. We woke feeling celebratory, so we decided to treat ourselves to brunch.

"Let's eat at the Mystic Diner," Claire suggested.

"Can we go to Rise instead?" Alex asked, consulting his phone. "They have vegan and gluten-free options for me."

"Plus, Rise is a better name. It will remind us of Fenway. Let's go," Claire agreed, humming the lyrics, *Rise up, come together, come together, come together.*

By the time we reached the restaurant and were seated, we were all starving. Because there was no lot scene at Mohegan, there was nowhere to get hot food after the show, and the microwaved bowls of macaroni and cheese we prepared at *Suby* weren't entirely satisfying. My noodles still retained a bit of a crunch, and powdered cheese has never been a top favorite of mine.

While we waited for our food to arrive, I stepped outside to call Aunt Karen. I hadn't spoken to her the entire time we'd be gone. Of course, we had corresponded with texts, but I'm sure she wanted to hear from me, and I wanted to listen to her voice, too.

"Have you been eating?" Aunt Karen asked, almost immediately after we had said hello.

"I'm actually at a restaurant right now," I said. "We're waiting for our lunches."

"And you'll be home tomorrow?" Aunt Karen asked.

"I'm not sure. I don't think we'll get to Maywood until Friday, actually," I said. "It's a twelve-hour drive, so I guess it depends on how soon we leave tomorrow."

"You're planning to drive straight through?" she asked.

"Alex, Chris, and Claire will take turns driving," I said. "They take shifts and in between, can nap in the RV. We will be fine."

"And it's been good? I mean, the shows. The experience. Being with them? Good?"

I smiled. "More than good. I'll tell you more when I get back home."

"I'm counting on it, kid," she said. "Text me when you're on the road so I can have food ready for you. Be safe. I love you."

"Love you, too," I said as we hung up before I realized I hadn't thought to ask her about her work. I know the show she was preparing for Chicago was important. She said it was the most prestigious gallery she had ever shown her art. I made a mental note to be more considerate when I got home to Maywood. Home. Just that thought was enough to make my heartache, so I decided to focus on the present and worry about that later.

When I returned to the table, our food had just arrived. I laughed to see three plates and a cup of coffee, a glass of water, and another glass of orange juice in front of Claire. For a girl so thin, she always ordered so much. "Because I like to taste," she would say, passing whatever plate for me to finish, causing me to smile, reminding me of my mom who liked to share plates, too.

After lunch, Claire wanted to visit the Mystic Museum of Art, but we reminded her of PhanArt, so we went back to *Suby* to gear up for our last show. Although the PhanArt show was small, it was excellent, mainly because there was no scene on the lot. Vendors set up tables to sell pins, painted denim, stickers/decals, posters, posters, and more posters, ties and donut sport coats and helping friendly hemp salve. We even met the phinancial guy and learned about Groove Safe, a group committed to protecting women's rights to attend shows without unwanted advances. Although Claire and Taylor already had their pair of Baba Cool shades, we stopped by their table.

"That has to be her," Taylor whispered to Claire and me.

"Do we dare go up and say hello?" Claire said.

"Who are we talking about?" I said. "I mean, about whom."

"Bella," Claire whispered, pointing subtly. "That's Trey's daughter, Bella."

"Phish royalty," Taylor sighed, which cracked us up.

I looked over to the small woman holding what looked like a monkey in her arms.

"Is that a monkey?" I asked.

"That's Coco," Claire said. "She's the monkey on tour. Come on, let's just say hello."

Bella could not have been kinder and more gracious to us when we introduced herself. She posed for pictures and even let us take turns holding Coco, a stuffed monkey that belonged to one of Bella's friends. In return, Claire gifted Bella with several of our Uno cards. Bella complimented my red hunting hat with a smile. "I read *The Catcher in the Rye*, too," she said.

When we walked away, Claire squealed, "I cannot believe we just met Bella and Coco."

"It's how you know we're ending tour," Taylor said. "It's manifest destiny."

Claire linked her arm through Taylor's and said, "Until next time. Only until next time."

We found our seats just before the band took the stage. I looked around at the thousands of people in the theater in amazement. These were my people. It would become the community in which I'd orbit and connect for the rest of my life. Or at least, for as long as I was able to attend shows, but judging by the older phans who called themselves 1.0, I had a feeling my desire to connect with the band would remain strong well into my adult life. When they launched into *Drift While You're Sleeping*, my soul resonated in response. To think how far I'd come in just a few weeks by following a girl around in an RV to chase a band, seemingly random and simple actions had profoundly altered my reality. I would always remember my mother in small ways like when Claire orders too many dishes or when I hear specific Grateful Dead lyrics, and that was important. I didn't need to hide one small picture of her in my sock drawer. I carried her in my heart. Thinking about her and talking about her was how I would keep her spirit alive and honor her life. I didn't need to lock this all away. I could let it go because I was no longer alone. I was part of something bigger than myself, connected by love, *it's love and it always was and it is and it always will be love.* I could forever picture her as a child, barefoot in a patchwork dance, twirling around to the Grateful Dead. Because I now understand time to be more fluid than the linear construct of seconds stacking into minutes culminating into hours shaping individual days, I know that my mother and I will always be connected when I lose myself to the music. When I embrace the concept, *surrender to the flow* as more than a slogan or bumper sticker, her time and my time would temporarily exist together. I'd discovered my legacy, learning more about my mother through experiencing a similar adventure of valuing the power of music, and the energy that resides within expanding and bouncing until it reaches every last person gathered together for the same intent. I would not have to visit Gramercy Park to speak to my mother. She would be with me in any venue, any city I chose to see Phish, a fact that comforted me immensely as the waves of grief still reverberated in my soul. I could miss her, but I had finally found a way to honor her.

When we filed out of the venue, Chris said, "Let's drive now. I mean, there's no reason we shouldn't start the trek back home now, is there?"

"I'm fine," Alex said. "I'm with you. Let's drive."

So, we loaded into *Suby* and made our way back to home to Maywood. The drive took over fourteen hours, as we stopped for gas when we wanted and took breaks to change drivers. I texted Aunt Karen to expect us early afternoon. When we pulled up to the Calico House, she was waiting for us on the front porch. It felt good to hug her.

"Welcome home," Aunt Karen said. "I'll bet you all are hungry. I've got food. Come in."

We all traipsed into the kitchen where a pot of chili simmered on the stove. Cornbread kept warm under a cloth napkin in a wicker basket, and rice was steamed and ready. A wood bowl held a large green salad. She even had a second small pot of beans only for Alex. Chris smiled when he heard the music and teased Aunt Karen. "JRAD?" he said.

"I'm trying to expand my musical horizons," she replied with a smirk. "I've even been listening to Phish to keep up. Now tell me all about the shows."

We ate and laughed and told stories from the road until the last bowl was scraped clean, and Taylor and I began clearing and washing dishes. Aunt Karen brewed tea and brought out a plate of oatmeal cookies with raisins. When everyone rose to leave, Aunt Karen reminded them about my birthday party.

"Get lots of sleep so we can celebrate," she said as we walked them back to *Suby*. "Tuesday. The party is Tuesday. Today is Thursday."

"Thanks for the reminder," Alex laughed. "It's hard to reorient. Especially since we didn't plan to be back until tomorrow."

"I'm glad we drove straight through," Chris said, yawning. "An extra day to sleep."

Claire and I kissed quickly. She murmured, "I'll call you later tonight, yes?"

"Or I'll call you," I said. "Get some rest."

After they left, I thanked Aunt Karen and asked her about her art. We talked at the kitchen table for about an hour before I couldn't stop yawning. Aunt Karen laughed. "Get some sleep, kid," she said. "Then come to the studio tomorrow, and I'll show you the pieces I plan to show." I hugged her and retreated up the stairs to my room. Even though it was still light, I fell into a dreamless sleep, grateful to be home in my bed. It would now and forever be my home.

33

On the morning of my birthday party, the skies were overcast, and it looked like rain. Aunt Karen reassured me it would pass and that by the time guests would arrive, the weather would be perfect for the gathering. I spent the first part of the day stacking wood with Luke for the bonfire that would surely be lit for the drummers and poi dancers while Aunt Karen worked in her studio. The day before, she had taken me on a tour of the paintings she planned to show in Chicago, and they were incredible. I asked her why she hadn't included the Chagall-like painting of the chickens.

"Because that painting is for you," she said. "I plan to hang it in your room whenever you come back home."

Claire promised to come early to help set up. Since we'd been home, she had launched into the installment for PhanArt in December, so we hadn't seen each other, and I was missing her. She and Taylor arrived as Luke, and I finished setting up the tables outside for Aunt Karen.

"Happy Birthday," Claire said as we hugged.

"Thank you. I'm so glad to see you both," I said as I hugged Taylor, too.

"Taylor already started her common app," Claire said. "Can you believe it? She's such an overachiever."

"Wait," I said. "It's open? I didn't think it opened until August."

"It doesn't," Taylor reassured me. "It opens August 1, but you can start the process now and then just transfer everything over. I'm merely getting everything ready. Like the essays and stuff."

"You have nothing to worry about. You are such an overachiever," Claire said. "She had near-perfect ACT scores. It's crazy. How about you, Sam? Are you done with the ACTs?"

"Yes, so I'm good for applying to NYU and Columbia, I hope. I mean, we'll see, but I have the minimum requirements to at least apply," I said, wanting to change the conversation. "Let's go see what Aunt Karen needs us to do."

As we hung the paper lanterns and draped table clothes, Claire pushed again. "What score did you get, Sam?"

I stopped and looked at her. "What does it matter?"

"It doesn't," she said, looking puzzled. "What's wrong? Did you bomb them or something?"

I sighed. "No, I didn't bomb the ACT. I got a thirty-five."

"Help!" she cried jokingly. "I'm surrounded by geniuses."

"The only genius around here is you," I laughed. "Tell me about your new installment piece. I want to hear everything."

As we finished setting up for the party, Claire launched into an elaborate explanation for her new piece. It was amazing to me how she even thought of these projects, and I loved the way her brain worked. I would never get tired of hearing her talk about her art. She, Taylor and I took iced teas to the Siberian elm and sat in the shade together for the rest of the afternoon watching the ducks swim on the pond until Chris pulled into the driveway and walked down to join us.

"Where's Alex?" I asked after we had bro-hugged hello.

"His dad needed him in the restaurant," Chris said. "He'll be here later tonight, though."

Aunt Karen's friends arrived, and there was more food than we could ever need piling up on the tables because nobody came empty-handed. Scattered arrangements of daisies in mason jars and Phish playing from the speakers created a festive atmosphere. Before long, people were drinking, smoking, and eating. Some folks perched on the porch. Others gathered in the kitchen and living room. It was much like the first gathering of the summer. It was nice to stop and chat with people I had met before, who were eager to ask about my experience at the shows.

"Phish? Phish sucks," this big older guy named Phil said. "You kids don't know about Jerry Garcia, but there will never be a better band than the Grateful Dead."

"That's because you've never seen Phish," Chris said.

"It's useless trying to convince Phil," Mason, the banjo-playing French translator I met at the last gathering, said. "Phil doesn't see anything but the Dead."

"That's because there is nothing better than the Dead," Phil insisted. "Phish is a wannabe."

"Wannabe, what? Great?" Chris replied. "Because if that's the case, then yeah. Phish is a wannabe."

"Phish will never be as great as the Dead. No matter how hard they try, they will never be the Dead," Phil said. "There was and only will be one Jerry Garcia."

"They aren't trying to be the Dead," Chris said. "That's the whole point."

"Don't they just cover Dead tunes?" Phil said. "I mean, a band who makes that much money just playing Dead songs is lame."

Chris and I burst out laughing. Phil was so misinformed, it was funny.

I tilted my head and said, "You've never even listened to Phish, have you?"

"I saw Trey play with the Dead in Chicago, and that was enough," he said.

"I hate to burst your bubble, man, but Phish is not a Dead cover band. They're their own band with their own songs and their own music," Chris said.

"Listen, man. Let me tell you about a show I went to in 1979," Phil said before Aunt Karen interrupted him.

"1979? Phil, I was eleven years old in '79," she said, teasing him.

Phil turned to Karen and leered at her. "I would have hit that eleven-year-old. I would have been all over *that* eleven-year-old," he said. He continued even though his comment was met with stunned silence. "Anyway, it was the week after Thanksgiving, and it was cold as hell in Cleveland."

Claire interrupted him and barked, "You what? That's disgusting. What the hell are you talking about? You would have hit on a child?"

"Listen, I was just trying to compliment Karen," he said, holding his hands up as if to ward off blows.

"How is threatening to assault a child a compliment?" Claire said, holding her ground. "Men like you are what the entire problem is with the community. Phish, Dead. It doesn't matter. You're all a bunch of pigs."

Aunt Karen reached out to Claire and put her arm around her to steer her out of the kitchen. "Thank you, Claire. You're right, but this is a party. Let's go outside and get some air, shall we?"

I looked at Phil, who just laughed and said to Mason, "Women. Am I right?"

"No, man. You are not right. Sometimes you need to stop and think before you speak," Mason said. He walked out of the kitchen back into the living room, pausing to shake his head at me.

Phil turned to Chris and me, but before he could speak, Chris said, "Let's go outside and check on Claire. See you, man."

I turned to Phil on my way out, "By the way. The music you've been listening to all night is Phish. Just for the record. Phish." I slammed the door in anger. I couldn't help it. What a fucking asshole.

"Exactly," Chris said.

"Wait," I said, shaking my head. "Did I say that out loud?"

"What a fucking asshole?" Chris said. "Yes. And I agree."

We joined Claire and Aunt Karen, who were sitting on the porch swing. Claire managed a small smile when I approached her, so Aunt Karen excused herself so I could sit next to her. Chris patted Claire's hand before he went back into the house to find Taylor.

"That guy was awful, Claire. Don't feel so badly," I said. "You were amazing, though. You told him off. I'm proud of you."

"Thanks," she sighed. "Obviously, you know this is a hot topic for me. You saw my Barbie doll installation."

"I did," I said. Then I took a deep breath and asked, "Did this happen to you?"

"No," she said. "I was never abused, thank God. It never happened to me, but it happens to too many girls. Have you ever heard of the writer, Laurie Halse Anderson?"

I shook my head in response. She continued, "She wrote two books Taylor and I read. The first book, *Speak*, was about a girl who was raped, but her second book was a book in verse called *Shout*. I created my art in response to her books. See, you aren't the only one who is inspired by the books you read."

"So, I see," I smiled. "I'm not familiar with her books, but that's no surprise considering I attend an all-boys school, I guess."

"That's just it," Claire said. "It should be required reading for boys. We need to train boys not to rape, not just train girls to be safe. Our society is just so fucking ridiculous, but look. I don't want all of my art to revolve around this one issue. It's not even really my issue, per se. What has inspired me to create these installments around the Phish community is to build positivity, not just to create art to expose ills in society or make huge feminist statements if that makes any sense. I don't want to be known as the crazy child abuse artist or whatever. It was just one project, not my entire life's work. Or at least, what I hope to become my entire life's work once I get to college and continue making art."

"*I contain multitudes*," I quoted in response.

Claire smiled, "Whitman. Yes. I may not be large in stature, but I am large in spirit, and I also contain multitudes. Thank you for understanding but listen, I don't want your entire birthday party focused on one unfortunate incident. Can we just move beyond and enjoy your party? He's a fuckwit. We can't change that, but it doesn't have to ruin our entire night, does it?"

"Of course not. As long as you're fine, that's all that matters. Look," I said, pointing, "They're starting up the bonfire and drumming. Want to join in?"

"After I give you your gift," she said. "Let me get it. Stay here. I'll be right back. I just need to go to my car."

Taylor and Chris stepped out to the porch as Claire walked to her car. She returned with Alex, who was holding a plant in a terra cotta pot.

"Happy Birthday," Alex said as he handed me the plant. "This is a Christmas cactus. If you take good care of it, it will bud and bloom in December right before we meet up again at Madison Square Garden, kind of like an advent calendar of sorts only you're counting down to New Year's Eve."

"Thanks, Alex," I said, wondering if my dorm room had enough sunlight even to keep a plant alive, but the gesture was so thoughtful, I was touched. Aunt Karen and Luke joined us on the porch with gifts in their hands.

"Me next," Claire said as she handed me a small package wrapped in white paper tied with a green ribbon. Scrawled, in her handwriting in green ink across the white paper, was a quote that read:

Life can only be understood backwards, but it must be lived forwards.— Søren Kierkegaard.

Inside the box was a double frame connected by hinges. When I opened the frames, one picture captured Claire in mid-dance, her arms spread above her head, and the other looked like Claire again, spinning with her arms out wide. Both figures were wearing the same skirt. I furrowed my brow, trying to figure it out.

"This is me at SPAC," she said, pointing. "This is your mother at a Dead show. This was her skirt that I borrowed from Aunt Karen. When I saw this picture in the photo album, I knew that I wanted to get a picture of me dancing so you could have both us of caught doing what we love the best, dancing at a show. I didn't have the same top, but I tried to get as close as possible, so we matched. Do you like it?"

"I love it," I said, holding back tears caught in my throat. No longer would I hide away my one picture of my mother in my sock drawer. This double-framed picture would sit on my desk for me to see the two women I loved the most, captured joyfully in mid-dance whenever I wanted.

Aunt Karen held out a small wrapped package tied with a blue ribbon to me. "I hope you like it," she said. I unwrapped it to find nestled in cotton, a gold medal on a chain. "It was your grandfather's. It's a medal of St. Stephen. You know that Grateful Dead song, right?

It was your grandfather's favorite, and he wore this necklace all the time. Now it's yours."

I lifted the necklace from the box and unhooked the chain to put it around my neck, smiling up at Aunt Karen in gratitude. Luke held out his palm to hand me three blue stones.

"These represent the three stones used to martyr St. Stephen," he said. The stones were smooth in my hand. Before I could say anything, Chris handed me a small glass jar. Inside was a perfect bud with a little red ribbon around the stem. "This gift needs no explanation," he joked.

"Indeed," I said as we laughed. "Thanks, man. And thank you, Luke. I appreciate this."

Finally, Taylor handed me a scroll tied with a yellow ribbon. "I wrote you a poem," she said.

"Would you read it to me?" I asked.

"I already did," Taylor said. "It's the poem I wrote at SPAC that afternoon."

"I didn't know you were writing it for me," I said.

"I know," she said. "But when you asked me to read, then, I didn't want to ruin the surprise, so I just read it to you without explaining it was your birthday poem."

"Thank you, Taylor," I said. "Thank you, everybody. This is the best birthday I've ever had."

I didn't notice Aunt Karen had slipped away until she returned, holding a birthday cake full of lit candles, a stream of people from inside following her as they all launched into song. Everyone clapped when I blew out the candles. Chris held up a hand and said, "Listen." Over the speaker played *Backwards Down the Number Line.*

"Good timing," I laughed. "Seriously, everyone. Thank you. Thank you so much."

Aunt Karen took the cake to the tables and began serving. Taylor and Claire helped by adding berries to each slice of cake from a bowl. Aunt Karen explained, "Cake and berries are so much better than cake and ice cream. Don't you think?"

"I think it's incredible," I said as I tasted the vanilla from the cake and the sharp sweetness of the blackberries from the vines that grew on the side of Aunt Karen's studio. A perfect combination of tart and sweet. After we had eaten, we all joined the circle around the bonfire to finish the evening, listening to the drummers and watching women dance poi and with hula hoops. I was content as I've ever been in my life, Claire leaning against my chest, my arms wrapped around her tight.

34

Don't you see anything that you'd like to try

"Theme from the Bottom"
Anastasio & Marshall

"Hold this for a second, will ya?" Claire asked, handing me her cone. "Are you sure you've never had butterscotch-dipped cones before? Try mine."

"No, thanks," I said. "I'll stick with my chocolate."

We were sitting side-by-side at the scarred wood patio table outside the Dairy Queen. Claire pulled a folded-up piece of paper from her back pocket, opened it up, and smoothed the creases. At the top of the page, she had written *Maywood Adventures, A Three-Week Journey.* She uncapped a green felt pen and crossed off *butterscotch-dipped cones at Dairy Queen. In the Sun.*

"Why in the sun?" I asked.

"Because ice cream always tastes better in the sun. It's best eaten during the day," she said. "Trust me. This list includes important life experiences not to missed and only to be found in small-town Americana. And we can't send you back to school and then back to the Big City without experiencing some quintessential middle-American adventures, now can we?"

"I definitely do not want to miss out on everything the Midwest has to offer," I teased.

"Too bad it's already past Fourth of July," she said, frowning. "You haven't lived until you've seen a small-town parade."

"That's okay. I've been to the Macy's Day Parade in Thanksgiving," I said.

"Not the same," she said. "Completely different league altogether. Our parade does not have huge balloons, for one. We do, however, have the local beauty queen in her sash riding on a convertible, waving. And the high school marching band, of course. Some floats. And lots and lots of old guys dressed in their military garb followed by almost every little kid in town riding their bicycles decorated with red, white and blue crepe paper."

"You're right. I can't believe I'm going to miss that," I deadpanned, making Claire laugh.

"And you've already been to the country club to drink Bloody Mary's," she said.

"Not necessarily a Midwest thing, though," I said. "I've been to country clubs before. My grandparents belong to a club. We go every Easter with them."

"Right. Okay, eat up. We've got places to be," Claire said. "We're running against the clock, Sam. Time is not on our side."

I followed her to the car. She kept the windows open and blasted The Talking Heads while driving, her hair whipping around, sunglasses in place. We drove out of town down country roads, spotting cows and horses in the fields around us. She pulled into a gravel driveway to a large barn.

"Do you see that?" she asked, pointing to the barn. "That's what's called a barn quilt."

Above the entrance of the barn was a square painted to look like a square of a patchwork quilt.

"There are lots of different styles," she explained. "Once you've seen one, you'll start paying attention and find lots of others. But now, welcome to the Maywood Flea Market. Have you ever been to a flea market?"

"I have not," I said. "This is a first."

"Let's go. There are treasures to be found," she said, putting her hand into mine as we entered the barn. Inside were individual booths set up, which created a maze effect as we wandered around, inspecting the wares. There was a lot of furniture and houseware items, but also toys, books, clothes, and other oddities. Claire lifted a Raggedy Ann doll. "I had one of these," she said before returning it to the table.

"I always thought those dolls were a little spooky," I said. "Something about the face reminds me of a demented clown."

I wandered to a book booth and began sorting through the old paperbacks. I picked up a copy of *The Portable Nietzsche* from 1955. Claire unearthed a large black book.

"Look at this!" she exclaimed. "I can't believe I just found it. Oh, I've been searching for a copy forever. Wait. Let me check if it's the right edition."

The title of the book read *The Last Whole Earth Catalog* featuring an image of the earth as if from space, partially eclipsed. "I'll take it," she said.

We wandered around a bit longer with our books in hand. Claire was ready to leave when she spotted a crystal doorknob. Both sides of the doorknob were attached. Its price tag read three dollars. "Bit steep, but I'm going to treat myself," she said. Before we turned away, she spotted a key ring holding a set of old skeleton keys for five dollars. "And this," she said.

"Big spender," I teased as we brought our items to the front table where an older man in denim overalls sat at a table with a cashbox and paper receipt booklet.

"Hey, Mr. Dabbelt," Claire said as she piled our things on the table.

"How ya doing, Claire honey? Find everything you need today?" he said as he tallied up our purchases.

"Yes, sir," Claire said, unearthing a twenty-dollar bill from her back pocket. "Thank you so much. See you soon."

"See you soon, dear," he called after us after he had given Claire her change.

As we pulled out of the driveway to go back to the Calico House, I said, "You didn't have to pay for my book, Claire."

"It's a gift, Sam," she said. "Besides, I can afford to splurge three dollars on you, can't I?"

Back at the house, Claire pulled *The Last Whole Earth Catalog* on her lap as we settled next to each other on the porch swing. Aunt Karen was down at her studio working, so Claire and I were alone.

"Okay, this is also a gift for you," she said. "I want you to open it up and look at the bottom right corner of each page."

I scanned the small square at the bottom of the first corner and then turned the page. As I began to understand what I was reading, I flipped the pages more quickly and then looked back up at Claire with my eyebrows raised, waiting for an explanation.

"This is how Gurney Norman first published *Divine Right's Trip*," she said. "As installments within the catalog. Cool, huh?"

"This is very cool," I said. "But, you should keep it."

"No. You gave your copy back to Cosmic Charlie. I want you to take this with you."

"Thank you, Claire," I said and reached over to kiss her. When our kissing got more heated, Claire asked, "Do you think we could sneak into your room? I want to be alone with you."

I stood up and offered her my hand as we walked into the kitchen and up the stairs. I closed and locked the door behind me.

When we heard Aunt Karen return to the house a few hours later, we emerged and joined her in the kitchen where she was preparing dinner.

"Hello, Claire," she said. "Will you be joining us for dinner tonight? Sam, would you set the table, please? Luke should be here soon, and then we'll eat."

The four of us sat down to yet another feast Aunt Karen prepared, using tomatoes, herbs, and zucchini from her garden. There was grilled salmon in lemon dill sauce and jasmine rice as well as a basket of freshly baked biscuits.

"I like to cook a huge meal after painting all day," Aunt Karen explained. "It allows me to think about what I've accomplished in the studio and what problems I still need to solve."

"What problems?" Claire asked.

"I see my art as a series of problems to be solved. You add one color. That's a problem when deciding the next. Composition. Balance. Form. All problems to be solved," Aunt Karen explained.

"I've never thought of my art as problems," Claire said. "That's fascinating."

"What did you two do today?" Luke asked.

"I took Sam to the flea market," Claire said as she unearthed her list from her back pocket. "We have much to do in these last three weeks if he is to experience the bounty the Midwest has to offer. See?"

As Luke examined the list, Aunt Karen set the kettle for tea, and I cleared the table. She turned to tousle my hair. "I can't believe it's almost the end of summer. I'm going to miss you, kid," she said.

"I'm going to miss you, too," I said, but turned away when tears threatened to well up past the knot in my throat. I was dreading going back to school. I wished I was a little kid and could throw myself down on the kitchen floor in a temper tantrum. Instead, I drank a glass of water to compose myself.

"Hey," Luke said, pointing to the list. "When are you going to do this one? Maybe Karen and I will join in."

"Tomorrow night," Claire said. "Yes. You and Karen are totally welcome, of course."

"Welcome to what?" Aunt Karen said, putting mugs, lemon and the sugar jar on the table.

"The drive-in," Luke said. "When's the last time you've been to a drive-in?"

Aunt Karen laughed. "Oh my. That would have to be a million years ago, at least. What's showing?"

"Drive-in, as in drive-in movies?" I asked, preparing my tea with lemon and looking around for the honey. "I didn't think those things even still existed."

"They do in Maywood," Claire said. "I'll come over early to make the popcorn. We have to make it and carry it in a brown paper grocery bag, so the butter stains the paper and the salt all falls to the bottom. That's how my family always did it. Do you have a paper bag, Karen?"

"I think so," Aunt Karen said, getting up to look in the pantry. "Here's one. I'll set it out for you."

"We're all going," Claire said. "Chris, Taylor. Even Alex asked for the night off. The whole crew. It's going to be awesome."

"Do you know what's playing?" Luke asked. "Not that it matters. When's the last time we went to the movies, Karen?"

"I think they're playing that *Yesterday* movie on one screen and *Toy Story 4* on the other. There are two screens. One for the kids and the other for the grown-ups," Claire explained.

As it turned out, Aunt Karen and Luke weren't able to join us. Luke had a last-minute furniture order to fill, so Aunt Karen decided to get some work done in her studio. She said she felt pressured to finish everything before her Chicago show. Alex had to cancel as well. He got called into work, so that left just Taylor, Chris to pick me and Claire up in Boot's SUV. I pulled on my red hunting hat in a gesture of premature nostalgia for this summer. Taylor and Chris filled the cab with blankets and pillows as well as loaded in camping chairs we set up after we backed into the designated space at the drive-in. There were even old-fashioned speakers you could put on your car window, but Chris said he would use the radio station to tune into the sound instead. Claire and I brought the bag of popcorn we popped in Aunt Karen's kitchen and after we went to the concession stand to load up with sodas and candy, Chris pulled out the flask to doctor our drinks. The movie was a little corny, but I like the Beatles, so I enjoyed the soundtrack if nothing else.

"This is so *The Outsiders*," I said. "I keep thinking we're going to see Pony Boy and Two-Bit."

"I always wanted to be Cherry Valance," Claire sighed as she leaned against me.

"*Stay gold, Pony Boy*," Chris said. "I can't believe you've never been to a drive-in before."

"I have never jumped from a trestle either," I admitted. "Or have gone to a Phish show or climbed a tree."

"Good thing you came here this summer. You seem to have led a sheltered life," he said.

I laughed. "I'd like to see any of you negotiate the Manhattan subway system, find your way around the city. I mean, have any of you ever been to MoMa or the Guggenheim, even? Rockefeller Center or the Empire State Building? Been in the back of a smelly cab? Eaten good pizza and I mean good pizza? It's a matter of perspective."

"Hey guys," Claire interrupted. "I'm taking Sam to the sunflower field to walk the labyrinth next week. You in?"

Taylor said, "Of course. I haven't been all summer. The sunflowers should be in bloom by this time of year, don't you think?"

"I'm counting on it," Claire said.

None of us were very interested in the film. Christopher and Taylor sat together on folding chairs. It was apparent they were back together as a couple, and in a romantic phase reconnecting. Claire and I got into the back of the SUV to recline, feet out. I wasn't paying much attention to the movie, though. I kept thinking about how Aunt Karen's opening was in precisely two weeks. That was all the time I had left in Maywood. Dad called. He was back from China, so he planned to meet us in Chicago, and then I would fly back to school from there. How had summer gone by so quickly? As I squeezed my arm around Claire, I felt a pang of heartache. I was going to miss her. It was time to start thinking about the ending.

I whispered, "You read *Catcher in the Rye*, right?"

Claire said, "Yes. I told you that. Why?"

"You know Holden saw that Castle guy commit suicide?"

"Weird. Are you sure? I think I forgot that detail," she said.

"Yes, I'm sure. The boy jumped out of a window after a bunch of bullies did unspeakable things to him. It happened at one of the schools he got kicked out of. I don't remember which one, though. Not Pencey."

She sighed. "That's horribly sad. You and Holden were suffering loss. I saw the novel as a story of grief. What I remember is him missing Allie so much. He's your literary angel of sorts, don't you think? I mean, when you become a real writer and all." She snatched off my red hunting hat and pulled it down on her head and smiled at me.

"Only, I won't suddenly choose to become a deaf-mute, but end up in a psych hospital because I met you. Because I came here this summer. I mean, I could've cracked up as he did, you know?"

"But you didn't. Also, you didn't run away from your problems like Holden. The whole novel is about running away. You confronted your issues. You sought your truth," Claire said.

"Holden didn't have an Aunt Karen and a Calico House. I think that's what makes the difference. All of this makes the difference. All of you." I kissed her. "You can keep the hat to remember me."

Claire put the hat back on my head. "I don't need a hat to remember you. And there's no way you're going back to school without it. Especially now that you know what it means."

"What does it mean?"

"We're survivors. Ready for all things. We might be a bit broken in some ways, but we are in omnia paratus."

35

Trapped in time and I don't know what to do
These friends of mine, I can see right through

"Mike's Song"
Mike Gordon

Before we went to the sunflower field to tour the labyrinth, Claire and I sat together at the kitchen table with her mostly crossed-off list. We had eaten ice cream during the day, explored the flea market, gone to the drive-in movies. We went back to the trestle although we didn't jump in this time. We swam in the pond and ate a picnic under the elm tree. We walked barefoot in Dream Creek, the stream in the backyards of her neighborhood. Claire pointed out the place she and Taylor once created a Tree World, using leaves and branches to assemble an organic structure she and Taylor spent hours in until the weather destroyed it naturally. She had even taken me to her favorite merry-go-round at Hill Top Park, her childhood playground, but nothing could prepare me for this next adventure.

The Seven Wonders of the World should include sunflower fields, or at least this particular farm should be. I've never seen anything like it before. We drove several miles outside of Maywood, past fields of corn where Chris, Taylor, and Claire yelled in unison, "Knee-high by the Fourth of July" for whatever reason and gazed at clusters of cows and horses secured behind fences before we pulled up to their friend, Mr. Lackey's farm. He was an artist who was a printmaker and painter, as well as a creator of short films. Claire said she was surprised I had never met him at one of Aunt Karen's gatherings as most of the artists in Maywood knew each other, and he and his wife, Jenny, were known to grace the Calico House.

As soon as we turned into the columned stone entrance, the sunflower field opened to what looked like acres. Rows and rows of sunflowers, some bent and others facing the sun; all taller than any of us. Chris slowed the car so I could see the flowers. I understood why Claire and Taylor insisted I ride shotgun. They didn't want me to miss anything. A small sign that read, *Homegrown Press,* announced the entrance. We followed the unpaved, gravel lane that led to Mr. Lackey's farmhouse. There weren't any other houses. Just a big barn behind an old, white-painted farmhouse. He had a wrap-around porch, much like Aunt Karen's Calico House, but that's where the similarity ended. No crazy rainbow colors here. We climbed out of the car and greeted Mr. Lackey, who was sitting on the porch. There were dozens of books stacked all around his chair. He stood, hugged Claire, and invited us to a glass of iced tea. Claire politely declined in her haste to get into the sunflower fields.

"Mr. Lackey, this is my friend, Sam." Claire introduced us. I shook his hand. He was an older gentleman with a grizzly beard, but his eyes were sharp and focused as he shook my hand.

"Nice to meet you, Sam," he said. "John Lackey."

After we gained permission to walk the sunflower field, Claire pulled my hand, leading me across the lawn into the sunflower field. She put her fingers to her lips to silence me as we began our trek through the sunflower field. Reverently, we started our journey through the path created by the individual rows. Many of the flowers stood taller than us. It was like walking through a giant's garden; the scale was so large. We spent a long while just walking through the sunflower field, which felt like a dreamscape of sorts.

Then, Claire pulled out her phone and started snapping pictures. I didn't want to pose for any, but she said it was important we have some pictures of our summer together. Once she said that I realized we hadn't posted many images from tour or from anywhere else for that matter. So, once Taylor and Chris found us, we took turns taking pictures of each other in groups and pairs and even some "selfies" so we could all be in the photos. We joked around, the girls made "duck faces," and Chris and I pretended to be sword fighting with sunflowers. Later, I would print and tack some of these photos over my desk in my dorm room at school to look back at that magical moment in Mr. Lackey's sunflower field. I especially love the one where Claire suddenly jumped on my back, and our faces are peeking through the stalks.

"Ready to walk the labyrinth?" Claire suggested.

Chris said, "Absolutely. Sam needs to see it." We turned from the sunflowers and walked across a grassy meadow. "When they built the farm, they had the foresight to create a labyrinth with the rocks they dug from the ground when clearing the fields, instead of just stacking them up and hauling them away."

"What exactly is a labyrinth?" I asked.

"Exactly what it says. You'll see," Claire said.

We hiked up a small incline of the meadow until we reached the top where we could see the rock labyrinth below. Pale gray and brown rocks formed a concentric circle path, which was as large as a football field. There were so many rocks. It was amazing to think each one was excavated from the ground and placed here so purposefully. The whole endeavor must have taken forever. We stood quietly, looking down for a moment before we trekked down and stood at the one side.

Claire said, "Ready to enter?"

We nodded and walked silently around until we reached the center where a tower of flat, round rocks was stacked, magically balanced. Claire called it a cairn. Once I saw the large cairn, I realized I had seen several smaller ones on our walk around the perimeter of the labyrinth.

"Traditionally, they're used as markers for mountain bike and hiking trails. Although there's a saying, *two rocks do not make a duck.* But they're also used for meditation. Very sacred. Would you like to make one before we leave?" Claire offered.

"I think we should. Let's each find our place and leave behind our mark," Taylor suggested.

"That's a good idea," Chris said and reached for her hand.

"Okay, set your intentions," Claire said. "For each stone, there is an intent. Like a wish or a prayer. Let's just take a moment to think about that before we set off." Chris lifted his hand clasped in Taylors, and kissed her knuckles. We stood silently for a few minutes before Claire raised her fingers to her lips and then touched the cairn as we turned around to wind our way out. Nobody took any pictures. The space seemed almost religious, definitely spiritual. We were all quiet for once, not horsing around and talking smack like usual. Taylor found her spot first, and Chris stopped to stack his cairn next to her. Claire and I continued. There were plenty of smaller stones arranged with the big rocks that made the labyrinth. We both knew exactly when to stop and begin stacking. It wasn't as easy as it looked, as you needed to find the right balance with the right rocks. Of course, Claire's cairn was taller than mine, but they looked good. The point wasn't the result, of course. The process was the meditation, according to Claire. I just liked the feeling of sunshine on my neck, the smooth stones I cupped in my palm before I considered its placement and the spicy geranium perfume of Claire, kneeled next to me.

"You didn't know they hunted doves?" Alex asked the next day after we had settled into Aunt Karen's car for a driving lesson. I had asked Alex to teach me to drive before I left. Meanwhile, I told him about Mr. Lackey's sunflower field and the labyrinth.

"I don't know if I remember even seeing any doves," I said. "Are you sure?"

"Yes, I'm sure. That's the irony of the sunflower field. The fields are peaceful, almost surreal, you know. But the sunflowers attract doves. That's the whole point. To go dove hunting. The sunflowers are called a baited field. The doves are attracted to the sunflower seeds."

"That doesn't sound exactly fair, though," I said as I thought about this. Was nothing as it seemed? Was everything two-sided; multidimensional? A metaphor of life, perhaps?

"What hunting is fair?" Alex said. "Turn here. Listen, I used to think deer hunting was barbaric until I saw what happens when they restrict the laws. The deer starve, so they flood the suburbs, destroying everyone's gardens to eat. So, what's better? Starving deer or deer population controlled by hunting? At least people eat venison."

"Okay, but like, what do they do with the doves? Eat them?" I asked.

"Yea, I guess. Like quail, I would suppose. Okay, pull over. It's time to practice parallel parking again. Once you've got that, you're ready to get your permit." Alex had borrowed orange cones and had arranged them so I could practice.

"Are you sure these cones are spaced far enough apart?" I asked after knocking cone after cone over in my attempt to park.

"You're the New Yorker. Do you think parking spaces are easy to maneuver into there? I mean, you've gotta be able to get into tight spots."

After I tried again and again, Alex cheered when I finally was able to park without hitting a cone. But that still wasn't good enough. He insisted I do it at least five times correctly. I was damn near sweating by the time we had finished. What a fantastic feeling, though. I could drive. If I got my license, I could have freedom. I'm just so glad I asked Alex to teach me. What I wanted to do was drive fast, though. Like, really fast, but Alex said no.

"Dude, you don't even have your permit. There is no way we're heading out on a highway for you to blast down and get busted. No way, man. We're breaking the law as it is."

"So, in Ohio, kids just get their permits and then start learning to drive?" That didn't sound very logical to me.

"Exactly. And they're not allowed to drive without a licensed driver in the car with them at all times, and then, there are other rules for teenagers, I think. But yeah, that's pretty much how it works. After a few weeks or so, you take the real test, and if you can drive, turn, park, etcetera, they issue you a license."

"Well, I appreciate you teaching me, Alex," I said as we pulled back to the Calico House.

"No problem, man. I'll see you soon." Alex waved as he got into his truck and drove off, but I felt sad waving back. I knew it was just an expression, but I wasn't going to see Alex again soon after we said good-bye for the last time tomorrow night. It was time to leave for Chicago, whether I was ready or not.

36

In time we'll weather this storm inside together
You'll see the change when the sun shines through

"Joy"
Anastasio & Marshall

My last night in Maywood, Claire, Chris, Taylor, and Alex
came to the Calico House after dinner to say good-bye.

"Are we going to climb the tree one last time?" Alex asked.

"Do!" Claire said. "I'll take pictures of you up there."

"It might be cool if we all climbed the tree and got a picture of
everybody up there," I said. I wanted to remember this tree as not just
where my mother's ashes were scattered, not just the place I went
alone to read and think, but as a place where I found friends. Friends
I could count on for life. Well, and okay. I'll admit. I wanted to also
remember it as my first time with Claire. It was a sacred tree. I don't
think any guy doesn't remember his first, and I know I wouldn't. I
would carve our initials inside a heart on the tree if I could.

Alex and I climbed first, and Claire took our picture. Then,
he climbed down so he and Chris could help the girls first before
Chris climbed up. Alex struggled with Claire's phone but managed to
snap a few pictures of the four of us in the tree before the sunset
entirely on the pond. From this vantage point, I also caught sight of
the blue heron one last time. I tried to point it out to Claire but almost
lost my balance. I looked down at the distance and had to shake my

head to rid myself of a mental picture of Castle, lying there dead on a sidewalk, still wearing Holden's borrowed shirt. I held firmly to the branches before we all carefully made our way down from the tree and returned to the porch.

Claire put her head back and sighed. "I wish you weren't leaving."

"I know," Taylor said. "We joked around on the drive here about ways we could kidnap you and keep you here forever."

"There is no forever," Chris said. "This time next year, we'll all be leaving for college."

"But we'll be together, right?" Taylor asked Chris.

"Right," he agreed and kissed her. "Have you two talked about this? Can you make plans to, at least, apply to the same schools?"

Claire and I looked at each other.

"We could make a plan," I said.

"We will make a plan," Claire agreed.

Aunt Karen stepped onto the porch, looked at our faces, and said, "It's not the end of the world, guys. Sam is just going back to school. He'll be back."

Claire asked, "You will come back, Sam? Won't you?"

"Of course, I will," I said. "This has been the best summer of my life."

Aunt Karen leaned down to hug me and whispered, "You are my family, Sam."

"You are mine, too," I said.

Alex came up to the porch to say good-bye, "Get that license, Sam. Stay cool."

"Thanks for everything, Alex," I said. "You're a great guy."

After Alex mounted his bicycle and rode off, Taylor and Chris stood up to say good-bye. I almost got choked up when I half-hugged Chris, the way dudes do. He was indeed my first best friend. I kissed Taylor on the cheek and whispered, "Take care." There wasn't anything else to say. Of course, Claire stayed behind with me, and after they left, we made our way back to our tree.

37

We stayed up all night to watch the sunrise, lying on a blanket at the base of the elm, my arm wrapped protectively around Claire, and her body pressed lengthwise against mine. Claire used her phone to play *Blaze On*. She pulled up the lyrics because she said it had chosen this song, hoping we'd have this last quiet moment together. *Climb that hill, stay on your feet/Scramble for your footing when it gets too steep/You're on the highway now with higher hopes/While all around are rolling eggs with living yolks.* I had a feeling I'd hear the refrain, *So now the band plays on, you got one life, blaze on* in my head for days.

When the song ended, she said, "This tree is so complicated, isn't it? I mean, this is where we made love the first time, not knowing your mother's ashes were scattered here."

"It doesn't freak you out, does it? I mean, it was three years ago, so it's not like we were rolling around in her ashes or anything. Okay, that's gross."

"Do you think she would have liked me?" Claire said.

"I know she would. Aunt Karen likes you. I like you," I said.

"I like you, too. I like thinking that your mother's spirit is here. Do you think your dad will like me?" she asked, frowning a little.

"Claire, I haven't even met your dad, and it's been all summer, but yes. Dad will like you."

"I know. Daddy is just like that. He ignores us all. Not just me. Boots, even. I shouldn't be so hard on her. She's just doing what she thinks she has to do to get Daddy's attention. It's sad. It's like he's just resigned to how his life turned out, and so all he does is work."

"My dad escapes into work, too. But that's not such a bad thing. If he hadn't gone to China this summer, I wouldn't have come to Maywood at all."

"I'm happy you did," Claire said and began to cry. I held her and stroked her head until she stopped and lifted her face for a bittersweet kiss. We made love quietly one last time, pulled our clothes back on, and sat together until dawn.

"What are we going to do?" Claire whispered.

"There isn't anything to do. I mean. We wait. Will you wait?"

"Of course. And we can text and video chat, but you'll write me real letters, too?"

"I'll write you real letters and stories, too," I said.

"I'm counting on that. But, after? We don't have a plan or whatever."

I sat up and took her hands in my hands. "Let's plan to apply to at least one common school. How does that sound? Or maybe we'll go to schools that are near each other. But Claire, you have to do what's best for you. If you get into NYU or wherever else you are accepted, that's where you have to go. We've got to be adults about this. Right now, I don't want any other girl in the world. I love you. This summer has been perfect. Let's take it one step at a time and hope for the best."

"Ya, I hate it when you're reasonable. I love you. You're right, though. It doesn't stop me from missing you already," she said, wiping tears from the corners of her eyes.

"You have no idea how much I'm going to miss you. At least you'll still be in Maywood. I have to go back to St. Philips and believe me; they're all a bunch of goddamn phonies. All of them."

Claire laughed. "Don't be such a crumb-bum."

"I wondered how long it would take you to call me that."

Because the pond faces west, we turned to walk toward the pink streaks of sunrise on the other side of the Calico House. I stopped to gaze at the house, the garage, the chicken coop, and Aunt Karen's studio. My home. I took Claire's hand to lead her to the coop to collect eggs. I wanted to make my farewell breakfast, so we quietly slipped into the kitchen with our basket of eggs. Claire brewed the coffee and cut fruit while I scrambled eggs and heated muffins. Aunt Karen emerged and smiled when she saw the table set.

"Well, isn't this lovely. What time did you two wake up?" she said, accepting the cup of coffee Claire offered.

"We never slept. We stayed up all night for the sunrise," Claire said.

I served the eggs and brought the warmed muffins to the table, and we ate.

Aunt Karen yawned. "Up all night. Egad. That makes me tired just thinking about it. But, when you're in love, every moment together is precious."

I wondered how I would be able to eat an egg at school ever again. Who would have thought a stupid yolk would make me choke up? I realized it was yet another thing I was going to miss. I stood up to hide my tears. Claire helped me clear the table, but Aunt Karen shooed us off to say good-bye. It was time for us to pack and head to the airport, so I walked Claire to the driveway. We hugged tightly. Even though we were both crying, I gave her a long, sloppy kiss. When we broke apart, she laughed. As she got behind the wheel and rolled the window down, she called out, "Letters, remember?"

"And stories," I answered back. "All of my words."

38

Was it for this my life I sought

"Stash"
Anastasio & Marshall

The gallery was teeming with polished, sophisticated, well-dressed people. I guess that was a good thing since Aunt Karen needs rich people to buy her art. She looked spectacular in her flowing dress and eyes lit up with excitement. Aunt Karen can charm anybody, and her art looked awesome installed on the stark white walls. I watched as people moved more closely to see the details and then jostle people behind them to move back to watch the compositions come back into focus.

"What are you smirking at?" I turned around to find my dad grinning at me. We hugged the back-slapping kind of hug. He said, "You look well, Son. Good summer?"

"Amazing summer," I said. "How was China?"

"Chinese." He laughed at his joke. "Some crowd, huh? It's great for Karen. She deserves it."

We watched as she greeted one person after another, being led around by her agent. Dad and I munched on canapés servers brought around on silver platters. When we made our way to the bar, Dad raised an eyebrow when I ordered a vodka tonic. With lime.

"Learned to drink this summer?" he asked.

"Well, it's Ohio, you know. Nothing left to do but drink and run around cornfields," I said.

He asked, "What else did you learn?"

I pulled on my tie to loosen it a bit. After this summer, wearing my school tie felt constricting. Not to mention my blue blazer, khaki pants, and real shoes. I wished I had the nerve to wear my red hunting hat.

"I met a girl," I mumbled, taking a large gulp from my drink.

Dad sighed and sipped from his martini. "Serious?" he asked.

"Serious enough. Her name is Claire."

"Well, then, I look forward to meeting her."

I looked at my dad in surprise. "We're going to write letters. Maybe she'll come to the city this fall to do a college tour of NYU. The New School is her first choice, but she knows she wants to be here; to live here in the city."

"That will be nice. She must be smart if she's looking at those schools."

"She is," I said. "She's incredibly smart."

"And beautiful, I assume."

"Botticelli beautiful," I said, which made Dad laugh. Then he leaned in, brow wrinkled. "I assume you were safe?"

"Yes, Dad. You can be sure of that."

He shook his head. "Okay, Sam. Well, listen, you turned eighteen, so it's not like you're a kid anymore, I guess. Happy Birthday, by the way. You got my card?"

"Yes, thank you," I said, remembering the generous check he included.

"It's too crowded in here to continue this conversation. Let's say we split out of here and go grab dinner, just the two of us?"

"But what about Aunt Karen?" I asked.

"I have a feeling she's going to be here a long time. Let's talk to her. We can meet her back at the hotel after. I mean, look at this. This show is going to sell out before it's over."

I followed him because I was curious. It was the most Dad, and I had spoken in a long time. I wanted to tell him about my summer. I wanted to talk to him. But first I had to speak with Claire, so I excused myself to make the call. It wasn't much quieter on the street, but I turned the corner into an alley. She answered on the first ring. I described Aunt Karen's show because I knew she'd be excited, and she was. Then, she told me about her day. She was in a hurry to get as much done on her installation piece for the PhanArt show on New Year's Eve before school started again, and she would focus her attention on the common apps for college. Her excitement for art still delighted me, even as I felt a pang from missing her so much already. I was glad we hadn't FaceTimed so she couldn't see me hold back tears when we said good-bye.

I went back into the gallery just as Dad opened the glass door to leave. We walked a few blocks before finding a steak house, Dad knew. He ordered a glass of wine, but I just stuck with a Coke. I don't think the restaurant would have served me anyway. Having a cocktail at the gallery was one thing. It was a private reception. Also, I wanted to stay alert. Over rare steaks, baked potatoes, and salad, I regaled him with stories from the summer. It was weird. I don't think I had ever talked this much to my dad before, but I guess I had a lot to say. I wanted to connect with him. Have him understand me better, maybe. From across the table, Dad seemed engaged for once. He never even put his phone on the table, which is saying something. Maybe there was hope. Perhaps we could forge a new relationship now that I was an adult. By the time the server cleared our plates, I felt relaxed enough to say what I had been thinking.

"I forgive you."

Dad blinked. Then, he just sat back against the booth. "That makes one of us, at least. Sam, I will never be able to forgive myself." He signaled the server for coffee and cognac. "I have to give it to Karen. She could have vilified me, yet she chose not to."

"That's just not her personality," I said. "Is that why I've never been to the Calico House before?"

"What? No. Well, not entirely, at least mostly because it's just too painful for me. Too many reminders. But I never meant to keep you away from your family, Sam."

"I know, Dad. But it is my home now. I'm going to go back to visit," I said.

"I think that can be arranged," he said as he pulled out his wallet to pay our bill before we walked back to the hotel. Aunt Karen and Luke were just getting out of a cab as we approached.

"I sold out, Sam!" Her face was flushed. I pulled her into a big hug. Luke introduced himself and shook hands with Dad. We all went into the hotel bar, where Dad ordered a bottle of champagne to celebrate.

"I've had way too much to drink tonight, but what the hell," Aunt Karen said after the server uncorked the bottle.

I looked around the table as we laughed at the stories Aunt Karen shared about people she met at the gallery and watched how animated and excited she was. Then, Aunt Karen straightened her shoulders, raised her glass and toasted, "To Maggie."

They all joined. "To Maggie."

I said, "To Mom." After we drank, I kissed Aunt Karen on the cheek and said, "Thank you for the best summer of my life."

"You're welcome, Sam."

Luke cleared his throat. "I was going to wait, but there doesn't seem a better time than this." Then, he kneeled, reached into his pocket and pulled out a box. When he opened it to reveal an engagement ring, he asked, "Karen, will you marry me?"

"Yes!" Aunt Karen cried. Dad and I clapped as they kissed, and Luke slipped the ring onto her finger.

"Congratulations," Dad said.

"I'm so happy for you both," I added.

"Now, I guess you have a reason to come home again," Luke said. "For the wedding."

Aunt Karen laughed. "I don't think he needed a reason to come home again, but yes. I guess we're planning a wedding soon."

Luke looked directly into Aunt Karen's eyes. "Very soon."

The next morning was a scramble. I barely had time to hug Aunt Karen and Luke good-bye before Dad hailed a cab to take us to the airport. They were staying in Chicago a few more days to wrap up the show and meet with her agent again. I teased them. "Promise you won't run to the courthouse and elope."

"We won't! The wedding will be at the Calico House, of course. We wouldn't get married without you," Aunt Karen said, hugging me one last time.

I watched them standing on the sidewalk, holding hands as our cab pulled away. Once we boarded the plane and settled into our seats, Dad picked up my copy of *The Portable Nietzsche.*

"What's this?" he asked. "I thought you were reading *Catcher in the Rye?*"

"I was, but that was a million years ago." Then I asked him, "So, Dad. Have you ever seen a sunflower field?"

NOVEMBER 1, 2019

DEAD AND CO

MADISON SQUARE GARDEN
New York, NY

SET 1: Cold Rain and Snow, Hell in a Bucket, Row Jimmy, Ramble On Rose, Mississippi Half-Step Uptown Toodeloo, Mr. Charlie, Friend of the Devil, Bird Song

SET 2: Scarlet Begonias> Fire on the Mountain; He's Gone, Smokestack Lightning, China Cat Sunflower> I Know You Rider, Drums> Space, Althea, Morning Dew

ENCORE: The Weight, Brokedown Palace

39

Took me a long time

"Back on the Train"
Anastasio

Winter Break arrived before I knew it, but at the same time, Fall Semester was the longest of my life as I bided time completing my common application, corresponding with Claire and trying to keep up with my classes in between. I felt impatient on the train ride from school into the city where Dad met me at the station. Things between us were better than they had ever been, and we found a natural rhythm to our conversations now, which launched with our first talk in Chicago at dinner when I told him about Phish tour.

"I'm glad you had that experience," Dad said. "How many shows did you see?"

"Twelve," I said. "We're going to meet up again at Madison Square Garden for New Year's Eve. That's when you will meet my friends. May they stay with us?"

"Of course," Dad said. "I look forward to meeting them. You know I saw the Grateful Dead with your mom. This was before your time. When Jerry was still alive."

"I didn't know that," I said. "You saw the Grateful Dead?"

"Yes. Your mom and I met in undergrad. We saw lots of shows back then. Grateful Dead, Neil Young, Steely Dan, The Rolling Stones. Whenever we could, we would catch a show. She was devastated when Jerry died, of course," he said. "By then, we were already living in New York and newly married. We were happy back then. Wait, why are you smiling?"

"I guess because I'm trying to picture you at a Dead show," I said. "Takes some getting used to. Did you wear a coat and tie?"

"Very funny," Dad said, but he was smiling, too.

I could not have been more surprised to find a driver at my dorm room Friday, November first. I had just returned from classes when the driver knocked on my door, announcing that Dad had sent him to take me into the city. Dad scored tickets at Madison Square Garden to see Dead and Company that evening, so I quickly changed out of my school uniform into my favorite *Read Icculus* t-shirt and jeans before pulling on my red hunting hat. I texted Claire in the car what was happening. She said she was jealous of seeing Dead and Co since she had yet to see them, but glad Dad and I would see a show together. The driver let me off right in front of the venue, directing me into the food court area on the first floor of the arena.

When I walked in, I saw Dad right away. He was wearing a grey hooded sweatshirt with a steal-your-face that read, *Yes, I May Be Old, But I Saw The Grateful Dead On Stage* and jeans, which both stunned and humored me. We hugged hello, and Dad directed me to get food from the different booths while he got a beer for himself and a soda for me. While we ate, we caught up about school and the common apps. When I told him I applied to NYU, Columbia, UVA, Kenyon, and Yale, as a writing major, he seemed pleased even though he was a Harvard grad. Our tickets were club seats, of course. These were corporate tickets Dad got from work. Waiting in line to enter the venue, I paid attention to the crowd. Not so dissimilar from Phish, in that, they were all hippies, but that's where the similarities ended. I was one of the youngest people there. Most of the crowd were old white guys who looked like any other dads, which made sense to me since I was with my dad. There were as few women as there were at a Phish show. Men did outnumber the women in the jam band scene. There was no doubt. I wondered if Deadhead women had a group like Phish Chicks. If they didn't, they should. Claire and Taylor always felt connected to their community of women at shows.

We settled into our club seats, which had access to the 360 Club and Bar and Grille. Dad ordered two beers, slipping one to me. We sipped our beers and chatted until the band took the stage.

"Why is Bob Weir wearing a kilt?" I asked Dad.

"Because Robert Hunter just died," he said. "I'll explain more at set break."

Although the tempo was slower than what I was used to listening to old Grateful Dead shows, the first set was incredible, especially *Bird Song*, driven with a funky beat by the keyboardist, Jeff Chimenti. A woman I did not know named Maggie Rogers the stage to add her vocals to *Friend of the Devil*, one of Aunt Karen's favorite songs. And although I wouldn't say Dad danced, he swayed a bit as he stayed on his feet for the whole set.

Second set was better for me as I loved almost every song and knew the lyrics by heart. Dad threw down for *The Weight*, which cracked me up. Who knew the old guy had it in him? When they closed the show with *Brokedown Palace*, I had tears in my eyes, thinking about Claire, *by the waterside, I will lay my head* reminding me of her love for when earth touched the water. I consoled myself thinking that we would be together in this same venue in just a few short weeks.

Dad arranged for a driver to pick us up after the show, asking him to stop to pick up a pie from our favorite pizzeria on the way home. Dad opened a couple more beers, and we sat together, eating pizza, drinking beer, and talking well into the night. He told me about Robert Hunter, who I did not know was a descendent of Robert Burns. He shared stories about the shows he and Mom attended and talked about his experience in a fraternity and at college, hoping I would choose to pledge next year. He even told me stories about pranks he pulled when he boarded at St. Philips and about the summer he and Mom backpacked around Europe, staying at youth hostels and traveling with their Eurail passes.

When I couldn't hold myself up a minute longer, I rose and said, "Dad, this was the best night I could have ever asked for. Thank you."

"Thank you," Dad said, pulling me into a hug. "I feel like something has reconnected between you and me, of course, but also to my younger self, as well. I forgot how much I enjoyed going to shows with your Mom. I'm glad you guided me back, son."

I finally collapsed in my old room and slept in until the late afternoon. Dad and I spent Saturday walking the Hudson after breakfast at our corner spot in the neighborhood. That evening, we ordered in Thai and watched movies, both of us with our feet kicked up on the sofa. By Sunday afternoon, I was back at my dorm studying for a history exam and texting with Claire all about the show.

I pleaded with Dad to return to Maywood for Thanksgiving, but he invited Grandma and Grandpa for the holiday, explaining he had to fly to Los Angeles the day after for business. I reluctantly agreed to stay in New York because I knew my grandparents missed me, and I hadn't seen them since Spring and because Dad didn't give me any other choice. So, I was beyond ready to greet Claire when she, Chris, and Taylor drove up for New Year's Eve. They had to travel via car instead of flying because of Claire's installment. She was delighted to have been accepted to the PhanArt show the day before New Year's Eve. They left Ohio for the ten-hour drive Friday the twenty-seventh. I wasn't worried about the trip from Ohio to New York, as the weather cooperated, and there weren't any storms predicted. What I worried about was after they came through the Lincoln Tunnel and had to navigate through Manhattan traffic. Dad had arranged guest passes for them to park in our building's garage, but they had to get here first. I had nothing to worry about as they all popped out of the car with huge grins on their faces.

"Welcome to New York," I said, my arms spread open wide. After we had hugged hello, we pulled their bags out with the help of our doorman before giving the keys to the valet.

"Fancy," Claire teased me. After I showed them around the apartment and guided them to the guest rooms to drop their stuff,

Claire stood at the windows in the living room, gazing at the park. I held up my key in response.

"Would you like to go now or wait until tomorrow when it's daylight?" I asked.

"I can wait," she said. "I want to see everything,"

"You will," I promised. "We have a week together. An entire week."

Dad arrived home early from work to meet Claire, Chris, and Taylor. He made reservations for dinner, so we followed him the few blocks to our favorite restaurant, our neighborhood Italian place where you ordered several different dishes to share family-style which delighted Claire, of course.

"I'd like to make a toast," Chris said, holding up his water glass. We held ours in return.

"Congratulations to Taylor, who just received early-acceptance to Kenyon," he said. We clinked glasses and echoed our congratulations to her.

"That's fantastic, Taylor. Wow. Early acceptance," I said. "You threw it all in, didn't you?"

"What does that mean?" Dad asked.

"When you apply for early acceptance, you are saying it's your first and only choice. If they accept you, that's where you go without negotiation for grants and scholarships and whatever," I explained. "But it was Taylor's first choice, so it all worked out."

"That was very brave of you, Taylor," Dad said. "Well done."

"Thank you, sir," Taylor said. She was still smiling, and a bit flushed from the attention.

"Call me Drew. You may all call me Drew," he said, raising his glass again. "Welcome to New York."

DECEMBER 29, 2019

MADISON SQUARE GARDEN
New York, NY

SET 1: Turtle in the Clouds, The Moma Dance > Kill Devil Falls, Yarmouth Road, The Wedge, Beauty of a Broken Heart, Fuego > My Friend, My Friend > Birds of a Feather, While My Guitar Gently Weeps, Walls of the Cave

SET 2: Carini > Back on the Train > Bathtub Gin > Golden Age > Also Sprach Zarathustra > Sneakin' Sally Through the Alley > Chalk Dust Torture, Harry Hood

ENCORE: Show of Life > Run Like an Antelope

40

And the days turn to years
And it hasn't stopped yet
The memories we shared
I will never forget
No, I will never forget

"Miss You"
Anastasio

The New Year's run started Saturday and ran the four nights.
We had our tickets for New Year's Eve only, which fell on a Tuesday.
We knew we would miss Monday's show because we would be busy
helping Claire with her installment, so that only left Saturday and
Sunday. When I proposed spending all day Saturday sight-seeing and
just trying for the Sunday show only, everyone agreed. We started with
cappuccinos from Café Reggio in Greenwich Village, drinking them in
Washington Square Park, where we hung out with the buskers,
homeless, and tourists. We then took the bus to MoMa, which
everyone loved. We walked midtown to see the tree at Rockefeller
Center and the front of the NBC studios, and we wandered around
Times Square and down Broadway. It wasn't until we returned to the
apartment late afternoon that I turned to Claire with my key to show
her the park while Taylor and Chris decided to catch a nap before we
left to walk Little Italy and then eat in Chinatown for dinner.

Claire and I held hands as we toured Gramercy Park. I
pointed out the pagoda birdhouses and showed her the Edwin Booth

statue, where we held the memorial for my mom at the great Shakespearean actor's foot. Claire especially liked the Fantasy Fountain best, of course.

"I wish you could have seen Janey Waney, the Calder sculpture that was here forever," I said. "They just moved it to Paris last year. You would have loved it."

"I've seen pictures," she said. "I'm sorry it's gone, but this park is incredible regardless. It's magical here."

We planned to leave the venue early to score tickets Sunday until Dad surprised us with corporate tickets. "They're not clubhouse like for the Dead, but they're free tickets," he said as we thanked him profusely.

Because I had just been there with Dad, I felt like a pro leading everyone into the venue. He may not have gotten us club tickets, but nobody was complaining about the general admission floor seats where there were no seats. We were thrilled. Because we got there early, we sat down and began building community with the folks around us. We met a man who had flown in from Alabama for the shows, and even though he was a weird loner, he was friendly. The guys behind us were fraternity brothers, and the group to our other side were older. Hell, everyone was older than us, something we were quite used to by now. About fifteen minutes before the band took the stage, we were no longer sitting, but our garbage bag that held our winter coats and the girls' bags marked our dancing island. Suddenly, a seven-foot woman and her eight-foot man stepped right in front of

Taylor and stopped. We waited a few moments for them to move on before Taylor tapped the woman's shoulder and said, "Excuse me."

Chris chimed in, "Move on, please."

The woman turned around and snarled, "I'll stand where I want. It's a show for fuck's sake."

"Not in our area," Taylor said, holding her ground. "We've been here for an hour. See, this is our garbage bag. This is our space. Just move a few steps over, please."

"Is this your first show?" the woman said. "You do not get to take all the room on the floor. You don't have to be so rude."

Taylor took a deep breath and spoke in a tone I've never heard her use before, "That's right. I'm rude. I'm a fucking bitch, actually. Do you really want to spend your show with a bitch? Because that just doesn't make any sense. I'm a total bitch."

That stance worked, or the look on Taylor's face was so ferocious, the mean seven-foot woman and her eight-foot man walked away, much to our relief. I couldn't believe it. Taylor, with her quiet demeanor and tiny stature, was as non-confrontational as any hippie I had ever met. I was proud of her for standing up to a woman who was not only much taller than Taylor but older. The dudes behind her were also paying attention because they cheered and applauded Taylor's bravado. With that, the lights lowered, and the band took the stage. The highlights of first set for me were *Wedge* and *My Friend, My Friend.* It was cool being on the floor because it felt intimate like the entire crowd was only us on the floor in front of the band. I had to remind myself to look around the venue to see we were merely one of twenty thousand bodies dancing and connecting to every note.

At set break as we sat back down on the floor, one of the fraternity guys behind us leaned forward to get our attention. "Look," he said, pointing backward. On the back of the seven-foot mean woman who was sitting behind them, someone had slapped a bright orange sticker on her back that read, *Don't Engage Me. I Chomp!!!!* We could not stop laughing at the bitch karma could be. "Guess I wasn't the only person she freaked out on," Taylor said. It was hysterical.

I took opportunity with the *Carini* opener to wind my way from our space to the back of the floor to find the restrooms and to restock our waters since we didn't leave our space during set break. Maybe I just won't ever understand that song. The whole Lucy's dead thing freaked me out. However, the *Harry Hood* and then the *Antelope* closer far made up for one unlovable song. We walked out of the venue, animatedly discussing our predictions for New Year's Eve with anticipation for whatever goodness lay ahead. A couple of slices to go, and we were back at the apartment in bed by midnight.

41

Navigating Claire's installment from my father's parking garage to Hotel Pennsylvania proved to be less of a logistics nightmare than we anticipated. We were able to drive Chris's car, and park it in the hotel's lot to unload the installment from there, much to my relief. I didn't know how else we would lug it on a bus or subway across Manhattan. It wasn't so much big as cumbersome as the installment consisted of five poles and stands from which triangular flags were hung and then attached to the floor. With the use of luggage carts, we were able to load everything and get it up to the eighteenth floor where PhanArt was setting up. This structure was not a web, but more like an umbrella of sorts. Claire called it her Love Fountain. No wonder she was so taken with the Fantasy Fountain in the park yesterday.

Four poles stood in a square between a center pole that held a light-up neon scrawled sign that read *LOVE*. Below the sign was a fountain of thin metallic strands that held their shape to cascade down in a dramatic flounce, much like the tassel on the hat of a marching band drum major. The four poles that made up the square held the triangles that opened in an arch to the floor. Whereas Claire's webs were all white, this piece screamed bright colors. Transparent, loosely woven patchwork panels made from plastic created the triangles. Woven within the panels were seemingly random objects like Matchbox cars, doll heads and torsos (sometimes not all connected), jacks, marbles, LEGOs, Lincoln Logs, skeleton keys, miniature cups and saucers, plastic trucks and cars of various sizes, numerous plastic balls of every color, deflated balloons, wands for soap bubbles, Slinkys, and Army figures. There was even a Jack-in-the-Box on one panel and a creepy Raggedy Ann hanging from another. The overall effect was whimsical in a carnival way, a bit chaotic but fun to see. Each panel was assigned its color, but there were multitudes of shades and tints of that same color woven together to make each form. Claire had used a strong plastic tubing to shape the arch of each panel into an elegant curve from the top of the center pole to the floor, like a bird's wings in flight. There was no text in this work except the *LOVE* sign at the top. Each arch was tall enough for people to walk under, and they intended for people to also walk around it. The center pole was woven with the same material as the panels, mixing all four colors. Claire guided us to secure the pole stands with gaffer's tape so they would be strong in the event some wook stumbled into them. As we taped and tested poles, we joked with each other, "Is it wook-worthy?"

PhanArt was a reunion for us, not just with each other, but with folks we met that summer, like Tim and Kristin, the couple from Kentucky who home-schooled their kids.

"It's time we exchanged names," Tim said when we shook hands. However, we didn't have much more to talk after he and Kristin looked at Claire's creation before they were swept in the tide of old friends from their college days in Philadelphia. "We've all been friends for twenty years," Tim said as he waved in apology for the abrupt interruption.

I saw Willow and nudged Chris. "I'm glad Alex isn't here," I said.

Before he could respond, Tippy and Plums surprised us. They had driven in from New Jersey just that afternoon.

"Hey guys," Chris said. "Do you have a booth here?"

"Nah, man. I got out of the game. Too much of a hassle and too busy getting ready for fucking college and graduation and shit," Plums said.

"Do you know where you're going?" Chris asked Tippy, who launched into his own story of the college application game. Taylor was lucky to be done. Smart, more like it.

I turned my attention back to Claire, whose face was animated, hands talking, dramatic explanations of her art as only she is wont to do. She was charming, and her last two installments reflected that much more than the first Barbie doll show. I shuddered to remember it, so I guess that meant that it was good, by virtue of being disturbing. Powerful, I think. I liked these two last pieces so much better if you valued art on its aesthetic beauty and not just on its message. The elegance of the lines in the cobwebs and the lines of these four arched panels reminded me of Bernini's sculptures.

I walked the booths, inspecting the art. This PhanArt was much bigger than the one at Mohegan, and there was a lot to take in. The booths offered stickers, t-shirts, hats, postcards, jewelry, and clothes. I lost track of time watching a guy work on a live-action painting. There were even yoga sessions offered by Surrender to the Flow. I splurged on a donut tie for Dad from a booth called Sec. 119.

It was expensive because it was silk, and I knew he would appreciate it. I wanted to find a piece of jewelry to gift Claire, but nothing seemed right because I had another idea tugging at the back of my mind. I would have to pursue it tomorrow morning if I could slip away for a bit, maybe while they were all sleeping.

The afternoon slid by quickly. Before we knew it, it was five o'clock; time to deconstruct the whole thing and pack it back into Chris's car.

"That's one thing about actually selling art, Claire. You don't carry out as much as you load in if you're doing it right," Chris complained. It took us several trips to load everything back into the car, parked in the hotel garage.

Nobody was in a good mood once we had navigated traffic to park in front of my building, so I suggested finishing the evening by ordering in and hanging out at the apartment watching movies, which everyone gratefully accepted. Claire was delighted like I hoped when I pulled out the take-out menus Dad and I still kept in a kitchen drawer even though everything would be ordered with an app. on my phone. He had left a note on the fridge. He'd be out for the evening, and we could order whatever we wanted.

I unearthed a bottle of vodka from the freezer and poured cocktails with cranberry juice and wedges of lime while we waited for the food to arrive. Claire and Taylor had commandeered the remote and scanned for a movie they wanted to watch. I was so happy to have my friends in my living room; I didn't care what they chose even as Chris half-heartedly bickered with their decisions like always.

It was a great night. We ate too much food and watched *Fast Times at Ridgemont High* and drank vodka. We went out on the balcony to smoke a joint and then had a dance party, blasting Pigeons Playing Ping Pong and STS9 until my dad returned home. He wasn't mad, but he shut down the evening, claiming it was a Monday night at midnight, and we needed to rest up for tomorrow, New Year's Eve.

DECEMBER 31, 2019

MADISON SQUARE GARDEN
New York, NY

SET 1: Martian Monster > Buried Alive > AC/DC Bag > Halley's Comet > Prince Caspian > Sparkle > Axilla, Maze > Fluffhead > Rise/Come Together

SET 2: Punch You in the Eye > Wolfman's Brother > Light > Twist > Soul Planet > Mercury > Possum

SET 3: Send in the Clowns, First Tube, Auld Lang Syne, Sand, Drift While You're Sleeping, What's the Use?, You Enjoy Myself

ENCORE: Tweezer Reprise, Rescue Squad

42

I hope this happens once again

"Guyute"
Anastasio

When I returned from my early morning, errand, Chris, and Taylor were up drinking coffee in the kitchen.

"Morning," I said as I opened the cabinet for a mug to pour my cup. "Where's Claire?"

"Still sleeping, I think," Taylor said, yawning, so I retrieved another mug and made a second cup of coffee to bring to her, adding the sugar she liked. She smiled when she saw me enter the room.

"Were you sleeping?" I asked as I handed her the steaming cup.

"I just woke up," she said. "Good morning."

I sat on the corner of the bed, pulling a robin egg blue box from my coat pocket and handing it to her. "Happy New Year."

"What's this?" she asked, smiling with recognition at the box.

"A gift," I said. "Open it."

I got the response I was hoping for as she squealed with delight, holding up the silver necklace that spelled *Love* in Paloma Picasso's handwriting. She put it on immediately and thanked me with a kiss.

"I love it," she said. "Thank you."

"You're welcome," I said. "I love you. When I saw your latest installation, I knew I had to get this for you, so I went out this morning."

"Just now?" she asked. "How did you even know about this necklace?"

"My mom still gets Tiffany catalogs, and I saw it," I said. "Dad should probably discontinue the junk mail and magazine subscriptions, but he hasn't yet. Maybe never will."

"And because you read everything in sight," she nodded. "Makes sense."

We joined Chris and Taylor in the kitchen and decided to get dressed to get some breakfast and some fresh air. We ate, then walked and window shopped.

"How far is Central Park?" Chris asked.

"About fourteen blocks," I said. "Why? Do you want to go?"

He looked at me and said, "Not today. I just wondered. Maybe next time," which made me smile, thinking there would be a next time.

Of course, the girls demanded extra time to get ready for the show. "It's YEMSG!" they insisted. Chris and I hit the cart and opened beers to pass the time. Dad wouldn't be coming home. He planned to work late and then to drive to his parents' house for the evening. We had the apartment to ourselves.

Our seats were in the 200 section, but in the center of the venue, which was perfect, and we wouldn't have to worry about seven-foot mean women harshing our groove. Three sets divided the show.

Trey's pan story completely lost me, but the *Fluffhead* was so amazing, I soon forgot to even ask anyone about it at the first set break. Second set yawned a bit for me after the always satisfying *Punch You in the Eye*. When the band came out in costume to launch the last set with *Send in the Clones*, we freaked out a bit. They were wearing the same four colors Claire had used in her Love Fountain. It was uncanny. There were dozens of kids, an entire youth choir, costumed as color-coded clones who danced and sang on stage as the band members got on four individual platforms suspended above the stage. We all hugged and kissed at midnight when they dropped the balloons, which were all the same color scheme. It's so weird when things like this happen, and they seemed to happen all the time when it came to anything to do with Phish. But even when it became apparent to everyone that Trey might actually be stuck up on his platform, they made our whole night by pushing through to play *Drift While You're Sleeping*. Tears were streaming down Claire's face as she sang about love and leaned over to kiss me repeatedly. I thought it was brilliant to choose *What's the Use?* for the next song. The clones held these round metallic discs that reflected lights throughout the venue. It was wild.

Finally, Trey admitted he was officially stuck on his platform, still suspended above the stage. It was both awesome and awful. Even for encore, he joked this would be when the band left the stage and returned, so they would just finish the show, and he would get down after we all left. But, of course, nobody in the audience was going to leave until the Rescue Squad got on Fishman's platform and safely got

317

Trey from his. As the platform lowered, Trey picked up the drumsticks and started playing, while leading us to chant, "Rescue Squad. Rescue Squad" until they safely returned to the main stage. He bowed, walked off stage, and a moment later, the house lights went up. Chris, Taylor, Claire, and I linked arms and walked into the night together.

Acknowledgments

I'd like to thank the members of Phish: Trey Anastasio, Mike Gordon, Page McConnell, and Jon Fishman. I am eternally grateful for your music. I have carried you with me through my entire adult life, through marriage, maternity, and beyond. Your songs serve to heal my soul. It was the delight of my days to set my characters on tour with you. Thank you, Peter Conners. *Growing Up Dead: The Hallucinated Confessions of a Teenage Deadhead* was an inspiration in the journey of writing this book. I am grateful to Gurney Norman, who helped me launch this process and mentored me with such kind encouragement. Thank you to Wolf Lant, who found the RV that became *Suby Greenberg*. Elva Rangel, you are so kind as to help me learn Spanish. Special appreciation for my principal, Joe Gibson, who supports me in my writing career as he leads me as a teacher and likes to chat about all things Phish in between. This book would not be as rich with authentic details of the lot scenes if it were not for the kindness of the Phish Chicks and Phish Hens, who eagerly shared their stories with me. Adrienne DeVos and rainbow sunshine, I will forever remember your kindness. I am grateful for my Chalkdust Torturer colleagues and the darling Little Rager families. Shout out to my monkeykats of the past and the present. Our days dancing at shows and running wild on Shakedown are the memories that fuel the scenes of this book. Kat O'Sullivan, thank you for allowing your Calico House to live in the fictitious world of Maywood, Ohio, and for allowing your photograph to grace my cover. I feel such gratitude for Alecia Whitaker, who guided me with her wisdom and valuable time in the editing process and whose notes launched a revision process larger than we could have anticipated and for which I am satisfied. Jay McCoy, partnering with you in all things poetry means everything to me. I don't know where I'd be without your careful eye and brilliant mind. Thank you to my son, Carter Neumann, who designed the cover of this book and to my husband, Kevin Neumann, who patiently assists me in everything I do, including taking off with me to Phish shows. There's no one else with whom I'd rather waste my time.

Resources

The Catcher in the Rye by J.D. Salinger

The Goldfinch by Donna Tartt

Growing Up Dead: The Hallucinated Confessions of a Teenage Deadhead by Peter Conners

Charlotte's Web by E.B. White

Divine Right's Trip by Gurney Norman

The Funniest Things Overheard At Phish's Two-Night Stand At The Gorge by Kendall Deflin

Wook hunters bag and tag our smelliest invasive species by Reilly Capps in "Rooster"

Phish lyrics from Phish.net

Set Lists researched from Jambase.com and Phish.net

Made in the USA
Middletown, DE
15 June 2020

10002449R10196